THE LONG-LOST LOVE LETTERS OF DOC HOLLIDAY

DAVID CORBETT

SQUARE TIRE BOOKS
Austin, TX

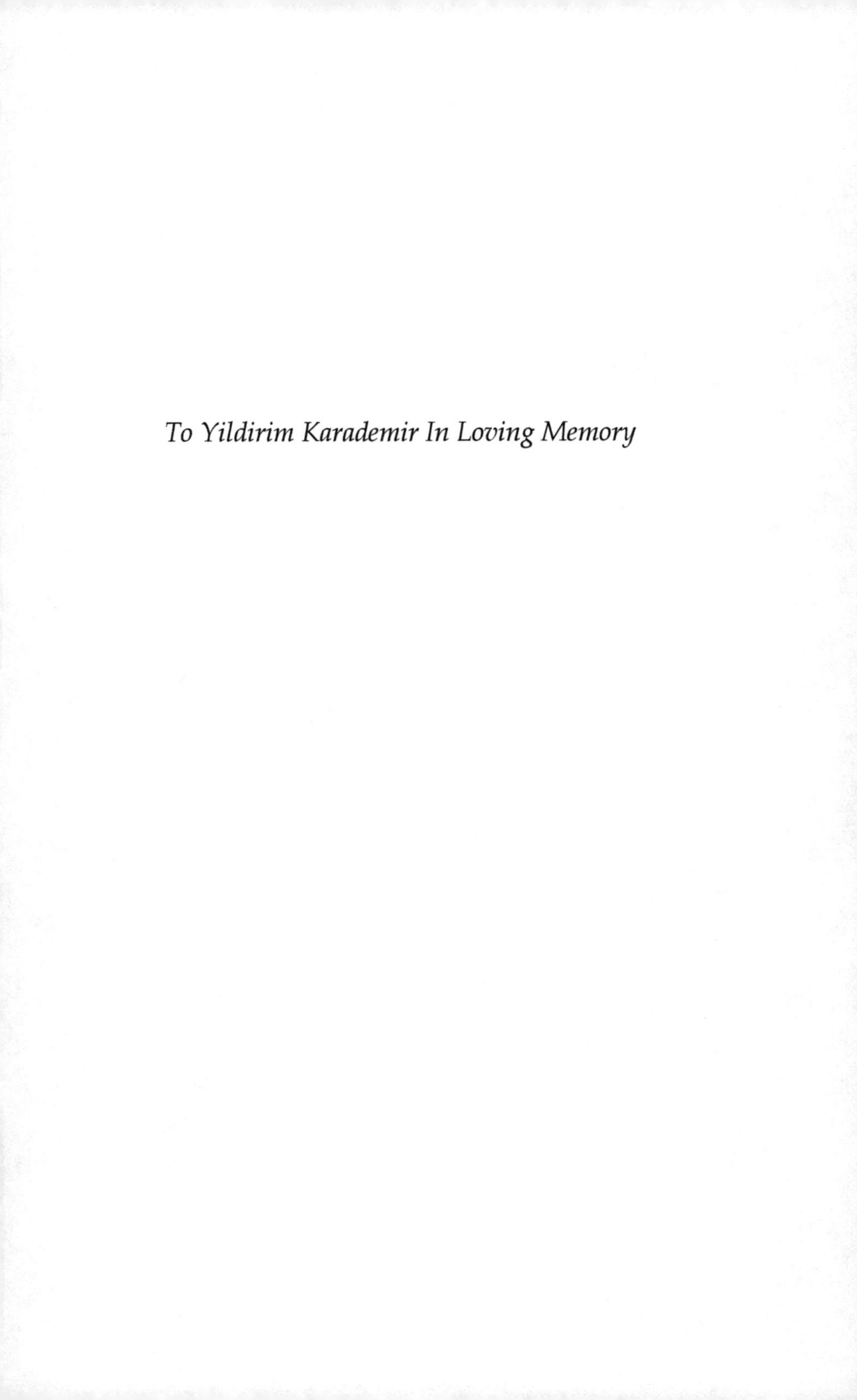

To Yildirim Karademir In Loving Memory

[H]istory repeats her tale unconsciously, and goes off into a mystic rhyme; ages are prototypes of other ages, and the winding course of time brings us round to the same spot again.

~ *The Christian Remembrancer, Volume 10,* October 1845

The artist must know the manner whereby to convince others of the truthfulness of his lies.

~ *Pablo Picasso*

PART I

All happiness or unhappiness solely depends upon the quality of the object to which we are attached by love.

~ Baruch Spinoza

~ 1 ~

DON'T look for the innocent here. You won't find them. Start with Lisa Balamaro.

Prodigal daughter, born into what many would consider American royalty, she had no use for that old canard that there are no second acts in American life. Though only twenty-eight years old, she'd already been obliged to crawl out from the wreckage she'd made of herself.

In her first year of law school, after an all-night party upstate in the Hudson Valley, she foolishly chose to drive all the way back to the Bronx at daybreak. Blind drunk, she fell asleep at the wheel and careened off the Taconic Parkway into oncoming traffic, narrowly missing an airporter van, and only coming to rest upon impact with an old-growth hickory.

The airbag saved her, nominally: a separated shoulder, both cheeks broken, a gaping wound above her right eye — she still bore the scar — plus a broken rib, a punctured lung. Even so, she lived.

For a middle child already seen as the family letdown—
father a revered jurist, mother a force in Philadelphia charity
circles, golden-boy older brother clerking for Justice Breyer,
beautiful younger sister serving an internship in Brussels
with NATO—this particular disaster (it wasn't the first)
proved transformative.

Coffin, meet final nail.

Ironically, as her family turned away, she found new
direction within. And so she knew it could be done, knew
what it took to make it happen: to change. It explained her
preference for misfits, outcasts, the failed and forgotten—
why else represent artists?

Why else feel so committed to a man like Tuck Mercer?

His face—deeply lined from the sun, with that chiseled
roughness that speaks of the West—possessed the watchful
patience of a man who's earned each and every one of his
forty-three years on this earth. And yet a wistful humor
abided in his eyes as well. That hint of charitable grace
provided the wary a reason to loosen their spines, unbuckle
their shoulders, and return his smile.

An aura of loss hovered about him as well, an
impression intensified by his limp and the occasional
reliance on a maple walking stick with an ivory lion's head
grip.

The irony of this impression, with its palette of hard-
earned toughness and wise, affable charm, lay in the fact that
most people, if they knew what's commonly referred to as

the truth, would have considered nearly half his life wasted.

How else to regard the eight years in prison, or the decade before when he earned the right to his cell?

To Lisa's way of thinking, that all just added further testament to his capacity for self—transformation, for in truth Tuck had reinvented himself not just once, but twice.

Up until age eighteen, he'd been an up-and-comer on the rodeo circuit, earning side money as a sketch artist, exhibiting no small talent in either realm. But then the door to the future he'd been scheming got slammed shut for good, after which, through two hard years of dogged patience and meticulous practice, he transformed himself into an art forger.

Not just some slapdash hack, either. They would come to call him The Man Who Forged the West, for he could claim responsibility for over two hundred fake Blumenscheins, Blakelocks, Schreyvogels, Catlins, even the occasional Farny or Remington and one wildly convincing Georgia O'Keefe, a fair share of his pieces still gracing the walls of mansions, galleries, and museums throughout the world, the great majority in China.

Nothing lasts forever, of course, especially in matters of crime. Tuck was betrayed, apprehended, prosecuted, all of which eventually produced his second transformation.

Since leaving prison, he'd "gone legit," working with the same galleries, foundations, and auction houses he'd bamboozled for a decade, now consulting on the provenance of artwork depicting the American West, pieces that came into their possession through purchase or bequeathal or estate endowment.

He'd uncovered not a few creditable fakes and confirmed a handful of genuine finds. Lisa helped negotiate that transition.

He'd been one of her first clients when she'd uprooted herself from the east coast, hoping to escape all its backsliding ghosts, and relocated to San Francisco. She'd staked her fledgling reputation on the irreversible nature of Tuck's turn toward legitimacy and reliability, which helped explain the strength of the connection between them.

It wasn't just a case of client and counsel, or even troubled saint and gifted sinner. They'd established a genuine rapport in their work together, grown close over long walks in Golden Gate Park, leisurely lunches and dinners at Greens and The Slanted Door, late night talks about the addictive power of hatred, the strangely liberating silence of God, the inscrutable allure of romance.

That closeness explained the walking stick. Lisa found it while wandering antique shops in the tiny outposts of rural Sonoma, and instantly recognized the elegant, simple instrument as a fitting gift for her newfound friend, for she knew Tuck's limp was not feigned or exaggerated, a ploy to inspire pity—or trust. The injury was real and had never truly healed.

Which returns us to what cut short his earliest dreams, slamming the door on that long-lost future.

He'd been eighteen, showing off for a girl he had no right to love—a sixteen-year-old whose portrait, clothed and otherwise, he'd secretly sketched or painted dozens of times. At La Fiesta de Los Vaqueros in Tucson, he chose to ride a bucking longhorn named Crater Maker, who showed him where dreams end. And nothingness begins.

The rodeo clown trailing them from the chute had failed to turn the bull away from Tuck's riding hand. The steer bucked him off, but a suicide wrap delayed impact—the animal dragged him one-armed a full thirty yards.

When he finally did break free, the bull turned before he could scramble to his feet. Its hooves crushed his ribs into splinters. One horn, despite the dulled tip, plowed deep into his pelvis, butchering muscle, ripping arteries like thread.

Tuck dropped into unconsciousness then coma, lying near death for days. When he finally blinked awake in the ICU on the third night—lying there alone, packed tight in gauze and strapped to a thousand tubes—it took several moments for the situation to register.

He lay like that for some time, eyes open in the dim smeary light, taking in that unique smell every hospital has, the fragrance of bad luck, nothing but his howling mind for company, while the room maintained its terrible welcoming silence.

Even then he knew he'd crossed some crucial border, the dividing line between the cowboy career he'd lost for good, the love the fates had stolen back with it—her family would make damn sure she never saw him again—and the lonely, angry years of deceit ahead.

But now, twenty-five years on, three years since walking out of Leavenworth, he sipped from a glass of his favorite whiskey, Knappogue Castle 14, and entertained his young brunette lawyer-cum-*amiga* with her distinctive scar, arcing around her eye like a wicked red whiptail.

They sat across from each other in the third-floor studio of the Queen Anne Victorian he'd purchased with honest money, refurbished with his own hands.

Meanwhile, in the leather wingback armchair across from him, Lisa nursed her tea and wondered at the reason she was there. He'd said he had a surprise, one that would "knock her over."

Secretly, she enjoyed the idea of being knocked over — no one changes that completely. And as she sat there, watching him, listening to his gravelly voice, patiently waiting him out, she found herself wanting nothing so much as to have him put down his glass, gather his cane, cross the space between them, and ravage her.

~ 2 ~

"CLOSE your eyes for a sec."

She obeyed with a smile, trembling, and imagined him leaning down, lifting her chin as she closed her eyes—better yet, clutching her hair in his fist and pulling her head back, not rough or mean.

Riderly.

Then a long, stubbled, hungry kiss . . .

"Like I said, got something here to show you."

With that, he finally rose from his chair. She could hear the taut leather creak and sigh as he gained his feet.

She clung to her hope for a kiss but then he passed, heading toward the cluttered workspace behind her, trailing a brusque whiff of cologne and Irish single malt.

Her heart tripped over itself for a second, wondering if she'd misread the signals. She'd kept her longings under wraps for some time now—or hoped she had. As a lawyer, she'd developed an expertise in keeping secrets—at least, those of others.

A soughing groan beyond the door, a rustle of cloth—he tugged up his trouser leg to kneel, she thought, the groan a giveaway. Then the ticking sound of the whirling tumblers on his vault, the crunch of the lever, the heavy door gliding open.

He has a present for you, nimrod—a necklace, a bracelet, a sketch he made, maybe provocative, possibly nude. Something precious. Something in need of hiding.

After a moment she heard the vault door close again and another small moan of nagging effort as he regained his feet.

Her pulse shivered in her wrist like a minnow. Something soft dropped invitingly onto the engraved copper tray, perched atop an antique quilted bench, that served as a coffee table.

"Go ahead," he told her. "Look." She did so, blinking for a moment.

"Have any idea what you're looking at?"

A packet about the size of a handbag, wrapped in weathered velvet and tied with frayed ribbon, rested between them on the copper tray.

Lisa began to reach for it—an innocent impulse, intending to inspect its distinctively angular sag and bulge more closely—but then felt a sudden reluctance. And disappointment. It wasn't for her. Not in the way she'd hoped.

"If I had to guess, I'd say . . . letters?"

Tuck smiled. "Not just any letters. Most infamous love letters in the history of the United States."

You Nighted States.

Lisa regarded the packet more mindfully, still resisting the impulse to touch.

Pouring himself another two fingers of whiskey. "Sure I can't tempt you?"

She offered a wan smile then leaned across the coffee table, reached for his hand, pulled it toward her, and inhaled from the glass. The aroma conjured peat smoke, warm caramel, and a prom dress spackled with vomit—one of her other disasters.

"How heavenly." She sat back, collecting her mug of tea. "But you understand."

Tuck offered a sweet, heartbreaking smile. "Course I do."

Her cheeks warmed. "So—these letters, how did you happen to come upon them?"

He cocked an eyebrow. "Suspicious?"

"We're way past that. Call me curious."

"Tell you how they got here in a minute. First, guess who wrote them."

Lisa possessed one of those rare lawyerly minds not inclined to a fondness for riddles. "I can think of nothing more tedious."

Tuck, swirling the whiskey now. That southwestern drawl: "You're no fun."

"You have no idea how often I hear that."

"Oh for the love of mud—they're the letters Doc Holliday and his cousin Mattie, the one that became a nun, wrote back and forth after he left Georgia."

The packet exerted its gravity more seriously now. Lisa couldn't help but stare at the humble ribbon, the worn velvet.

"I thought those letters didn't exist."

"They don't. They were burned. Too scandalous, too much a threat to the family's reputation—or the nun's. They got destroyed by Sister Melanie herself — that's the name she took when she signed up with the Sisters of Mercy."

Lisa had more than a passing acquaintance with nuns. Not so much gamblers or gun-toting dentists. "That's beginning to ring a bell. The whiff of scandal, I mean."

"The name Melanie's kinda intriguing on its own. Nuns usually take the names of saints, or did prior to Vatican II. There's only two saints named Melanie, and one of them married her first cousin. Interesting choice of name, then, don't you think, given the rumors she and Doc were sweethearts?"

Lisa stared into her tea. As a girl, she'd memorized the canon of saints and their grim biographies the way boys learn by heart the stats on baseball cards. She remembered a Melania the Younger, but wasn't the marriage against her will?

"There's more," Tuck said. "Ever read *Gone with The Wind*?"

Lisa snapped to. "Read? No."

"Seen the movie?"

"Naturally."

"Well, Scarlett O'Hara's sister-in-law Melanie was based on guess who. Margaret Mitchell, the woman who wrote the book, was kin to the Hollidays."

Lisa settled a bit deeper into her chair, a girl getting told a story. Not quite the same as being ravaged, but . . .

"Apparently, when Doc died in Glenwood Springs, someone gathered up his belongings and shipped them back to Atlanta. Specifically, to Mattie, who was Sister Melanie by then. She'd entered the convent four years before. Some think it broke Doc's heart. To finally realize: no, it would never happen, they would never be together. Not in this life. There's some evidence he converted to Catholicism near the end, as though to get himself ready for a second chance to be with her in the beyond."

How utterly Romeo and Juliet, Lisa thought. And kind of creepy.

"Among Doc's things were the letters Mattie wrote to him all those years. But the good sister felt so concerned about propriety she refused to go to the train station in Atlanta to pick up the trunk when it arrived from Colorado. She sent her uncle instead."

"Southern gentility."

"Hypocritical pride, more like."

Tuck rose uneasily from his chair, collected his whiskey in one hand, walking stick in the other, and shambled over to the window. "Whole damn family was jittery as June bugs when it came to scandal. Some of them even denied Doc was any relation. Rest just chose not to discuss him."

Every family has its black sheep, she thought. Ahem.

"Then around the 1930s, not too long before Mattie died, a few new books about Wyatt Earp came out, stirring up all the old rumors."

"And mentioned Dr. Shoot-em-Up, I imagine."

"He didn't come out miserably, but he hardly got canonized, neither. Virgil Earp's wife, Allie, openly despised him. Even Josie, Wyatt's wife, referred to him as 'an irascible tubercular' and 'the misanthropic dentist.' Said his devotion to Wyatt was more liability than benefit and the friendship only survived out of pity."

Friendships don't survive out of pity, she thought. If only.

"But that was nothing compared to the blowback from the anti-Earp contingent back in Arizona. The kindest thing Doc got called was a touchy drunk. Before she died, Mattie confided that if only people could read Doc's letters, they'd know he wasn't the sick, heartless bastard everybody made him out to be."

Lisa, flinching inadvertently at *touchy drunk*, said, "Shame she destroyed them then. The letters, I mean. Unless . . . "

Tuck turned back from the window, pointing with his glass at the ribboned packet. "Exactly. She *said* she destroyed them. What if our dear Sister of Mercy lied?"

~ 3 ~

TUCK had already identified a motivated buyer through channels he'd established in the world of western art and artifacts—a retired judge and noted collector who owned a ranch at the edge of the Dragoon Mountains northeast of Tombstone—but when it came time to make the call he put Lisa on the line for the pitch. The judge agreed to a rendezvous. "Why not tomorrow—there any problem with that?"

Given the need to move quickly, Tuck had insisted she not just take the letters with her but read a few, acquaint herself with their texture, their smell, the script, the words themselves, the better to assess their value.

"They've been boxed up tight for a good long while," he'd said. "Won't be no worse for wear if you leaf through a couple. Just take reasonable care. Besides, they're not real, remember? They don't exist."

On the drive across town to her office, Lisa suffered the relentless temptation to pull over, oblige Tuck's suggestion. At

15

times she even imagined voices whispering to her from within the small black Pelican case in which he'd secured the letters.

Finally, her resistance crumbled. She pulled into the parking lot of the Asian Art Museum and mustered the gumption to venture a peek.

Tuck had given her several pairs of cotton gloves, the kind experts preferred when handling rare documents. She supposed it made her look as though she intended not to read the letters but palpate them. Or express their anal glands.

She unlocked the small hard-shell case and stared for a moment at the knotted ribbon, the worn velvet cloth. Inside, the antique envelopes bore three-cent George Washington stamps and postmarks from the late 1870s, early-to-mid 1880s, and she selected one at random.

The envelope was brittle, addressed to Martha Anne Holliday from John H. Holliday. The pages inside were worn and soft but sturdy, about seven inches by four, with rough edges indicating they'd been cut by a knife from larger sheets — not recently, from what she could tell, though only an expert could determine that for certain.

The cream laid paper gave off an indefinable scent, neither musty nor perfumed. The ink was reddish brown, not black, an effect of oxidation, typical of iron-gall, a distinctive ingredient of the time. Tuck had explained all this, as well as the blurring from corrosion and the mirror-image tracings of some of the writing caused by cellulose degradation.

The penmanship had an elegant precision, and the folds in the pages were deeply creased, just short of tearing, suggesting the letter had been frequently, even obsessively read and re-read.

And as easily as that, she thought, we're prepared to believe.

⸻◈◈◈⸻

November 8, 1881

Dearest Mattie:

Be forewarned, my news is not good.

I killed a man, and but for luck would have killed another, for which it now appears I will likely hang.

Three men in all died in the affray. Make no mistake, the violence was mutual. We defended ourselves. More importantly, though hatred enflamed both sides, a fact I cannot deny, those responsible for the mortalities, myself and the Earp brothers, two of whom took bullets as well, acted under color of the law.

That now, however, appears to matter little, for the forces aligned against us, men without principle or honor, who treat the truth like a rag to polish their mendacity, will say or do anything to watch us swing.

Small surprise, I suppose, for if history teaches us anything, it is that men can always produce attractive arguments to justify their disgraceful actions.

Then again, that is precisely what is being said of us. That we used the law to justify butchery.

It is not true, Mattie, I swear that to you.

This turn in events has me wishing that I could not just write to you, but speak directly, openly, as we so often did long into the night at the house on Cat Creek, or that summer I hid away with you and your family in Jonesboro.

In particular, I find myself revisiting over and over the evening when we left the house and walked beneath a threatening sky, with silent lightning flashes in the distance, talking as we trudged toward shelter in a windbreak of pines.

You told me that night that you felt you knew me better than anyone else on earth. In particular, you understood not just the elemental, intemperate fire in my spirit, but its causes — Mother's horrible sickness and ugly death, my father's insidious betrayals, the degrading occupation with all the scum and scavengers it legitimized.

More importantly, you told me that you loved me. We embraced and kissed, and you let me press my hand to your heart, so that I might feel the fury of its beating.

It is that remembrance that has intensified and clarified my feelings of regret tonight. Your face rose up in my mind's eye with such shocking vividness as I sat here, hoping to tame my thoughts, that I nearly wept with longing for your presence.

I will admit, I am afraid. But I need to assure you, I did not kill easily or casually. Once the smoke cleared and the damage could be assessed, I returned to my hotel room, put my face in my hands and could not help myself from muttering over and over, like a penitent before the altar of Judgment, "This is awful. Just awful."

I found myself praying for the men we killed and shuddered at the haphazard course of misjudgment that led to so much blood.

Worse, I understood the ancient curse of wrath in a way I previously had not, drawing from the well of rage more deeply than I ever imagined a man could.

What I tasted when I drank was the sin of Cain.

I do not say this out of some perverse extravagance, or to placate your piety, nor to seek from you once again the grace of understanding or, even more impertinent, forgiveness.

I say it to claim the truth about my own nature. The greatest sin is not murder but hypocrisy. I saw myself clearly, too clearly. I am not a good man, and absent a deluge of grace from God, that never will change.

That is the terrible truth of sin, the absence of escape.

I know you will pray for me and remind me of the Lord's mercy. I am grateful for all such kindness. What I am trying to confide is that I know now, as I have never understood before, just how little I deserve such a blessing.

I will end here, except to say that, sobered by the prospect of malicious judgment and immanent death, as well as the fact I may never get the chance to write you again, I have never felt more keenly the affection for you that I carry in my heart.

Please know that, despite all the meagerness of spirit I have exhibited, throughout all my misspent wanderings, you have remained my true north. That will continue until my final breath.

It is well past midnight, but not quite dawn. An hour, I suppose, that has defined my life. For it seems I have spent the vast majority of my days enveloped in darkness, waiting for that first show of light.

With all the love in my heart,
Your devoted, John Henry

~ 4 ~

THE offices of Barragan & Balamaro—"Creative Law for Creative People"—took up the whole first floor of an ivy-covered, bay-windowed Italianate mansion overlooking Fay Park on Russian Hill. The house belonged to Nico Barragan, Lisa's partner.

They'd met during her first year of law school at Fordham. A graduate assistant at the time, he led a symposium on art and the law at the Brooklyn Museum that basically changed her life. Good God, she'd thought. Being an attorney can be *fun*.

She soon developed a walloping student crush, but as the dashing bachelor professor tended to prefer the wild, the beautiful, and the damned—angry poets, wastrel painters, fringe musicians—she contented herself with studying under him, learning from him, volunteering for law clinics, helping out with his quirky practice.

When an eccentric aunt left him the San Francisco property, he decided to pull up stakes and head west. Unable to imagine needing the entire place for himself, he'd built out the downstairs for offices, the second floor for his residence, the third for guests and visitors, and hung out his shingle.

When the business began to take off, he contacted Lisa and asked if she'd consider relocating. For the sake of the flattery alone, she would have said yes. And sobered by the prospect of malicious judgment, as it were, she recognized the wisdom of placing a continent between her new career and her reckless past.

⚬⬦⚬

Letting herself in at the mansion's front door, she spotted a light from the kitchen in back, beyond the offices, and ambled down the high-ceilinged corridor toward it.

A toasty aroma greeted her as Nico, nursing a glass of white wine, turned as she entered and offered a smile—rugged man-boy in the prime of life, a cyclist's build, strong and slender, ponytail, soul patch, jeans and plaid flannel. The hip lawyer at home.

"Roasting eggplant and jalapeños for a tapenade," he said. "I would've done it upstairs, but the thermostat on my oven's still on the blink." He set down his wine. "You're working late. Make you some tea?"

"That would be lovely." She set the hard-shell case on the center island, scooched herself onto a stool. "I have a few things to square away before I head off tomorrow."

"Really." Scouring the cabinet, searching through tea tins. "Head off for where?"

"Arizona."

"Good God, why—penance?"

"Tombstone Territory."

"Ah!" He turned from the cabinet. "Golden Assam, yes?"

"Did you hear what I said?"

"Of course." He put on the kettle, triggered the flame. "Tombstone. Arizona. Land of cowpokes and cacti and immigrant-bashing homophobes. My question stands— why?"

She nodded to the Pelican case. "Let me tell you a story."

He glanced up, met her eyes. Something registered, as though at last he'd intuited her seriousness.

"Mind if I make a salad while you do? I'm famished."

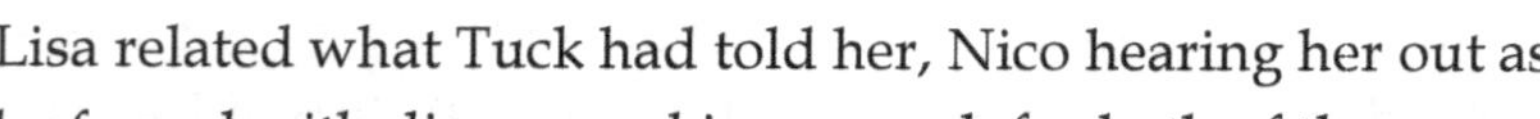

Lisa related what Tuck had told her, Nico hearing her out as he fussed with dinner, making enough for both of them.

"So apparently, instead of burning the letters like she said she did, Sister Melanie, Doc's cousin, secretly handed them over to this former slave named Sophie Walton. She stayed on as a servant for the family after the Civil War and lived with the wife of one of his other cousins. There's a lot of byzantine family stuff I won't go into now—"

"Please," Nico said, plucking the tops off cherry tomatoes, "don't."

"—but the long and the short of it is that the nun trusted Sophie to both save the letters and also keep them secret, at least until the generation that still felt scandalized by Doc had died off. But before she could do that, Sophie herself passed away. Her name was Sophie Walton Murphy then, though no one seems to know who Murphy was."

"Men," Nico offered, turning toward the sink to rinse his tomatoes.

"The letters got stuck in a safe deposit box at a tiny African-American bank in Brooklyn that went under in the Great Depression. The U.S. Comptroller of the Currency collected up all the unclaimed boxes, and the letters just sat in a warehouse somewhere until 1985 when—again, I'll skip the details—a woman named Savannah Murphy Royster claimed a kinship to Sophie and, after a lot of rigmarole, took possession."

"Happy ending," Nico said, "tra-la-la." He'd moved on to the cucumbers, the Persian variety, small and crisp, slicing them onto a bed of greens in a large wood bowl.

"Kind of. Turns out Savannah was a bit of a squirrelly bird herself. Hoarder type, house a labyrinth of dusty junk. Did nothing with the letters, didn't even look at them, apparently, for thirty years. Then, after a stroke, she decides to see if they're worth anything. Finds out about Tuck, learns he pretty much knows everything about the Old West—"

"Phony or otherwise," Nico said. Glancing up, he added, "Sorry."

"Savannah hands them over to him to authenticate, intending them as a present for her favorite granddaughter, a young lady named Rayella Vargas."

"Sounds like a kickboxer," he said. "Or a bride of the revolution."

"According to Tuck, she's barely more than a kid, hasn't had much luck in life. This could be her ticket. But before Tuck can get anywhere looking into the letters, the grandmother has a second stroke and dies."

"Oops." Nico glanced up. "Let me guess. She didn't have a will."

Lisa waved him off. "It was a pre-death gift, apparently, or that's how Tuck understood it. Regardless, that's not the point. The Holliday family will never concede that these letters are genuine, especially given what's in them."

Finally, she had his full attention. "You've read them?"

"One," she admitted sheepishly. "On the drive here. Wouldn't you?"

"Oh hell yes."

"Getting back to the problem—the family most likely will dig in their heels, stand by the nun's story that she burned them, and file suit."

"Under what cause of action?"

"I don't know, false light, publication of private facts, specific performance if nothing else."

"The nun's the one with standing, not them. And to restate the obvious: Sistuh Melanie, she dead."

"You're missing the point. Again. Rayella's broke. She can't afford the legal fees even if the lawsuit goes nowhere. Or pay to authenticate the letters. No known independent samples of either Doc's or Mattie's handwriting have apparently survived. These letters are it."

"Maybe she can use them for wallpaper."

"Tuck let her know that there are people willing to buy them, even without authentication. The money's not inconsiderable."

Nico shrugged. "Black market for everything." He returned to the sink, rinsed off his knife and cutting board. "And Tuck's going to arrange that for her?"

"Sort of. He's identified the buyer. But given his past, it just seems wise for him to stay in the background. Rayella needs somebody else, somebody beyond reproach."

Nico slowly turned back from the sink. "I see."

"No," Lisa said. "Not you. Not the firm. Just me."

$$\sim 5 \sim$$

NICO wrapped up his preparations, adding strawberries and anchovies and cayenne pecans, a hearty drizzle of olive oil and balsamic, the juice from a whole Meyer lemon, tossed the lot and divvied it up into individual bowls.

They ate in silence for a while.

Finally, he said, "Not to play the spoil-sport, but the whole thing sounds a bit screwy."

"I know." Even to herself, her voice sounded a thousand miles off.

"So . . ."

She speared a slice of grilled red pepper. "Just how it is. Like I said, I'm heading off tomorrow. We're flying to Tucson. I'm meeting the client, Rayella, at the airport."

"That quick."

"Seems so."

He took that in, nodded. In a conciliatory tone: "Probably a lot of Old West nuts around there. Well, okay, not nuts. That's rude. Aficionados. Connoisseurs. And such."

"Yeah," she murmured, thinking: *motivated buyer.*

The silence returned. In time, it felt like a river running between them.

"Know what?" He waited until she glanced up, looking at her as though she'd flunked some essential test. "Just going on attitude, okay? Body language. I don't think you're all that keen on this. You're pissed. You're afraid Ol' Hunk Forger is lying."

She set down her fork. "I wouldn't say *lying.*"

"What hasn't he told you?"

"How could I possibly know the answer to that?"

"What do you *think* he hasn't told you?"

"It isn't that he hasn't told me anything. It's just the situation altogether."

"No, it's him. It's Hunk."

"Please don't call him that."

"You've got an utterly obvious crush on the man."

"I do *not.*"

"Client crush, then. Slightly more innocent. No less dangerous."

"He hasn't been a client since I drafted his consulting agreement with Christie's. Technically."

"Now *that's* reassuring."

"He's my *friend.*"

"All the worse if he's playing you."

"He's got too much to lose. Everything he's built these past few years. He's made a reputation. The money's good, better than good. Why lie? Especially about this."

"Well, if you're going to revert to your old ways, might as well swing for the fences. You have to admit, if those letters are a hoax, it's a doozy."

She tossed her napkin gently onto the countertop, appetite gone.

He regarded her a moment. The brownest, warmest, hardest eyes, like those of a saint in a medieval tryptic. "I don't want you getting hurt."

"That's not an issue."

"Yeah? Who is this clown willing to pay good money for a bunch of letters he's got a pretty good idea are fake?"

"I told you—"

"No, really, think about it. Who does that?"

"The guy who bought some of the most laughable forgeries ever made was a mathematician and astronomer. Smarter than the average bear. And yet it never occurred to him that letters written by Cleopatra, Mary Magdalene, and Lazarus wouldn't be written in French. People want what they want."

"Wow. There's a newsbreak."

"Nico—"

"What if this yahoo gets his nose out of joint when it actually dawns on him: 'Hey, this is bullshit.' What if he's got a screw loose, takes the whole gunslinger thing way too seriously? Thinks collecting stuff is a contact sport."

"It's Arizona, Nico, not Westworld. I realize our specialty's 'creative' law, but you're sounding a little . . . I dunno . . . overboard."

"It's called being concerned. I'm *concerned* about you. I'm *concerned* that this thing could go sideways. And slam into a rock."

"I can look after myself."

"Said the blind girl."

"Oh, come on — seriously?"

He collected their bowls. "Just come back in one piece, okay?" At the sink, he started scraping leftovers into the compost tin.

Lisa stared at his back for a while, then in the gentlest voice, "You know the hard part, right? It's not thinking this is all a scam. That's easy. Anybody can manage that. The hard part's allowing yourself to accept the fact that those stupid letters might just be real."

"You don't think they are?"

"I honestly, truly: Do. Not. Know."

"Dangerous enough if they aren't," he said. "Remember the weapons of mass destruction in Iraq? They weren't real. Look what happened."

⸻◈⸻

An hour later, she sat at her desk, once again wearing the white cotton gloves, feeling a need to inspect at least a few more of the letters. The impulse went beyond mere curiosity — she needed to determine for herself whether the letters rang true, seemed credibly authentic — real. After shuffling them into what appeared to be proper chronological order, she selected the very first one, from Mattie to Doc, and gently opened the envelope.

——⊰◈⊱——

June 20, 1873

My Dear John Henry:

As I pick up my pen to write, I feel a terrible apprehension that every word that appears on the page will be wrong, confessing a meaning I do not intend, or perhaps intend too much.

I would have written you much sooner, but I lacked confidence you would wish to hear from me given the harsh words we shared shortly before your abrupt departure. I assure you that I have confided the content of our quarrel to no one, nor have I allowed myself to be drawn into the endless speculation as to the true reason you found it necessary to leave us in such haste.

There is considerable gossip on that point, mind you. Tongues have been wagging at both ends as to which young lady you robbed of virtue, which powerful man you insulted, cheated, or shot.

Uncle John has tried to stamp out the grassfire by telling any and all with a mind to listen that the trip west was in hopes of an improvement in climate, given the consumption that has come upon you, just as it did poor Francisco and, of course, your precious mother.

Not that this has silenced all murmurings. The family is not alone in realizing that, if it was salutary environs you desired, you could have easily decamped to Hamilton County, to live with Uncle James and the rest of your mother's family. The local springs, they say, rival those of Saratoga.

If not there, then Atlanta near Uncle John and Aunt Permelia, where the Ponce de Leon Springs are famous for their curative powers. Your condition, to anyone who bothered to give the matter a moment's thought, cannot explain your sudden need to flee us, your family.

Fortunately, people credit Uncle John for truthfulness, given his standing and his honorable nature, and so many have decided the more scurrilous rumors are just so much bosh. As for the others, what can be done?

Your father is silent on the matter, which surprises no one, given the hardness between the two of you since your mother's passing, and his remarrying so shortly thereafter. As for that woman, the one he wed, she and her kin cannot slander you enough, telling anyone who will listen that you are nothing but a scandalous drunk.

If what I hear is true, she reminds her little circle of rumormongers as often as possible that Uncle John, the man who now speaks so charitably of you, in fact turned you out of his home given your inability—or refusal—to rein in your more unruly inclinations, or distance yourself from disreputable company.

Regrettably, there is also the unfortunate incident at the washhole near Uncle Tom's property in Troupeville, which continues to generate talk. Depending on the unrestrained extent of the taleteller's imagination, you either fired over those colored boys' heads, shot one in the back, or murdered them all.

Uncle Tom has managed to keep a watchful eye on the matter, and so far, it seems, no reports of the incident have found their way into the papers, nor has anyone from the local Negro garrison or some scalawag from the Freedman's Bureau come snuffling around.

I do not believe, however, given the constant level of tension throughout the region and the ongoing injustices of the occupation, that anyone in the family feels confident that this misfortune has been put to bed once and for all.

Thus is the general nature of what is said regarding your journey west. But you and I know the real reason you left.

If you only knew how many hours of every day I sit by myself and remember your unannounced visit here, and your shocking, stammered proposal. If you only knew how often I see again the heartbreak in your eyes as I whispered my answer, then suffered your hurtful words and watched your abrupt retreat from the house before I could compose myself and articulate my reasons.

I assure you, I do not invoke my faith out of some perverse inclination to trump your love with God's. The simple truth remains, however, that the Church forbids marriage between first cousins, no matter how profound and true their love.

Nor, as I suspect you might secretly believe, was it disdain that prompted my refusal, disdain at the wastrel turn of your nature. Yes, I could detect the air of spirits coming off your person that day, and noticed the haggard redness of your eyes.

These, however, I could forgive, thinking you needed to brace up your nerve with liquid courage. Such are the forgiving deceptions women in love indulge.

Finally, do not entertain for an instant the notion that your affliction in any way influenced my heart. On the contrary, I sometimes wonder if your consumption is not a kind of stigmata, like that bestowed on God's most beloved saints, as testament to great sacrifice made in the name of holiness — I speak of the heartfelt concern and care you showed your lovely mother as she lay in prolonged agony, awaiting her death.

I wish I had words to express how greatly that sad and lonely devotion, the greatness of heart you demonstrated in such a despairing time, carved out the place you hold in my heart. I cannot, however, turn my back on the doctrines my mother so devotedly instilled in me, in all her children. Even Father, moved by the passion of her faith, converted before he died.

I will not bore you with a recounting of all the travails she managed to endure during the war solely through the strength of her love for God, and the many benevolent signs from Him she received throughout her ordeals.

Of such small miracles and trustworthy blessings is a great faith forged. You cannot ask me to lay it aside no matter how much my heart breaks to refuse your offer of lifelong devotion.

In fact, I must confess that in your absence, my fondness and longing have only intensified. It is not just that I miss you. I fear for you, fear for your life and your soul. If I could convince myself that, as you suggested to Uncle John, your journey west was intended in part to escape the temptations that afflicted you here, and that you now intend to follow the path of rectitude, believe me, I would kneel before you like the Magdalene and wash the dust from your boots with tears of joy.

Could I marry you? I would nurse you, comfort you, devote the whole of my life and my heart to you. Please believe it. Come home. I am waiting. As much as I confide, believe me, there is always more, depths beneath the depths.

Yours forever,
Mattie

September 30, 1873

Dearest Mattie:

Please excuse my delayed response to your letter. I have moved from Dallas to pursue opportunities some eighty miles north in a railhead town named Denison. It took a while for the post to follow.

Thank you for filling me in on the general jingling as to why I left Georgia. I suppose I should not be surprised at the willingness of so many to swallow the hogwash. As Professor Varnedoe might say, quoting his beloved Livy, "The populace is like the sea, motionless in itself, but stirred by every wind, even the lightest breeze."

The idea I would have made a path to Dallas for reasons of health is particularly laughable. How could anyone be so dull as to believe the air is better here? They suffered an outbreak of yellow fever only two weeks before I arrived, and they let their pigs roam free in the streets to scarf up the horse dung. Sadly, they lack a similar methodology for the filth the hogs leave behind. Such is the meaning of hygiene in Texas.

I was moved by your professions of affection, and your offer to nurse me to the end. I asked you to share my life, however, not ready me for the grave.

Regardless of how wretched I become on account of my condition, I want to live a life that feels like life, not an ambulatory wake, pacing death's anteroom. I cannot merely wait out the end, like my lovely, unlucky mother.

Nor could I bear the thought of having to look up into my father's eyes as I breathed my last, knowing the faithless coward would claim victory in outlasting his prodigal son. I have always known that, given the puny and deformed boy I was, he would have much preferred the Spartan method of childrearing, which is to say pitching me at birth into the chasm of Apothetae.

Nor could I bear feeling you so close to my hand and heart, and yet with that scolding interloper, Holy Mother Church, playing chaperone.

Such are my reasons, along with those you identify in your letter, for leaving behind the home I once knew and striking out for the edge of nowhere.

If I may be honest, I wondered if your rejection of my offered hand, followed by your delay in writing, were not meant to stir my doubts concerning your affection, and thus intensify my ardor in proving myself worthy.

Your behest that I rectify my ways and come home also served to further clarify my understanding of how matters stand between us. In my idler moments, I have imagined us beholding each other from afar, me on my weary horse, you atop your shimmering tower, before which you have so artfully arranged a thousand dragons. Plus a pope or two.

Do not mistake my candor for bitterness. Given your letter, however, I feel compelled to confess — that word the Roman faith so cherishes — that you will likely find wanting my news on the matter of self-rectification.

Make no mistake, I arrived with every intention of following through on my promises, to you and Uncle John and everyone else. I regularly attended services at the local Methodist church and joined the local Temperance Society. I humbly apprenticed myself to the esteemed Dr. Seegar, whose stern Baptist soul glows like a furnace with good old southern sanctimony. I feel certain that my father, though a modest Presbyterian, would no doubt find the *doctor's example equal to his own in its capacity for quick and pitiless judgment.*

And there, precisely, lies the problem. The path of righteousness too greatly resembles cowing to my father.

Or, to once again invoke Livy, let us say that I am the living embodiment of the maxim that we can endure neither our vices nor the remedies for them.

First came drink, for medicinal purposes initially—patients tend to get put off when the esteemed dentist cannot take control of his cough.

It is not just disease crackling inside my chest, however. Despair abides there as well. And so one drink becomes two, two becomes three, at which point the siren call of the gambling parlor grows irresistible.

Do not take that as blame. Accuse me of pride, fair enough, but I am not so shallow as to lay fault for the state of my soul at your doorstep. That said, I also refuse to concoct a dumbshow of virtue to please those who otherwise find me repugnant, undignified, or unworthy.

I have been dealt a bad hand, Mattie, and yet refuse to leave the table, for I am enchanted by reckless chance. The only eternity I seek is that of this very moment, which is the only truth of time I know. Give me the sacrament of immediacy, the unholy reckoning of the cards and luck.

If you were here, perhaps I could resist. Let me end, then, with that plea. Damn the scandal. Come. We will marry. Convert to Methodism, my mother's faith—would that be such a tragic sin? She converted back to that faith on her deathbed, doing so for my sake, wanting me to escape the heartless doctrine of election so central to Father's Presbyterianism. "Deeds, not creeds," she whispered to me so often in her final days, urging me to live. Live! Because our actions matter. Life matters.

Do you find it otherwise? If not, why not convert as well? I cannot imagine you would blaspheme my mother's memory by claiming she lacked for kindness or grace or virtue. So would you have me believe your God would cast her down into Hell for the sake of one baptism over another? Does the Almighty really take stock of such minutiae in culling the saved from the damned? Then he's an accountant, not a Deity, and like our dear, beautiful Confederacy, not at all what we imagined.

Forgive me if my words seem harsh. It is passion, not anger, inspiring them. Please believe that. Believe as well the sincerity of my plea. Come join me here, far away from the damning eyes of nicety. We can begin anew in this place beyond history. We can live this brief, unfathomable life together. We can, finally, love.

With all my heart,
John Henry

PART II

It may easily come to pass that a vain man may become proud and imagine himself pleasing to all when he is in reality a universal nuisance.

~ *Baruch Spinoza*

$$\sim 6 \sim$$

PRIOR to boarding the flight for Tucson, if anyone had asked Rayella Vargas what her life's motto might be, she would have answered: Aim Low. Then Miss.

The only child of a seamstress who did, indeed, always seem stressed—dead at age thirty, complications from diabetes—and her father some house painter that deportation took care of, Rayella had never enjoyed much in the way of stability.

Her kind and generous but extravagantly odd Grandma Savannah never took her in, so Rayella passed from uncle to aunt, the occasional family of a friend, her life packed into a single blue suitcase.

She'd never known the privilege of beauty, either. She'd spent her middle-school years in the vicinity of cute, and for one short but delicious year in high school she'd actually qualified as hot—exotic with her coffee-colored skin, her twist-out afro, her suddenly magnetic body. But then some things kept growing while others did not.

Her center of gravity lowered. Of course, some guys loved a girl with a little jam on the roll, hefty thighs, a killer badonkadonk. But she wanted to be sleek. Impossible, not just because of the chunkiness down low.

Her face had a moonpie shape, salvaged only by the deadly eyes, which were a tawny brown, like autumn pears. That earthy pale color made them seem especially raw and open, almost scarily so.

"Like your soul's right here," Rags told her once after making love, "not deep inside but inches away, every second I look at you."

Rags—Connor Trapnell, ex-marine, bit of a train wreck himself—had provided the one good thing in her life up to now. The one thing that didn't fit with aiming low. Or missing. Then again, she hadn't been the one aiming. He had.

With his war-torn body and tripwire mind, he'd been desperately searching for just one safe place. And he'd found it, he said. He'd found her.

Together they'd found a place away from damning eyes, found it in each other's arms, and at long last allowed themselves to love, to be loved.

But it wasn't Rags looking at her now, this moment. It was the attorney, Lisa Balamaro, sitting beside her in the aisle seat, trying to explain herself.

⸺◇◇◇⸺

"I'm lucky, I guess you could say. I have the luxury of being able to choose my clients. I don't really need the money."

Rayella couldn't take her eyes off the thin jagged scar around the woman's eye. "Meaning what," she said, "you're here out of pity?"

Boom. Like she'd been kicked. "Oh. No. That's not what I mean at all."

Her voice fell off at the end. Way it does, Rayella thought, when there's no denying you're the one better off. And not that much older than me, neither.

"I mean, yes, I suppose you could say I've done okay. And my parents were well off. I never really wanted for anything."

Like it could happen to anybody.

Pretty lady, not just because she could afford to look good. Little chunky in the calves, otherwise fit and classy and nicely put together, a glow in her skin, shoulder-length hair just so, a double-breasted suit, dark blue.

But that scar . . .

"Anyway, my practice centers on artists, all kinds—"

"Musicians?" Rayella once had dreams of singing. Who didn't?

"My partner is the specialist there. Represents almost every indie band in the Bay Area, plus a handful in LA, Portland, Seattle. He's also a major player in the Sundance scene, filmmakers, people like Ryan Coogler, Cary Fukunaga."

Like I'd know who that is, Rayella thought.

"I tend to focus on the plastic arts, painters and sculptors, but some designers too. Most have been struggling a long time and have no idea about insurance or contracts or derivative rights. It's one big reason I love the work, helping them make that step up."

"And that's how you see this thing we're doing," Rayella said, "these old letters. For me, I mean. A step up."

"I suppose so, yes. Hopefully. That's what I'm aiming for."

"But as for you, it's kind of a day off. Money-wise. You ain't taking a fee."

"Don't take that to mean I'm not motivated. I am. I'll get the best price I can for the letters. For you."

"Meaning what, exactly? You never wanted for nothing, said so yourself. So how come you figure you know what's best for me?" Rayella swallowed, a little scared at being so bold. But if not now, when? This young hotshot was in charge. No crime in making her prove she deserved it. "What I'm trying to say? You ain't making anything off me but you must be making it off somebody, or I don't get it. Your folks still paying your bills?"

For some reason, that made the lawyer smile again, but not as though she was amused.

"Not my place to pry, I suppose," Rayella said, breaking the silence.

"It's okay. You don't know me. I'm handling something of considerable value to you." She nodded at the small black case beneath the seat in front of her. The curious *old letters* Grandma Savannah had left. "I'm happy to give you a little background. Increase your comfort level."

One of the flight attendants bustled past, gloved-up to collect trash. They passed theirs over, notched up their trays.

The lady lawyer said, "Whatever you need to hear to help you make peace with me, with what I'm doing on your behalf, the whole situation, anything, just ask."

Seemed like a decent plan, Rayella thought. Make peace all around—with this woman, this business, Grandma Savannah's strange, bats-in-the-attic love, not to mention the gift she left behind. Make peace with things finally breaking your way, the luxury of that. Join the Death Made Me Lucky Club. For once in your life, aim high.

BY the time Lisa and Rayella reached the Whetstone Inn—twenty miles northwest of Tombstone, at the end of a winding dirt road pitted with rocks—they almost felt acclimated to the strangely intense February sunlight.

"Welcome to the middle of nuthin," Rayella said as Lisa slowed the rental car in a cloud of dust.

The building had the hand-built feel of Pueblo Revival—stucco walls painted sandstone beige with protruding redwood *vigas* along the roofline, rough-hewn window lintels, and porch supports.

The landscaping consisted of smooth brown pebbles scattered around isolated aloe and agave plants, plus a few mesquite and Palo Verde trees, here and there a tussock of chaparral sage.

"Yes," Lisa said. "I was expecting something a bit closer to civilization."

They got out of the car and hurried to the welcoming shade of the porch, then the vestibule within. The interior had a more welcoming feel—exposed redwood beams, sandstone pavers with Navajo rugs and brightly colored Mexican tile for accent. A wall-mounted coatrack fashioned from antlers crowned a rust-spotted mirror.

The narrow entry opened onto a large room furnished with low-slung leather chairs and sofas. Center stage, however, belonged to a long wood table of rough-hewn plank, at the shadowy end of which, backlit by harsh sunlight, a lone male figure sat.

"How do," the faceless stranger said. "Welcome to the Whetstone."

He rose from his chair and made way toward them, walking with an awkward forward lean, as though trying to catch some faint or distant sound. He wore a plaid shirt with western piping, the sleeves rolled up to his forearms.

He looked back and forth between the two women, offering an uncertain smile, then settled his eyes on Lisa. "You must be Miss Ballymaroo."

"Balamaro," Lisa said, offering her hand. "This is Rayella Vargas."

He shook Lisa's hand with a limp grip, nodded to Rayella, then turned toward the eastern wing of the inn and pointed the way. "Got a room here where you can rest a bit and freshen up. Judge called, said he's running late."

❖

Once in the room, Rayella dropped her purse on the floor and did a back-dive onto the bed, bouncing twice on the white duvet, arms outstretched.

"I feel like a big bag of dust."

"The desert will do that." Lisa pushed back her suit jacket sleeve, checked her watch. "I'm going to go out and wait for the buyer, this judge. Make yourself at home."

Rayella, still flat on her back, offered a listless wave. "Don't worry, I won't raid the minibar."

"Who said I was worried? Knock yourself out. If there is one."

Rayella shot up on one elbow. "I can get tanked?"

Lisa checked her phone for any missed calls or messages. "No. That wouldn't be wise. I'm going to need you sharp when we close."

"Sharp as a razor, bright as a laser." Rayella smiled wistfully, staring at the white linen curtains flaring with sunlight. "Grandma Savannah used to say that."

Back in the large open room off the entry, Lisa helped herself to water from a heavy glass pitcher swimming with lemon slices. Taking a seat in a low leather chair, she settled the Pelican case between her feet, opened her computer case, took out her laptop, and booted up. Stagecraft. Look busy.

Shortly the proprietor, if that was what he was, shuffled up from somewhere. "I can show you to the conference room if you'd like."

Lisa nodded at the long ancient table. "We won't be meeting here?"

"I'd imagine you don't want folks walking in on your meeting."

The place couldn't have seemed more deserted. "I didn't see any cars outside when I drove—"

"There's a couple from Cheyenne due in this afternoon. Can't tell when they'll show up. And knowing the judge, he'll want things private."

The man hovered over her. Dark hair cut close, a weathered face. "By the way, your name is?"

"You can call me Phin."

"Okay. Phin. Thank you. If you don't mind, I'll wait here, unless that's . . . "

"Fine with me. Judge knows his way around the place. Ought to, he paid for it." He headed toward the back door. "I'm gonna see to some things. Need me, just poke your head out the door, give out a holler."

———◇◇◇———

Ten minutes passed. Then fifteen. Finally, the sound of tires crushing gravel outside, a car engine throttling down into silence.

When the front door opened, the man who entered wore "lawyer" like a sandwich sign: moussed hair, Italian suit, Cartier sunglasses. A few years younger than Lisa had expected. Worse, instead of courtroom gravitas, he possessed the casual, chin-jutting pomp of a backwater narcissist.

Lisa closed her laptop and rose to her feet. "Judge Littmann?"

The man turned toward her voice. No smile. No movement forward.

So that's how this will go, she thought. Lovely. She put her laptop away, collected the Pelican case with the letters inside and walked over.

Extending her hand, she repeated, "Judge Littmann?"

The man offered a pained smile. "Name's Don Rankin. I'll be representing the judge in this."

That wasn't the arrangement, Lisa thought. Then a second man walked in.

This one was shorter, thicker—chestnut hair slicked back, tan linen suit with dark pinstripes, blue suede bucks. He wore several rings on each thick hand. His head narrowed near the top, as though the family gene pool favored jaw over cranium.

He sidled up next to Rankin and assumed position—spreading his feet, gripping one wrist with the opposite hand—staring straight into Lisa's eyes as though to say: C'mon, bitch. Gimme good reason.

Lisa, mustering as straight a face as possible, said, "And this is . . . ?"

"Mister Giordano is my associate," Rankin said.

How nice for both of you, Lisa thought. "I understand there's a conference room here, and you know where it is?"

Shortly the three of them were sitting in strangely incongruous chrome and leather swivel chairs, staring across a cherry veneer table.

As though to make up for the lack of thematic coherence with the rest of the inn, the walls bore posters from famous westerns—*The Far Country, Decision at Sundown, The Naked Spur*—while at the table's center, a tiny saguaro cactus rose like a bristly flagman from an earthenware cup.

Stretching out his hand, Rankin said, "Let's see the letters." Giordano, sitting to his left, swiveled mindlessly back and forth.

Lisa sat back, working through what she intended to say, what she intended not to say. She felt vaguely foolish not having seen this coming, wondering if Tuck had. And if so, why hadn't he told her about it?

"You did bring the fucking letters?" This from Giordano.

Lisa refused the clown so much as a glance. "Tell you what," she said, directing the words at Rankin. "How about we start this off with you convincing me I didn't waste my time coming all this way."

Giordano started snapping his fingers, like he was trying to wake her up. "You deaf? Don said it. I said it. Show us the goddamn letters."

Rankin remained silent, brushing away an imaginary tuft of lint.

It wasn't until that moment she noticed the flat, glassy absence in Giordano's eyes, as though he'd just come from the taxidermist.

"Okay," Lisa said. "Here's how it is. Mister Rankin, you tell your 'associate' here that Halloween's still eight months off, but if he really wants to trick-or-treat as Fredo Corleone, I can introduce him to the uncle of my senior prom date, Michael Lancelotti. You know, Mikey Lance, from South Philly? Help him raise his game."

Giordano shot up so fast his chair hit the wall behind him. "You think you can talk like that to my fucking face?"

"Mister Rankin?"

"I want to see the letters," Rankin said.

"You get this fool out of here, or I walk. Let Judge Littmann decide whose fault it is he lost his chance."

"You call me a fucking fool?"

Giordano looked ready to come across the table, but Lisa just sat there, looking at Rankin. Yeah, she was alone against the two of them in the middle of nowhere. But Nico knew where she was, the car rental company did as well, this meeting was no secret. These two couldn't afford to make that dumb a move.

Besides, she told herself, the Giordanos of the world, they're just noise. And she really did date Mikey Lance's nephew. Well, sort of. She got wasted with him at the Rittenhouse after the prom, and judging from the state of things when she sobered up, she'd had sex with him, too.

Not just him. Two of his friends. And his fiancée.

Finally, Rankin held out an arm, checking his partner. "Bobby? Do me a favor."

"Nah, nah, Don, c'mon, I'm not—"

"It's okay. Really. Wait for me."

Giordano took a deep frowning breath, then made a show of casually buttoning his linen jacket as he headed for the door, mad-dogging Lisa with those empty eyes the entire way.

Once the door clicked shut behind him, Rankin said, "If it were up to me . . . " A helpless shrug. "Now—ready to get serious?"

~ 8 ~

"**B**EFORE this goes any further," Lisa said, "I need to hear from the judge himself that you act on his authority."

Rankin offered an indulgent smile. "Fair enough." He began to fish around inside his suit jacket for his phone.

"Let's use mine," Lisa said, producing her cell. "I've got the number. The judge and I spoke last night."

She'd already entered the judge's information into her contacts file, programming the number for speed dial. Rankin watched as she thumbed in the code, waited for the connection. Fourth ring, someone picked up.

"Ms. Balamaro."

The miracle of caller ID. The voice was chesty and rough as a saw but educated. More to the point: familiar.

"Judge Littmann."

"Good to hear from you. I trust you arrived safely."

"Yes, I'm here with—"

"Don, I know. So sorry I couldn't come myself, but something came up rather abruptly here at Bristlecone. One of my best broodmares threw a shoe, and the loose nail dug right up high through the hoof. Had to wrap it in a gamgee, then turn her out to pasture for a bit, see how she walked. Been waiting for the farrier ever since, get a new shoe on her. Sorry to inconvenience you."

If that's all just a story, Lisa thought, it's a winner. "Will you be coming anytime soon?"

"There a problem?"

She looked across the table at Rankin, who was looking back across the table at her. Both smiled.

"I wouldn't say a problem. Call it a preference. I take it he's your lawyer?"

"Don wears a number of hats. My counselor, in the broadest sense. The point, as far as you and I are concerned, is that he has my total confidence."

The room seemed to shrink a little. "Does he now." Muffled background voices. Spirited nicker from a horse. The judge said, "I gather you don't share my opinion."

"It's not that. I just always prefer, in an exchange this significant, that buyer and seller meet face to face. Ms. Vargas is here."

More muffled noise, like the phone had been pressed against the man's shirt as he spoke to someone nearby. Then the judge came back on the line. "All right. Let me see what I can do. Like I said, I'm waiting for the farrier, and I know this may seem a little hands-on but this old girl won me a couple of purses, fat ones. Since then she's delivered nine good foals. I'm not handing her over to some sale-barn vet. Worse, a slaughter truck. Not my style."

"Should we wait?"

"No, no. Like I said, Don knows my business. You two kick it around a while, throw out some numbers. I'm sure I can step in and pick up wherever he leaves off."

Lisa ended the call, tucked her phone back into her pocket. Rankin, easing back and forth in his swivel chair, said, "Happy now?"

❖

Lisa placed the Pelican case on the table, thumbed in the combination, waited for the pop of the clasp. She removed two pairs of cotton gloves from inside the case, slipping one on, offering the other to Rankin.

He didn't reach for them, choosing instead to just sit there — gnomish smile, twiddling his thumbs, eyeing her like she was some carnival magician passing through town to hoodwink the rubes.

She removed the velvet packet from the hard-shell case, loosened the knot in the faded ribbon, and gently unbundled the letters.

"They're in chronological order," she said, turning them so the addresses and postmarks faced away. "Oldest, first."

Rankin wasn't looking at the letters. He was looking at her.

"Here's what I think," he said. "No way in hell those are real. Only an idiot would think so."

Neither of them moved. "The starting point of the negotiation," Lisa said finally, "is that authenticity can't be guaranteed. And is therefore irrelevant."

He chuckled. "You're dreaming." He sat forward finally and eyed the letters, but his gaze suggested he thought the real thing of value lay somewhere else. He still made no move for the gloves. "Can't believe the judge is wasting his time with this."

She smiled obligingly. "Yes, but unless I'm mistaken, that's not your call."

"First, the Holliday family says these don't exist, and no matter how many hoops the judge jumps through, how many experts he hires, how many tests they run — and all that costs money — it'll still be the word of a nun, a veritable saint according to the family, against a bunch of hustlers and pinheads."

Okay, she thought. Deep breath. "Perhaps even a nun," she said, "had reasons to shade the truth."

"My point," he said, "is all that front-end cost, paying the freight to figure out if these things are even old enough to be credible, let alone real, falls on the judge."

"I'm not denying that."

"Let's think this through for a minute." He clasped his hands behind his head, continuing to rock back and forth in his chair. "There are at least two ways I've come up with just over the past few hours as to who could have forged those letters and why."

"It's our position," she said, "that forgery is not at issue."

"First, the more boring of the theories, concerns the woman your client's great-great- grandwhatever worked for."

"You mean Sophie Walton Murphy."

"The slave."

"Former slave."

"She worked for a member of the Holliday family."

"Mary Cowperthwaite Fulton Holliday."

Rankin pointed. Bingo. "That's the one." Shaking his head. "Talk about a mouthful. Like names are wings. More you got, higher you fly."

"She was the wife of Doc Holliday's cousin Robert."

Tuck had mentioned this woman, who possessed her own peculiar intrigue.

She married into the family in 1884, long after Doc had departed for the West, and so only knew of him secondhand—what the family passed along, what she read in the papers. Her children and grandchildren remembered her being utterly appalled at having to acknowledge Doc even existed, let alone that there was some blood tie.

Then again, other facts seemed to indicate she wasn't scandalized at all. Quite the opposite. She was fascinated. Even obsessed. Though times were hard for a while after her husband died, by the late 1920s she'd come into money again and was living her dream, hanging out at the Algonquin in New York.

Rankin said, "She shot the breeze with all these snoots in New York."

"Eugene O'Neill," Lisa responded. "Among others." Like Dorothy Parker, Tallulah Bankhead, Noel Coward.

"And she had that Negro woman with her."

"Correct."

"She also had a granddaughter." Rankin began massaging his knuckles, as though it helped him think. "This granddaughter was engaged to a Swedish writer named Carl Olson—that's a fact, look it up—and this guy and Grandma talked about Doc Holliday day and night. Olson was fascinated, interviewed Grandma and the Negro, wrote it all down, and those notes became the basis for a biography."

"I know all this."

"Well, Olson and Grandma Holliday talked about writing a novel together, too. About her wicked dentist cousin by marriage."

"You think she and Olson wrote these letters instead of the novel."

Rankin shrugged. "It's a distinct possibility."

"Not as distinct as the reality," Lisa said, "which is my client inherited them from her own grandmother, who collected a safe deposit box that previously belonged—"

Rankin brushed past her. "Theory number two—you know Doc Holliday was related to the woman who wrote *Gone With the Wind*?"

Lisa sighed. The man had the world's most obvious mind. "Margaret Mitchell."

"Her second husband was a copy editor. First husband beat her, or so she said, but who believes a writer? Anyway, her and Hubby Number Two collaborated on a number of projects—dirty books, even—when they were scrabbling for money before she hit it big. The husband destroyed most of those papers after she died in that car accident."

"You're saying *they* forged these letters."

"For the money. And the husband intended to burn them later. But . . ."

"Boy, for a bunch of letters that are sitting right there, they sure have been through their share of fires."

"You're not listening."

"You think any of that's more plausible than what I've already explained about how these letters were discovered?"

"I'm saying that as long as there's that many plausible theories as to where these things came from, any value they have is a moving target, and the trajectory is down."

Lisa felt a vein in her neck start throbbing. Calm down, she thought. Be patient. The chucklehead's just maneuvering. "How far down, exactly, is 'down'?"

Finally, Rankin reached for the gloves but didn't put them on. He just fingered them, smiling, as though they were the punch line. "Five hundred, tops. And that's just go-away money. Because, like I said, only an idiot would fall for this nonsense."

~ 9 ~

A N hour passed and nothing Lisa said — no evidence she mustered, no logic she availed, not even a random reading from the letters themselves — could move Rankin off his laughable number. The man just kept circling back to the same old objections, the same stories, like a kid with his hands clasped over his ears yodeling gibberish.

She was about to call for a break, check in with Rayella — hoping she'd kept her word concerning the minibar, though given how much time had passed it would be easily forgivable if she hadn't — when a brisk knock came from the hallway outside.

Lisa presumed it was Giordano, coming back to tag-team — and, oh, how he'd been missed — but instead, as the door eased open, a taller, slightly older, more impressive man appeared.

From her research online, Lisa recognized the face, strangely at odds with his grizzled phone voice. The man had broad, handsome features, the skin smoother than she expected given the sun's brutality down here, with quick green eyes and a manly smile. His russet hair bore touches of gray, but nothing else about him suggested more than middle-age. He wore a plaid range shirt tucked into jeans beneath a tweed sports jacket. Loafers not boots, Lisa noticed, not sure what to make of that, given all the talk about thrown shoes and broodmares. Maybe they were barn loafers.

"Excuse my interruption." That incongruous rasp of a voice. The judge leaned across the table. "You must be Lisa."

"Judge Littmann." They shook hands. "Nice of you to come."

The judge took a chair beside Rankin and eyed the letters scattered across the table. Glancing up to Lisa: "May I?"

"Of course."

Rankin handed him his pair of cotton gloves, still unused, and the judge tugged them on. With gentle, meticulous care he picked up the nearest letter and eased up the flap, peering inside before nursing the small worn sheets of paper from their envelope. His green eyes warmed as he folded the pages back, began to read.

He continued in silence, moving on to the second page with a smile, whispering, "How marvelous . . . "

Lisa, heartened by this, glanced across the table at Rankin, who seemed to be drifting into a nap, slouching in his chair, eyelids shuttering.

The judge folded the pages over again, slid them back inside their envelope, then clasped his hands before him on the table. "So—where do we stand?"

Rankin sat up straight, blinking his way back from the land of nod. Lisa said, "We've so far merely agreed to disagree on the value—"

"That so?" The judge studied Rankin with imperious curiosity. Rankin shrugged. "Value," the judge said, turning back to Lisa. "How many letters in all?"

"Forty-six," Lisa said.

"Nice round number." The judge smiled broadly, but the warmth in his eyes had fled. "Let's be adults about this, shall we? These letters—I have to admit, they're more, well, charming than I expected—but what of it? They're at best a curiosity, a kind of party favor. Something you drag out over brandy for a laugh, like the fake jade cobras they sell the yokels on Patpong Road."

"I tried to tell her," Rankin said, backhanding a yawn.

Lisa felt lightheaded, as though gravity—and her pride—had lost their hold. "In that case," she said, "I'd say a meeting of the minds looks out of the question. Sorry to have put you to any trouble."

She stood and opened the Pelican case, began to collect the letters. The judge reached out and stopped her, a two-finger tap on the wrist.

"Give me just a moment."

He rummaged inside the tweed jacket and collected a phone, hit speed dial. Instead of putting it to his ear, he watched the display screen, squinting with concentration. When an image appeared, he nodded approvingly.

Passing the phone across the table, he said, "I trust you're acquainted with FaceTime."

Lisa took the phone and looked at the screen. The image puzzled her for a second, for though she recognized Rayella her head was lowered—until a hand yanked it up by the hair.

Several strips of red tape sealed her mouth. A florid bruise darkened one cheek, punctuated by a thin gash, possibly left by a ring, now seeping blood. Lisa couldn't make out whoever had hold of her—the phone was held too close to her face—but she had to assume there were two men, at least, there with her in the room. Giordano and Phin.

Or were there others here as well—if so, how many?

Tears had caused Rayella's mascara to streak. Her amber eyes, normally so vivid and huge, seemed hazed, almost sleepy, as though from denial or disbelief. Maybe she was dizzy from the punch to her head, maybe they'd drugged her. Maybe she just wanted to close her eyes, make it all go away.

"It appears," the judge said, "you were wrong about who you could fool."

Lisa shot out of her chair, but the judge, with almost preternatural calm, said, "Don't. You'll only get the girl hurt worse. That can be arranged, I assure you. Now sit back down, please."

Lisa, at a loss for what else to do, obeyed. Rankin stood up, the eager lieutenant, and began collecting the letters. "Thing you gotta love about these old places?" He offered a wily smile. "No surveillance cameras." Not bothering with the gloves, he tossed the envelopes into the Pelican case like so much trash.

"Those don't belong to you," Lisa said, directing the words at Littmann. "They belong to the girl you've kidnapped."

He responded, "Ms. Balamaro, if you haven't figured this out by now, let me make it plain. These letters don't even exist." The judge slipped the phone back into his pocket. "As for the girl, she's fine, I assure you. Nothing much disturbed but her delusions."

"Yeah, that's just what it looked like."

"Spare me the theatrics, Ms. Balamaro. Now I'm sure you'll think about contacting the sheriff. Just understand, I'm a man with considerable influence in this area. I have many friends at every level, and my word goes a long way. The same cannot be said for you. You and that spic-a-boo you dragged along for window dressing are outsiders. And though it blew up on you pretty badly, you came here, let's be honest, with criminal intent."

"That's pretty rich, coming from you."

"Nothing so clearly signals weakness," the judge said, "as a tone of indignity. Now wisdom would dictate you minimize your losses and go back where you came from— quickly, quietly. I trust I'm understood."

With that, he rose, gestured for Rankin to lead the way, and followed him toward the door.

The tiny two-armed saguaro in its earthen pot seemed to wave goodbye.

Before slipping out, the judge turned back and offered Lisa one last easy smile.

"You let your friend Tuck Mercer know, him and me? This is just a start. We're nowhere close to even."

August 11, 1876

My Dearest John Henry:

Something happened here today of which I felt you should be informed. Two men from the Pinkerton Agency appeared at Uncle John's house in Atlanta, hoping to confirm that a Denver man they know as Tom Mackey is, in fact, you.

They offered no information beyond that, veiling the exact nature of their inquiry behind the repeated statement that their interest lay merely in establishing whether you and this Tom Mackey are, in fact, one and the same man.

Well, as you know, though Uncle John prides himself on his manners, he is no fool. No one assumes a false name, even one as transparent to his family as the one you have apparently chosen for yourself, unless trouble is snapping at his heels.

While on the one hand wanting to offer as much cooperation as possible, and yet on the other wishing you no harm, Uncle John told the men they might be confused.

He informed them of your mother's brother, Tom McKey, who could not possibly be relevant to their interest as he has never traveled west of Cuthbert, Georgia, where he served with the Fifth Georgia Volunteers as the field hospital's ward master. He went on to explain that since the war's end Tom has lived on the Banner Plantation near the Georgia-Florida line. Indeed, he was married just this past March to a Miss Sadie Allen of Valdosta and resides there with his newlywed bride.

The agents indulged this bit of pettifoggery with stony patience, then asked if there might be a photograph of you in the family's possession that they might view in order to settle the matter conclusively.

Now, you may wonder how I come to know all this firsthand. As it turns out, I happen to be staying with Uncle John and Aunt Permelia at the moment. They invited me down to meet some people in their circle involved in the local schools, for they are aware of my own wish to teach.

Aunt Permelia offered to show the agents the family album. However, before she could rise from her chair, I insisted on retrieving it for her, so she could remain with her guests.

When I found it, I madly scoured the pages for any photograph bearing your image. There was but one, and I removed it, slipping it beneath my dress before returning to the siting room.

The two agents flipped through the album with Aunt Permelia looking on, providing names when they inquired. Though Uncle John withstood all this with stoical nonchalance, I could sense he wished that his dear wife would just bite her tongue. That was nowhere more evident than when she came to the page where your picture once rested, and now only a blank spot remained. I feared terribly she would blurt out something thoughtless, but she just squinted quizzically and then moved on.

Once they had scanned the album twice without success, she innocently confessed to a sense of puzzlement, for she felt almost certain that she and Uncle John had possessed a photograph of you.

That was when one of the agents glanced up and nailed me in place with his stare.

He was a hard man with a square face and blank, heavy-lidded eyes, normally so suggestive of low morals and scant intelligence. But this man's gaze was cold. Even though I knew he could do nothing — what recourse did he have, demand I strip in order to search my person? — my heart pounded so savagely within my breast that I felt certain he and everyone else in the room could not help but hear it.

Finally, the other agent handed the album back and thanked Aunt and Uncle for their assistance. Only then did Agent Square-Face turn away, doing so with an insinuating smile. Shortly after that, the two men left. As yet, they have not returned.

You can imagine our state when we were once again alone.

Aunt Permelia, whose sensitivity to scandal remains acute, could hardly contain herself, wondering what terrible mischief or even outright evil has ensnared you.

Uncle John came to your defense, if somewhat abstractly, leaning on family honor and reminding us all that you remain, after all, a Holliday.

I said nothing. I have, as you requested, told no one of your reckless misadventures, or what I know of them from your scant correspondence of late. Even your letters' existence remains secret, though it pains my very soul to admit such a thing.

My concern for you and the state of your life has become almost unbearable. I fear I am fooling myself, living not just a lie but a kind of bitter joke, where every noble inclination is corrupted by vain sentiment. What I think is devotion and honest love in fact boils with corrupting, selfish sin, to which I remain avidly unaware.

I cannot live like this. I cannot keep spinning about in place like a witless dervish. I need to reclaim my hold on truth, or go mad.

Do not take lightly the loving concern of your family — not just me but Uncle John, who so ably demonstrated this afternoon he still seeks to love and protect you, in spite of whatever misfortune such devotion may bring to his door.

You would be safe here among your own, even if you stay only briefly. We will not betray you, no matter how grave your trouble. Besides, wittingly or not, you have now enlisted us all in your affairs. Do you not owe us the grace of your company?

Regardless, I will always stand by you with steadfast faith and loyalty. There is nothing you could ever do to change that.

Your loving cousin,
Mattie

~ 10 ~

THEY stopped at a quickie mart to tend to Rayella's cheek—dabbing away the dried blood with a wet tissue, using hand sanitizer for an antiseptic. Lisa went inside hoping to find something to help bring down the swelling, settling in the end on a pint of Häagen-Dazs, since there was nothing in the realm of frozen peas to be had, not even tater tots, and the only actual ice available came in rock-solid five-pound bags.

Using a napkin to protect her hand from frostbite, Rayella held the freezing carton to her face as they continued south to Sierra Vista, the county seat, a sun-blasted grid of strip malls and tract homes and crumbling adobe hovels sprawled across the foot of the Huachuca Mountains.

Lisa intended to file a complaint with the Cochise County Sheriff, naming all of them—Rankin, Giordano, Littmann, the innkeeper Phin, plus John Does 1-10 for any co-conspirators yet to be identified—for conspiracy, kidnapping, robbery, aggravated assault.

The first bad sign appeared in the form of the deputy who took down their information—a face hardened by desert sun perched atop a landslide of flab, the gut overhang straining the lower buttons of his tan service blouse. Lardscrabble, Lisa thought, watching as, with ho-hum languor, he wrote out her words in childlike letters, the popping of his gum punctuated now and then with a chesty sigh.

The second bad sign came when they got led back to an interrogation room, not a detective's cubicle. Smelling of ammonia and something vaguely repellent not even disinfectant could disguise, the space was cramped, windowless, with yellow-gray walls.

Ever so faintly, in the pitted concrete next to her chair, Lisa could make out the words, written in pencil: *Wetback Penthouse.*

The third bad sign was the wait—half an hour, still nothing. Lisa was preparing to go out and raise hell, make a scene only an Italian girl from Philly can, when the fourth bad sign materialized.

He was a lanky man in a sport coat and slacks, white western shirt, no tie, his badge in a flip wallet tucked into his breast pocket. As though to assure them of his local bona fides, he also wore Tony Lama cowboy boots and a Stetson. Pulling back a chair, he rested the high-crowned hat on the table and sat.

"My name's Jim Preston," he said. Flinty voice, lupine eyes. His graying hair bore a deep oval crease, imprint from his hatband, a kind of southwestern halo. "I head up the

Investigation Division. You two ladies aren't from around here, that right?"

It went straight downhill from there. The man wasn't rude or dismissive or hostile, he just kept coming back to the same unhelpful refrain: "Given what I'm hearing, no offense, but this just seems to me like a civil matter, not criminal."

Lisa said, for what felt like the thousandth time, "Look—letters of historical, personal, and monetary value were taken by force from my client. Look at her face. She was bound and beaten, threatened verbally in the most disgusting, humiliating terms."

She stopped short of specifics, preferring to have a woman deputy hear out that part of the ordeal. Meanwhile, Rayella seemed adrift, staring at nothing as the voices buzzed around her. She'd tossed the melting pint of ice cream in the trash, but a shimmer of dampness remained on her dark puffy cheek. The razor-thin cut left by Giordano's ring etched a jagged line across the purplish, knot-sized bruise.

"The man who runs the Whetstone, this Phin person, went to her room pretending that I wanted her to join us in the negotiation. But once she cracked the door, he and this Giordano creature force their way in, coldcock her, bind her hands behind her back, and—"

"I read the report," Preston said. "But try to understand. There's just too much he-said-she- said for me to move forward. Judge Littmann maintains you came here to shake him down. That's also a crime, you know."

"You've talked to him *already*?"

"Miss Balamaro—am I saying that right?"

"I demand those letters back," Lisa said. "And, really, shake him *down*?"

"He says those letters are worthless. And that you know it."

"If they're worthless, why offer five-hundred—"

"And he says Ms. Vargas here was perfectly fine when she left the Whetstone."

"That's a blatant goddamn lie."

Ever so slightly, the lawman flinched at Lisa's cursing. "All the men who were there back him up."

"Ah, the men, yes. Men you know, I assume."

Preston leaned forward, elbows on the table, and narrowed his gaze into hers. Spreading his hands, as though to reveal the big ball of nothing they held: "Something happened, I'll grant you that, but I have two credible and irreconcilable versions of just what that was. I book one of you, I gotta book you all. And where does that leave us?"

Lisa sat back, arms crossed. "You know, he told me this would happen. Judge Littmann, I mean."

Preston gathered his hat, rose from his chair. "I got called away from a crime scene for this. Three illegals, one just a girl, burned up in a fire at a safe house just outside Gleeson. Coroner's people were waiting for the cinders to cool so they could go on in, bag up the dead, when I got the call to come here, sit with you all." For the first time, he looked squarely at Rayella. "Time I got back out there. Now I really do wish I could help you. But honestly? I think your best bet is civil court."

——◄◇►——

They drove back to Tucson, gazing out through the bug-smeared windshield in silence, just a brief discussion of the plan from that point on, such as it was. For the most part, Rayella said nothing, squinting into the sunset as the car sped west along I-10, the highway a blade of asphalt carving the relentless desert in two.

Lisa booked two rooms at a resort spa in the Catalina foothills on the northeast corner of the city, figuring Rayella could use a little pampering given what she'd been through. She seemed to be bearing up okay but those eyes of hers, normally so raw and availing, apparently made a pact with her tongue to keep everyone out, reveal nothing.

The resort grounds—trellised bougainvillea and potted bird of paradise, manicured beds of violet pasque flowers and California poppy—passed in a leaden blur as they trudged toward their rooms.

Lisa said, "Look, I mean it, anything you want—dinner in bed, facial, full massage—it's on my card."

Rayella nodded then vanished into her room, the immediate slam of the deadbolt making it clear what she wanted was to feel safe, nothing more.

——◄◇►——

In her own room, alone for the first time in hours, Lisa stripped off her clothes and stepped beneath a scalding hot shower, trying to scrub off the shame.

74

She'd only brought the one suit to wear, expecting to return home that night, so had nothing else but the terrycloth robe on the wall hook, a resort perk, to change into as she brushed her wet hair, then rinsed out her blouse, pitted and rank from nervous sweat. After hanging it up on the shower rod to dry, she repeated the routine with her undies. If they were still wet come morning, she'd hit them with the hairdryer. She'd done it before.

Barefoot, naked beneath the thick white robe, she ironed her skirt and jacket, to make sure she didn't look like some vagabond when she had to face the world again.

Finally, all these minor tasks done, she geared herself up for the thing she'd been dreading most. The phone felt like a lead pipe in her hand as she hit speed dial. Four trilling rings in the static hiss. Then the crackling snap of the connection.

"Hey, Leezle-Diesel! Wondered when you'd call. So how'd it go?"

Feathery tremble of her hand against her lips, trying to hold it all in.

"Oh, Nico," she whispered. "I screwed up so bad."

ONCE Lisa explained the full extent of the debacle, Nico told her to fire up her laptop. They'd hammer out strategy over the phone.

"Given what I've heard so far, you want nothing to do with the local courts."

"Pretty much, yeah. Extra points for understatement."

Phone tucked in her shoulder, she poured herself a tall glass of ice water, picturing Nico at the other end, sipping a Napa pinot blanc, dressed in frumpy sweats with holes at the knees, a T-shirt from some up-and-coming indie band he represented. The ponytail, the soul patch.

"You can sue in federal court as long as the tortious act took place in the district where you're filing."

"Tucson governs all of southwest Arizona. I already checked."

"You'll base your argument on diversity jurisdiction — defendants are Arizona citizens, but the plaintiff resides in California."

"For a second there, I could've sworn you said 'perversity jurisdiction.'"

"It's probably what I meant."

"I've checked the local rules, and it looks like I need to file a formal *pro hac vice* application, show my license is in good standing, blah, blah, blah, and it can take up to three days before—"

"Don't sweat it. I've had the thing granted when I just showed up with my bar card. Given what happened here, the risk of damage to personal property, and the fact you're seeking emergency relief, I can't imagine that won't get waived."

Assuming I'm lucky, she thought. It seemed like a very long time since she'd felt a favorable wind at her back.

"If you haven't done it already, you need to draft an ex parte application for injunctive relief, keep these yahoos from destroying the letters, selling them to someone else, whatever."

"That was the first thing I thought of. Yeah. Threat of immediate and irreparable loss or damage. It's pretty much done."

"Good. Great. You included a request for an escrow holder pending trial?"

"Yeah. Yeah." Don't get defensive, she told herself. He's not browbeating you.

"Okay, getting back to the complaint, jurisdiction, you'll need to argue the amount in controversy exceeds seventy-five thousand dollars."

She swallowed what felt like a thumb. "Between you and me? I have no clue what those letters are really worth."

"Get Hunk—I'm sorry, Tuck—get him to give you an affidavit based on his 'expert knowledge of historical artifacts' or whatever."

"We've been thinking it would be best to keep him out of this, given his background."

"Well, think again. If you don't bring him forward, they will."

She remembered Littmann's parting remark—'*You let Tuck Mercer know . . . We're nowhere close to even*' —still no clue what he meant. "Right. Of course."

"Remember, you're not just seeking the return of the letters, you're seeking damages—not legal fees, they're barred—but travel costs, airfare, car rental, include the hotel you're at right now, any—"

"Wait—I can't claim damages add to the value of the letters."

"That's not the issue. The value of the letters is only part of the amount in controversy. Damages is the rest. Including the cost of any medical treatment your client needs."

"She didn't want any. Made it sound like it's not the first time she's been hit."

"You may want to talk her out of that attitude. A blow to the head's no joke."

Lisa felt her heart sink a little more. "Will do."

"There's also an intangible property issue, based on what's *in* the letters. This is where you can pump up the intrinsic value of the letters themselves. The merger doctrine allows you to incorporate historical value, emotional value. More important, potential commercial value—the rights if they become the basis for a book, movie, TV series. Might be your strongest argument, especially if anything happens to the letters."

She gathered the robe more tightly around her, morbidly picturing one or two candidates for the anything that could happen.

"The letters were a gift from the client's—"

"Rayella's."

"—grandmother. Okay, Rayella, fine. Sorry. There's your emotional value. And the historical value's obvious."

"Even if they're fake?"

"I seem to recall a certain someone mentioning a brilliant astronomer who got hornswoggled into paying good money for letters written by Mary Magdalene in French."

"That's market value. People will buy anything."

"If market value's not relevant, what is?"

"I've got to prove this up before a judge. Not some motivated Frenchman."

"Let me tell you a story."

In the background, she heard the opening of the fridge, the quick squeal and pop of a cork on an already opened bottle, the familiar glug of a filling glass. It awoke within her a deep nostalgic longing etched with terror. The old days. The previous her. Always there, always waiting for the chance—

"I read about this just today online," he said, the thud of the closing fridge door for punctuation. "Your situation made me curious."

Situation, she thought. The word every girl longs to hear.

"Back in the eighteenth century, a man named James McPherson produced a manuscript in old Scottish Gaelic. He identified it as the work of an ancient Celtic bard who called himself Ossian, which is a variant of Oisín, the name of a legendary soldier-poet and the son of Fionn mac Cumhaill."

At the sound of the name, she unwittingly flinched, for it called to mind the hotel owner, Phin. The bitterness of the memory only intensified with the hip-sounding surname, which struck her ear as "McCool."

"For whatever reason," Nico went on, "the Celtic Britons left behind hardly any archeological evidence of their existence. There were oral stories transcribed by monks but nothing original. And so *The Poems of Ossian* caused quite a stir. Helped launch the Romantic Movement, took the blame for a few revolutions, too. Got translated into dozens of languages—Goethe did the job in German himself. Napoleon commissioned Ingres to paint *The Dream of Ossian* for the Quirinal Palace in Rome, but the Pope found it a little too salaciously pagan."

"I love that word," Lisa said. "Salacious, I mean. Pagan's not half bad either." Her thoughts were drifting. She doubted she'd ever felt more tired.

"Anyway, not everyone fell for the whole Ossian thing. Samuel Johnson came right out and called McPherson a fraud. People argued back and forth for about fifty years, but that didn't keep writers from gushing about it—or imitating it. Not hacks, either. Blake, Thoreau, Byron. James Fennimore Cooper claimed he *wasn't* influenced by it, but apparently he's as lousy a liar as he is a novelist."

"I kinda liked *The Last of the Mohicans*."

"The book?"

"Okay, no. Got me. I thought the movie was pretty okay. Nice love story."

Silence.

"Back to Ossian?"

"Sorry."

"Mendelssohn, Schubert, Brahms all wrote music inspired by the thing. German and Scandinavian royalty named their sons Oskar, after one of the heroes in the story. Oscar Wilde, same deal. Even Selma, Alabama—"

"I get it," she said. "The letters don't have to be genuine to have value."

"It's not your best argument, but it's one more thing to throw against the wall."

She pictured a particularly chaotic Jackson Pollock hanging in the courtroom. My argument, Your Honor.

"More to the point? These are all intentional torts. You've got malice, oppression, fraud. They lured you down there under false pretenses, perpetrated violence. Bottom line: on top of equitable relief, intangible rights, and incidental costs, you've got a serious claim for punitive damages. So the seventy-five grand threshold? Even with authenticity in doubt, I don't see it as a problem, unless you draw an utter bozo for a judge."

Lisa imagined the bailiff crowing, "All rise," then His Honor entering the courtroom on a teeny-weeny tricycle: garish yarn hair, a greasepaint frown. Giant red ball for a nose.

A sudden wave of static crackled on the line, snapping her back. "Nico?"

"Okay," he continued, "that takes care of jurisdiction. The civil cause of action for theft is conversion. You'll also argue assault, battery, false imprisonment—"

"Not kidnapping?"

"Kidnapping is strictly a criminal offense. The tort is false imprisonment."

"Huh." How did he know that? "So I have to prove up—"

"Willful and unlawful restraint with risk of serious injury or harm."

"Slugged, then bound and gagged and terrorized. Check."

She decided against specifically mentioning the vulgar things Giordano had whispered in Rayella's ear. Even victims have a right to privacy, if not their pride.

"Remember, your focus is emergency injunctive relief— you want those letters back. Yesterday. I had a case like this last year, band manager locked the group out of the recording studio, all their equipment inside, started making crackpot demands, fifty percent of royalties—retroactive 'to the beginning of time'—utterly nuts. Federal judges tend to have no patience for that kind of thing. Your hearing should be quick."

Don't bet on it, she thought, rubbing her eyes. "From what I've seen so far from these people, they're going to fight this like all hell."

"Of course they are. And you'll fight back."

His confidence in her, it felt more kind than convincing. Even so, for just an instant, she imagined resting her head against his chest, feeling his arms wrap around her reassuringly.

"Nico, say I do win, obtain an order to put those letters into escrow pending trial—what if Littmann just ignores it? Holds onto the letters, says 'come and get me.'"

"That's what the U.S. Marshals are for."

Just like Wyatt Earp, she thought. Or was it Virgil? She puffed out her cheeks, let out a sigh. "Looks like I've got an all-nighter ahead."

"Lisa. Don't hang up. Know why I took you on as a partner?"

She resisted the impulse to say, *Because I've got a nice pair of torts?* "Nico, I told you, I'm not putting the firm's name on the caption, just mine."

"Not my point. I saw what you did in the Fordham legal clinic for that digital art collective in Bushwick. They wanted to put in aquaponic tanks for an installation."

"I helped them get liability clearance."

"You helped them break their goddamn lease with that greedy mouth-breather from Yonkers—which never should've happened, but you *made* it happen. *Pro bono*, no less. As a second-year law student."

"I got lucky."

"He tried to shake them down for the whole lease term, which he kinda had a right to do. But you kicked and clawed and wore him down. That's not luck."

She caught her free hand trembling, made a fist to stop it. "I can't thank you enough, Nico. I'm so sorry to have—"

"Stop it! Stop being sorry. This point on, you're a gunslinger. Shoot to kill."

$\sim 12 \sim$

IT took two hours of typing with the focus of a concert pianist to get the pleading out. Next, she drafted Rayella's affidavit, laying out the facts of how Tuck got in contact, her grandmother's gift, then a blow-by-blow account of the Whetstone Inn ordeal.

She wrapped up just before midnight—not too late, she hoped, to knock on Rayella's door, get a signature. After that, she'd move on to Tuck's account of the facts.

The resort had an all-night business center she could access with her room key, but her blouse and undergarments still felt damp from their hand-wash. So, naked beneath her suit jacket and skirt, and choosing to go barefoot for the sake of quiet, she padded down the cool tile stairs and along the sandstone walkway past the beds of California poppies, slipped through the lobby to the tiny, glass-walled room, let herself in, plugged in her laptop, and printed out the document.

Upstairs again, Rayella's room, right next to her own, she knocked gently on the painted wood door. Less than a mile to the east, the Santa Catalina Mountains rose up like burly, hooded monks—or Klansmen—standing shoulder-to-shoulder under a gaudy moon.

A tense, guarded voice from beyond the door. "Yeah?"

Lisa placed her hand gently on the doorframe, as though to offer an oath. "It's me, Rayella. Hope I didn't wake you. I have something here I need you to sign."

The deadbolt didn't slide back immediately, so she added, "I'm alone."

Just to her right, she saw the curtain jerk back at the edge of the window, Rayella peeking out to make sure no one else was there. Her eyes looked blasted and bloodshot, her mouth a tight thin line. The curtain dropped back in place. The door opened.

"I'm sorry," Lisa said, stepping inside, "to come by so late."

"Like I could sleep." Rayella locked the door, sliding the deadbolt home again for good measure. Still dressed in the blouse and slacks she'd worn all day, now badly wrinkled, she dropped onto the bed, tucking her legs beneath the covers.

Lisa said, "I have something for the filing tomorrow I need you to look over, tell me if there's anything I got wrong or you want changed. If it's okay, just sign."

Rayella took the three sheets of paper Lisa handed her, glanced briefly at the suit-and-bare- feet ensemble, then leaned into the glow of her bedside lamp to read.

Lisa found a chair near the wall and waited.

The room, though it shared a wall with her own, had drastically different décor, less artsy southwestern with its pastel watercolors of wildflowers and the Sky Island mountains, more Old West kitsch: knotty pine paneling, wall-mounted steer horns framed with braided rope, a rodeo poster above the bed. She wondered, given all Rayella had been through, whether the knickknacks felt campy or threatening.

"I left out any mention of the gross things Giordano said to you."

"Noticed that," Rayella murmured.

"I just figured, given how you looked as you talked about it—"

"Rest of this is bad enough. What he said—it ever hits the Internet?"

"I'm drafting a motion for the proceedings to be sealed. None of this should ever become public."

Rayella glanced up at her as though she'd just said the dumbest thing imaginable. Then, returning her gaze to the document: "Yeah, what's here is good. Got a pen?"

Lisa didn't, but she found one atop the dresser with a notepad supplied by the resort. As Rayella signed, Lisa asked, "How are you doing? Your head, I mean."

"I'm fine." She handed the pages back to Lisa.

"I'm worried about concuss—"

"*Said* I was *fine*." Rayella lay back down in the bed, turned her back.

Lisa, feeling a little jilted, said, "We've got a strong case for emergency injunctive relief—immediate return of the letters. This won't take long."

She caught herself wanting to say how sorry she was—for everything. Given Nico's admonition, however, she simply rose from her chair with, "I should get back to work."

"Funny," Rayella said, still facing the far wall, "how something you didn't even know existed one day becomes the most important thing in your life the next."

Funny and terrifying, Lisa thought, but before she could actually work out something appropriate to say, Rayella added, "I called my boyfriend. He's driving all night, should be here early in the morning."

"That's great," Lisa said.

"Just felt, I dunno, like it'd be nice, having someone on my side."

"Rayella, I realize you must feel like I let you down, but I really do understand that whatever—"

"You understand?" Like that, Rayella shot back up, feet on the floor, one fist clenching the sheet. "Rich little princess, famous daddy, 'never wanted for anything'—that's how you put it, remember?" An acid laugh. Eyes to match. "I been passed door to door my whole damn life. Learned to keep quiet, clean up after myself. Got used to going last. Got used to pretending I wasn't even there." Wincing as she shook her head. "But you *understand*."

⸺◇◇◇⸺

As she left, closing the door behind her, Lisa heard the deadbolt and chain clatter instantly back into place. Then, turning toward her room, she spotted a figure at the end of the walkway materializing from the shadows.

Her nakedness beneath her suit suddenly felt more extreme. She glanced quickly behind her, looking for somewhere to run — then took note of the tapping sound, the cane's brass tip against the pavers.

Turning back, she noticed first the distinctive lanky frame, then, as he came nearer, the wary smile, the lonesome eyes.

"Woulda got here sooner," Tuck said, "but they wouldn't let me fly the plane."

~ 13 ~

INSIDE her room, Lisa felt caged with Tuck sitting there. She started to pace back and forth, talking through the legal issues, and for several moments he watched her like a dog in a state of amazement at the workings of a clock.

Finally, he reached out, snagged her hand. "Sit for a minute. Let's talk this over."

"That's what I'm trying—"

"Not that. I don't mean the legalities, that's all fine. I mean what you need me to say to you. Personally."

She stood there a moment, enjoying the rough feel of his hand, then broke free, sat on the bed, wondering if he could tell she had nothing on beneath her suit.

"Littmann mentioned your name," she said. "We spent all that time keeping you out of it, making it look like I'd found him on my own. Then he not only brings you up, he makes it sound like there's serious bad blood."

"What did he say, exactly?"

"'Tell Tuck Mercer we're not even close to even.' Something along those lines."

Tuck sat back, as though chewing on the words, then shrugged. "I've got no clue what he's talking about."

"I find that hard to believe."

"Lisa—"

"Why come up with him as a buyer? How did you even know he existed?"

"He's on a list I put together of names the various auction houses let drop here and there, people interested in the American West—art, memorabilia, that kinda thing."

"Why would you need a list of names?"

"Why did Savannah Royster come to me? People get in touch, wondering about something they found in the attic—what is this worth, do you think this has value? Like I'm the cowpuncher's *Antiques Roadshow*. I put them in touch with people willing—"

"No, no." Shaking her head, she stood up, forearms waving back and forth as though to fend off a handsy drunk. "You lied to me."

"I did not. I swear."

"It doesn't make sense."

"He's the one lying."

"About *what*?"

"How the hell should I know? Ask him. Maybe he bought one of my fakes. If so, it's news to me. Look, Lisa, please . . . "

He got up from his chair, followed her to where she'd taken up position near the window, staring at the curtains for lack of anything better to do.

"I would never stick you in the middle of something like that." He rested a hand on her shoulder. "You really believe I would?"

She started trembling—anger, shame, fighting the desire to be held. Fighting the desire to turn around and knee him in the crotch. Shoot to kill.

With the gentlest pressure, he turned her around. Before she knew it, her head lay on his chest, his arms wrapped around her, one hand stroking her hair as he said, "I'll make this up to you, I promise. Never shoulda happened, not this way."

His breath had a sour scent, that whisper of whiskey, which instantly made her crave a drink. Except one drink would turn to three, then five, then a cascade of happy booze and the next thing she knew it would be two days later, she wouldn't recognize where she was or the people she was with, and no matter how hard she concentrated she'd never quite work out how she got there.

He broke the spell of that reflection by lifting her chin. Their eyes met briefly before the kiss, which felt at first like a crush of stubble but then she gave into it, focusing on his lips, licking and nibbling, leaning into him as she placed her hand on his nape and gently pressed, wanting him closer.

His hand moved under her jacket, and he shivered with surprise, just a little, as his fingers met skin, not cloth.

He led her away from the window and onto the bed, unbuttoning her suit jacket, unzipping the skirt. Yes, she thought in a moment of abstraction, slipping both items off, I don't want to have to iron those again.

He ran his calloused hands across her body, from between the knees up along the thighs, her hips, the flat of her stomach, the rippled fretwork of her ribcage, caressing one breast, then the other, smiling with a kind of appreciative sadness.

"You are so damn lovely," he whispered, like he'd just found something he thought had been lost.

She helped him off with his own clothes, and they lay together, doing the horizontal dance — leg here, arm there, hands wherever — while kissing some more and readying themselves for the next thing.

They both had condoms, he opted for hers — she slipped it on him herself, then lay back and wrapped her legs around his waist as he entered her, a claim of possession — finally, she thought — encircling her arms around his neck, not letting him stray too far, wanting to feel the heat coming off his chest.

God knows I've earned this, she thought.

As his rhythm picked up and his breathing quickened, she rocked her hips in time, urging him on, and when he came inside her, she closed her eyes, cooing with pleasure as she held back her own, not wanting to give him that, not yet.

Instead, her mind drifted to that night she drove off the Taconic Parkway into that massive tree, her very own *arbor mortis*. Earlier that evening, before her memory faded to black, she'd seduced a circus performer named Lars.

Lying on his back, he'd lifted her naked over the bed with those godlike arms of his, one hand flat against her sternum, the other cupping her pubis — his term, curiously medico-technical in his jargon, that Lars—two fingers curled deep inside her, his palm deftly placed and gently undulating as she arched her back and spread her arms and legs, tilting right and left as though riding updrafts and thermals in a canyon of light. As her orgasm built, then broke—it didn't take long—she thought: I just came like an angel. Like Icarus. Behold my melting wings.

Is that too much to ask, she wondered, opening her eyes again, seeing Tuck hunched above her, steadying his breath. Just once more in her life, to feel that kind of weightlessness. And was it really only twenty-four hours ago she would have given anything in the world to share that with this man?

—◇◇◇—

As they lay together afterward, she on her side, him close behind her, the only pillow talk she could muster was, "I can't let myself fall asleep. There's still—"

"Shush," he whispered, kissing her neck, scraping her skin with his stubble. "I know."

"I'm worried," she said. "We need to make it clear there was no undue influence or incapacity. The grandmother, she was in her right mind."

Tuck stopped his caresses. Drifting away to lie on his back, he said to the ceiling, "The old girl was totally clear-headed when we met. She came to my office, got there on her own steam. Went on and on about how the letters were going to be a surprise gift for—"

"Not 'going to be,'" Lisa said. "Stick to just 'were.'"

"Okay." A chesty sigh. "Got it. That was the sense, absolutely. Like I told you, I wrote as much on my copy of the contract. 'Gift for granddaughter.' I brought that, by the way, the contract, figuring you might need it."

Yes, she thought, but when exactly did you write those words down—at the time? Last night? On the plane?

She rose from the bed, found her robe, shrugged into it and cinched the belt, resisting an urge to pick up the phone, dial Nico's number—and discuss what?

Tuck watched her from where he lay, naked, middle-aged-cowboy handsome.

She said, "We might as well get to work. Drafting your affidavit, I mean."

"You're not actually thinking of using my testimony."

"You're crucial—how the letters came into the grandmother's possession—"

"I'm no lawyer, but isn't that hearsay?"

"That's up to the judge. I also need you to work up an estimate of their worth, and then there's the whole gift issue."

"Can't you work around all that somehow? Just let Rayella say her grandma gave her—"

"I'm not suborning perjury."

"I'm not asking you to *lie*. I'm asking you to leave something out."

"Under oath? That's a distinction without a difference."

"Lisa—"

"Besides, Littmann already knows you're involved in this."

"He doesn't *know* anything."

"He suspects, how's that? The point is, if we don't bring it up, he sure as hell will, and that'll make it look like we've got something to hide. Worse, withheld evidence."

He looked at her as though the promise of just a few moments before was lost for good. "What if I refuse? I don't mean to be a hard ass, but I really think this is the wrong way to go."

I can't believe, she thought, you actually said that. "Don't do this. It's really not fair."

That seemed to hit home. He lay there thinking it through, hands clasped behind his head so the ropey muscles in his arms flexed and popped. "You said the pleadings are sealed, right?"

"I'm going to file a motion to that effect, yes."

"So word won't leak out."

"There's no rock-solid guarantee. Things happen, but I'll do all I can."

"I mean, whatever the judge ends up thinking, fine. But if this gets out into the public domain, things get chancy fast."

"You're worried about your reputation?"

"I'm worried," he said, "about yours."

She felt chastened by the warmth in his eyes. "Leave the drafting to me. Your past is behind you. You're a respected expert now."

He rose and sat up on the edge of the bed, body lean and hard as a crowbar as he coughed once into his fist, settling his feet to the floor. After a moment, his face broke into a smile. For whatever reason, that charmed her. Maybe, she thought, just maybe, there's still a chance that gravity won't win.

He rose to his feet, favoring slightly his trick leg. "All righty, Misty Meaner. You call it, I'll haul it."

$$\sim 14 \sim$$

As was her custom, Meredith Littmann rose from her narrow, solitary bed well before daybreak. Darkness would linger beyond dawn, though, for at least another hour, possibly more, given the vast swath of shadow cast across the ranch by the Dragoon Mountains, rising up less than a mile to the east like a massive stone wall.

The arrested light did not bother her. On the contrary, she preferred it. One might even say she'd spent by far the better part of her life in twilight.

It wasn't just the abeyance of first light that appealed, however. The silence did as well. Those first moments of yawning stillness enchanted her. She could hear her own bare footfall across the creaking hardwood floor, like a ghost alone in her dusty manor.

All too soon the roosters and dogs would fight over who rose first, with the coyotes mocking them both from the granite hills. Then the murmurings of the ranch hands and wranglers as they made way from their quarters beyond the corral and headed for the stables, where they'd be greeted by nickers and whinnies and snorts, the ruffled shake of un-brushed manes, then a racket of hooves across hardpan as the ponies cantered out toward their morning pasture.

Soon enough the pump engines would roar alive, then start chugging if the windmills lay still.

The day, with all its pointless, noisy enterprise, would begin.

For now, at least, awake in the tranquil dark, she had time for herself, by herself.

Gideon, who for years now had bivouacked in the far wing of the sprawling house, would leave her alone—for hours, if not days—preferring his own company, or that of the help or his henchmen. His security detail would not check in until breakfast at the earliest, and even then only to ensure she'd not tumbled over something and broken her neck during the night—not so much to grieve her passing as to make arrangements.

She secretly nurtured this impression of fragility. In fact, since the twins had gone off to college—Ben to USC, Nicola to Stanford—she'd done her best, through calculated missteps and subtle failings, to create the impression that her defects in vision had grown progressively worse, as though hysterical blindness intensified in an empty nest.

True, her right eye remained clouded to the point that, if she shut her left, the world dissolved into a milky gray haze crisscrossed by blurred, arching silhouettes and dotted with spectral floaters.

However, if she reversed the procedure—closing the right eye, opening the left—she could read clearly all the way down to the seventh line on a Snellen chart, something she kept hidden even from her ophthalmologist. And, of course, her husband.

Being infirm had made her a fiercely private person. And long ago, when her affliction first manifested itself—age sixteen, after witnessing the boy she loved get trampled and gored by a rampaging bull—she found that most people quickly wearied of her presence. A quick question as to how she was feeling, what she might need, and then they couldn't vanish fast enough.

That came to suit her. Solitude, like higher math or a dead language, provided hidden treasures to those attuned to its subtleties. As for loneliness, it tended to bother most those who felt terrified by death, or wanted to escape their own minds.

⚬◇⚬

She felt her way from her bedroom into the long corridor connecting her wing of the house with the central foyer, found the switch for the track lighting, and gently raised the dimmer until the paintings lining each wall materialized.

There were forty-two overall, varying in size from that of a book cover to a blanket, varying as well in technique and competence, palette and tone. But not in era or subject matter. All concerned the American West and spoke of that century when artists, if no one else, realized a way of life, a rare form of human nobility—and savagery—was vanishing forever.

100

Holding a hand over her clouded eye, she began her morning meditation.

The relative obscurities appeared first, desert painters like Bill Bender, Olaf Wieghorst, then the modernists and minimalists who followed them: Jimmy Swinnerton, Conrad Buff, Maynard Dixon.

The last of these, Dixon, remained her favorite in this group, for personal as well as aesthetic reasons. He'd abandoned two wives for the sake of his freedom, the second being the Great Depression's most iconic photographer: Dorothea Lang.

Perhaps that aversion to constraint explained his preference for tone and shape over exactness of line, at least at this late state of his development. This piece in particular, of an Apache family meandering across chaparral toward distant hills—retained the strange harsh blur of dusty sunlight so true to the desert, even when scanned by her workaday eye.

Turning toward the opposite wall, she encountered the classic cowboy painters: Clyde Forsythe, Ed Borein, Charlie Russell and, of course, Frederic Remington. These pleased her least, not just on formal grounds, though several demonstrated excellent command of technique. They so clearly sentimentalized their subjects, which reduced to the level of cartoon even the most accomplished drawing and brushwork—but that also, of course, accounted for their vast popularity, as well as their inflated dollar value.

Next, moving down that same side of the corridor, came the Indian portraitists, from the obscure William Victor Higgins with his bright bold modernist colors to Sharp and

Blumenschein with their Cezanne textures and palette, the more Impressionistic Berninghaus, then still further back in time to the true original: George Catlin, the Buffalo Bill of the lecture circuit with his stern, simple, mesmerizing Choctaws and Seminoles, Comanche and Sioux.

Turning around again, she encountered a typically expansive Bierstadt landscape, this one of a spring cataract in the Rockies. Like all of his work, it exemplified the idealized naturalism of the Hudson River School, itself indebted to Turner and Constable, translated to the rolling plains and stark mountain valleys of the Great West—lovely, yes, but a bit preachy, too, with all that sublimity crowding out the simply, humbly beautiful.

She preferred the Farny beside it, a study situated somewhere in time between the more famous pieces, *Breaking Camp* and *Nomads*, depicting a Sioux family's difficult existence on the winter tall grass plains. The inheritance from Bierstadt, the Düsseldorf school, and the British landscape painters remained, but with a new sense of outdoor light and life borrowed from the Barbizon group and French *plein-air* naturalism. If Corot had painted the West, she thought, it would look like this.

Which brought her, at last, to her three favorite paintings.

The first, a tonalist study for the more famous *Blowing Rock*, with the same wraith-like female figure in the foreground, the same ominous moonlit sky streaked with cloud—created by layering thin coats of oil paint and light-absorbent varnish to elicit the soft-edged color and glowing light—represented the only Elliott Daingerfield in her collection. The painter, relatively obscure, owed the better part of his fame to another artist, the one for whom he'd been both close friend and biographer: Ralph Blakelock.

Self-taught genius, schizophrenic pauper, the "American Van Gogh"—poor, mad Blakelock. He was the most unique of the painters in her entire collection, and thus the hardest to imitate well. And yet, ironically, he was also possibly the greatest single source of forgeries in American art—the result of his becoming wildly popular when defenseless in a Hudson Valley asylum—fakes outnumbering originals by some calculations.

None of those forgeries, however, managed to capture his magic. These two demonstrated the difficulty well.

The first bore a resemblance to the more famous *Apache Indians Breaking Camp at Daybreak*, except the lighting suggested dusk, not dawn. Beyond that, it possessed the same devotion to rendering twilight through arching trees, and a spare depiction of the foreground figures with jagged strips and odd drops of delicately shaped paint, conjuring their colorful blankets and headdresses through abstraction, not detail.

The second resembled *The Captive*, with its complete devotion to the wilderness night's utter darkness except for the figures illumined by firelight—the small circle of warriors near the campfire, the isolated, slouching prisoner bound to her tree.

Both displayed their scenes from a distinct remove, as though witnessed from a hiding place beyond the clearing, or by an invisible observer outside time.

Both also possessed the same silvery shimmer on an impasto background, with varying areas of thick and thin paint, the knife and brush patterns clearly visible.

His lack of schooling had created a wildly improvisational openness to technique. But that innovative spirit also led him to using unwise materials: the copal resin in his varnish, which turned dark and cracked — so that only a generation later his paintings seemed even duskier in tone — and bitumen, which never dried completely, and often caused the surface to crackle into an alligator pattern.

But as Daingerfield, his devotee, pointed out long ago, these shortcomings were grossly overstated, and time had proven him right. Overall, the paintings were stable.

If only most so-called experts and connoisseurs had half the appreciation for technique and materials as the man responsible for these two masterpieces. The same man who painted every other work here on these walls: Henry "Tuck" Mercer.

~ 15 ~

MEREDITH had learned of Tuck's arrest and prosecution through news reports and had followed the case with attentive devotion. The boy she watched get trampled and gored and left for dead had grown to a mysterious manhood.

In his plea agreement, he was obliged to confess to his methodology.

He had always been an expert sketch artist, making side money at rodeos at his easel, dollar a portrait. Meredith had been a star subject, both at the rodeo and more intimate settings, not just in pencil and charcoal but watercolor and oil and in various stages of naturalism.

Once his injuries slammed the door on any further rodeo work, he launched his formal education at a Los Angeles restoration studio with one of the most highly regarded conservators in the business, from whom he learned the subtle art and exacting chemistry of repairing and cleaning older works of genius.

Specifically, he came to recognize every type of canvas weave and stretcher type in use during the nineteenth century, every variety of wood panel—especially academy board, an American favorite—and every kind of crack pattern.

He learned to recognize not just the unique subject matter and obvious techniques of individual artists, he also developed the ability to identify their distinctive patinas, brushstrokes, edgework, use of varnish, thickness of impasto.

He discovered that, under ultraviolet light, a genuine antique varnish unerringly revealed a distinctive green fluorescence. Though this "green slime" effect could not be faked, it could be simulated by using solvent to remove the old varnish from a genuine antique painting, then wringing the solvent and varnish into a jar, transferring it to a sprayer, and coating the fake with the concoction.

He observed that "rotten stone," a superfine powder made of volcanic rock, worked miracles in conjuring age when dusted across a freshly painted canvas.

He noticed as well the frequent appearance, especially in paintings long ago tucked away in attics or basements or barns, of tiny, clustered black dots near the frames and corners, which he learned were fly droppings. The insects were drawn to the sugar in the varnish. He also found out he could simulate the flyspecks by using pinpricks of epoxy mixed with amber-colored pigment.

He learned how to make gesso from rabbit-skin glue and powdered gypsum from the White Cliffs of Dover, how to "age" its tint with raw sienna watercolor, how to create cracking through prolonged exposure to the sun, how to enhance that cracking through a wash of black watercolor and soap.

He came to see the value of evaluating not just the paintings themselves but their cove or wedge frames—an art in itself, as was finding them in antique shops—as well as tack marks (the rust had to be simulated), reinforcing battens, signs of repair on the backs of the canvases, and other incidentals that could enhance the air of age and authenticity.

With this education in hand, he ventured into imitation.

He began by collecting oddball portraits and landscapes from the period—worthless eyesores or even the work of madmen—for the sake of the canvas and frames, using acetone to get rid of the original paint.

Once it was time to decide who to imitate, he started with the lesser-known artists such as Wieghorst and Buff, selling them to backwater collectors for a few thousand bucks, if that. Gradually, though, he moved on with greater confidence and command of technique to the real money painters.

It was at that stage of the endeavor that he gained the assistance of a dealer he met during his days in restoration, a man named Danyal Sherazi.

It was Sherazi who foresaw the boom in demand created by China's nouveau riche, the so-called Bling Dynasty. Specifically, he understood their insecurity, their need to affirm their deservedness by learning what it meant to have class.

Although many of the *turhao* stuck to the basics—learning designer brand names and how to pronounce *foie gras*—others, especially those who once attended American universities, realized the special caché afforded to anyone with a nuanced grasp of local culture, specifically American art. Better still if you knew it better than the natives, which wasn't hard, given the general ignorance of the average homegrown bourgeois.

Tuck learned from Sherazi that excellent technique—both in imitating the original artworks and disguising the recent production of the work—was not enough.

It was the story behind the painting, how it had gone undiscovered for so long, tucked away in some cellar or attic or barn, that truly fascinated the marks.

And so a partnership formed. Tuck produced the work. Sherazi sold the story, and made sure Tuck's forgeries were offered in mid-week sales, which the cognoscenti typically avoided, an arrangement Sherazi finagled with his auction house knockouts.

The scheme was finally exposed when one of the *turhao* befriended a curator at the National Gallery, and learned that though George Catlin did gain fame for his portraits of Comanche chieftains, he did so no later than 1844, and therefore could never have painted as an adult the warrior chief Isatai—a name colorfully translated as Coyote's Vagina.

The painting's owner took the news hard, since the rendering was so reverentially dignified, a study in timeless proto-Asiatic nobility—for weren't the ancient Chinese and the nomadic tribes of North America genetic kin? That was, after all, why he paid $2.2 million for the thing.

The whole masquerade unraveled quickly from there.

Supremely motivated to expose the men who defrauded him, and well enough connected to put some real heft in his crusade, the burned owner of Isatai's portrait enlisted an army of investigators and experts, including the FBI's Art Crime Team, all of whom demonstrated a particularly relentless devotion to finding, exposing, and bringing to justice The Man Who Forged the West.

And they did. Meanwhile, Danyal Sherazi vanished—rumors put him variously in Montevideo, Shanghai, or Tehran—leaving his painterly sidekick to take the fall.

Obliged to disclose his techniques, Tuck educated law enforcement, the art world, and potential targets of fraud on how he managed to fool so many for so long, and why he grew more daring, which is to say reckless, near the end.

Then he proceeded to identify, to the best he could recall, every single forgery he painted—known as "bazookas" in the trade—as well as to whom they were sold, though that was Sherazi's end of things, and Tuck's recollection on that point often proved imperfect.

Though prosecutors intended for the catalog of paintings to remain confidential, in order to protect the reputations of those who were duped, the list became public almost immediately, the work of dealers who wanted to make sure they weren't taken in a second time. Once that all became public, other Sherazi victims stepped sheepishly forward.

It was through using that catalog and the disclosures afterward that Meredith identified the paintings she wanted, who to approach, and how much to offer.

Some held on to the fakes, hoping to fool their less sophisticated friends. Others demanded far more than the paintings now were worth — though "original Tuck Mercers" had a caché all their own. Enough, however, were happy to sell.

And now they are mine till I die, she thought, just as the door to the foyer opened, and her husband, Gideon, appeared.

~ 16 ~

As always, he entered with an unquestioned aura of ownership. And yes, of course, he had a certain right in that regard, but not to the degree he believed.

They both had married in accordance with their station, notable old Arizona families, descendants of pioneer lawyers who dabbled in ranching, prosperous and dignified in the desert manner. Her money owed no deference to his.

He appeared in her life shortly after the accident, the one caused when her eyesight suddenly, utterly failed as she careened down that back road toward nowhere.

Only an hour before, she sat in the stands with thousands of others, cheering Tuck on — sweetheart of the rodeo, his girl — only to watch him get bucked off that steer almost instantly, watch him get dragged around the ring until finally the animal stomped and gored and ripped him apart.

Better to be blind and die.

111

Except she didn't die. Her grand romantic tragedy took a different turn.

Her family found a private clinic miles to the south, specializing in afflictions of the rich, the better to separate her once and for all from that rodeo bum near death at St. Joe's. When she awoke, she heard a stranger's voice. Gideon's. And the courtship began.

And like many a cunning suitor before him, he realized the wisest course lay in wooing the parents, not her.

Not that he was an utter scoundrel. His redemptive qualities revealed themselves over time: sturdiness as a provider; confidence among men of all kinds, especially the ranch hands; a surprising generosity of heart as a father.

As a husband, however, he possessed all the nuanced understanding of a pipe fitter trying to repair lace with a welding torch.

As he approached from the end of the corridor, she noticed he was carrying something, a large rumpled parcel wrapped in worn velvet, tied with an antique ribbon. His expression seemed strangely boyish, even shy, and that anomaly, given the rangy girth and broad manly face she otherwise found so familiar, made her vaguely afraid.

"I figured you'd be up," he said, stopping a few feet away. He raised the parcel a little. "I have something here I thought you might find interesting."

"I was just heading back to bed."

His eyes narrowed, the suntanned crow's feet at each corner fanning as the coldness she knew and trusted hardened his gaze. He held the parcel out for her to take. "You're not the least bit curious?"

Perhaps, she thought. The very least bit.

"I sought them out with you in mind."

Not *for* me, she thought. Just with me *in mind*. "How considerate."

"Go ahead." That galling, sly arrogance. "They won't explode."

"Okay, fine." She crossed her arms, shivered the hair away from her face. "Why darling, whatever might they be?"

For the slightest instant, his stare detoured to her throat. "Let's be adults about this, Meredith."

"Is there any way for you to get through a single conversation without using that expression?"

Bobbing the velvet packet gently in his hand: "They're letters."

"Old ones, from the look of it."

"Very."

"From anyone we know?"

"In a manner of speaking." He glanced at one of the paintings on the wall then held the velvet packet out a little farther, daring her to take them. Demanding her to. "Seriously, I thought you'd find them fascinating."

"Why would you think that?"

He didn't answer, just stood there with his arm extended, parcel in hand.

Finally, she relented, took it from him. "What now?"

She expected him to turn away, leave, but he just stood there, an arm's length distance, his eyes curiously sad now. Or morose. She couldn't tell which. After all, she *was* half blind.

"Is it really so hard to imagine," he said, "that I'm not the horrible mistake you like to pretend I am?"

November 15, 1876

Dearest Mattie,

Once again, I am obliged to ask forgiveness for the delay in my responding to your most recent letter. I have no excuse except an inability to formulate how best to word my reply.

I am inclined to believe that only through some strange necromancy did your recent letter even manage to arrive. I refer to your awareness, prompted by the curious appearance of Pinkerton agents at Uncle John's home, that you needed to address your correspondence to T.S. Mackey, the name I have seen fit to use here.

I suppose I should explain that subterfuge, which in a roundabout manner will also explain the disturbing visit you described so well in your letter.

In my previous correspondence I have hinted at the distinct way of life out here, beyond the reach of civil order and respectful manners. Perhaps it is time for me to stop hinting and state the matter plain.

I live in a small, threadbare room above a place called Long John's Saloon. I earn my living running a faro bank and dealing cards for an affable rogue named Charlie Foster, who operates an establishment with the gloriously benign moniker: Bab's Variety House.

The variety in question concerns not just the array of temptations on offer, but the kinds of men attracted to them: saddle tramps, bullwhackers, fugitives, sharpers and cappers and sheer brute fools.

In such illustrious company, with whiskey readily at hand, I cannot afford to betray the slightest reluctance to accept a challenge to my honor or step up in a scrape.

The problem lies in the fact that many of these men overvalue luck's estimation of their merit. Thus, when they discover the cards (or their own stupidity) have betrayed them, their anger rises all too quickly to a rollicking boil. They can fathom no other possibility than that they have been cheated, and that I am the scoundrel to blame. Or at least the one in easiest reach.

When I try to educate them, explaining that freaks of chance are not determinable by calculation, they only jack up their spines all the more. Threats get made, all too often followed by the appearance of weapons.

As you can imagine, my condition only amplifies the danger. No one respects, let alone fears, a lunger.

As a consequence, I have been forced to rely on a certain abject savagery, making it clear that death has no dominion over my temperament, and I will not be intimidated by drunken loudmouths or bad losers.

Simply put, whether they hate me or not, men fear me. If that were not true, I would have been murdered long ago for the mere sport of the killing.

Admittedly, what I have managed to gain in terms of survival I have paid for in the coin of isolation. By and large, I lead a solitary life.

All of which is mere prelude to my explanation of what led me to flee Texas, and assume the name, somewhat altered, of my favorite uncle. That, in turn, will hopefully reveal the likely provocation for the visit from the Pinkerton yokels.

I was gambling in the Flats outside Fort Griffin when a colored soldier, finding himself at the wrong end of a large pot, rose to his feet, accused me of various sins, some involving the mistreatment of mothers and barnyard animals, then reached for his weapon.

I proved not just luckier at cards but quicker at locating my pistol.

I did not know at the time that the cavalryman was absent without authority, nor did I realize his wound was fatal.

What I did know was that the fort's commanding officer was a protégé of a colonel named Pratt, one of those insufferably preachy Yanks of the do-gooder ilk, flaunting his Negro cavalry regiment and Tonkawa scouts like he was Moses and they were his dutiful Hebrews.

Accordingly, I had little faith the wheels of justice would roll my way. And so I decided it would be best to head out of town as efficiently as possible — with my winnings, naturally.

I packed my belongings and headed for Denver, having heard it was a wide-open town, taking a wildly circuitous route via train with the hope of throwing off any pursuers.

I took up my new name and made myself as inconspicuous as possible. Or tried to. As I said, this region attracts a particularly thick and volatile breed of creature.

For example, a man named Bud Ryan.

He fashions himself a gambler, but whatever skills he might possess seem to vanish whenever he sits across the table from me.

The dullard could hardly hand up his money more readily if he simply let me grab him by the ankles, suspend him upside down, and shake until the coins come tumbling from his pockets.

Naturally, this has led to some rancor between us.

Nothing galls rough, stupid men so much as encountering a man of even modest intellect who, with seemingly little effort or concern, drags them to the woodshed — and leaves with their money.

I cannot prove any of what I am about to suggest, but I consider it possible, even likely, given the temperaments of the men in question.

Ryan has a few influential friends here, men wealthier if not wiser than he is. As I mentioned, I tend to keep to myself. This makes me an easy target for rumormongers.

I suspect Ryan, putting his finger to the wind and plucking from it whatever gossip served his purpose, especially anything sordid wafting from Texas, convinced some of his well-heeled acquaintances that I am a cold-blooded killer and should be held to account.

Inspired by this nonsense, I believe these men, on Ryan's behalf or at least at his behest, employed the Pinkerton agency to follow up.

Again, as I noted, I have no proof whatsoever this is true. Just an instinct. But I sense in Ryan's recent taunts, which increasingly refer to some reckoning he believes is coming my way, that the acrimony between us will shortly come to a head.

Meaning, perhaps, I may be leaving Denver sooner than originally planned — which allows me, at last, to turn away from the dreary business I have been describing and instead address other matters brought up in your letter.

Regarding family: I have reached out to Aunt Annaleeza in Kansas and have made preliminary plans to join her and her family for Christmas. I thought you would be heartened to know that.

Unfortunately, those are possibly the only cheery words I can offer on the subject of family.

Specifically, regarding my father and the issue of forgiveness — I am sure the good Major has prospered, as his nature always inclined him to frugality, industry, and hard-headed pragmatism.

But memory afflicts me with too many recollections of stern indifference and icy distance to make the prospect of his actual presence before me seem anything but a horrible mistake.

Not that he was cruel, per se. For the most part, I simply remained invisible to him, except as a target for reprimand.

Worse, Mother shared in my invisibility, especially once her sickness grew irreversible. I almost wondered if my incapacity to be seen by that man became a kind of contagion, passed on to her, for he could not avoid her sickbed enough during those hard last months.

You know the truth of what I'm saying, for you too witnessed my father's utter absence, which cannot be justified with the usual prattle of how the women were perfectly competent bedside, whereas he needed to make sure the family got sheltered and fed.

How quickly we learned the lie to that, for his vanishings could not be explained by the manly business of money alone. A mere three months after Mother's passing, and the Martin woman appears, barely seven years older than I. Father had been sneaking to her odious father's property just down the road to court the girl outside the eye of town and family.

That girl-woman became my "stepmother," a term handed down since the dawn of time in legend and myth as a cognate for witch.

No, if you want forgiveness for all that, turn to your Roman God, not me. I shall remain invisible, the better to render myself an easy object of sanctimony and scorn.

Forgive me. I hate to end on such a bitter note, but such lately is my turn of mind.

And no, you should not feel responsible for that, or suffer over the state of my life or my soul. Each night before sleep comes, I think of you, picture you in my mind, wish for your presence here. Please understand, I cannot return to Georgia. I have lost any sense of home there. Except in you.

I will stop now. Nothing I write feels worth reading. But I owed you a response to your lovely letter. I re-read it often, and thank you for it.

Your devoted,
John Henry

FULLY dressed—including, at last, her blouse and undergarments—and tottering in her heels from a mere half hour of sleep, Lisa quietly gathered the documents she intended to file at the District Courthouse downtown, shouldered her purse and valise, gathered the keys to her rental car, and tiptoed toward the door.

"Not even a simple 'goodbye'?"

Tuck rolled onto his side in the rumpled bed, squinting as he propped himself up on one elbow. Morning sunlight flared at the curtain edges.

"I'll brush my teeth quick," he added, "if that's the problem."

No, Lisa thought. That's not the problem. "I didn't want to wake you."

"Too late." He pulled back the sheet and sat up with a yawn, checking his watch. "Courthouse won't open for another hour."

"Giving myself time to get lost. And find coffee." She made herself smile. "Plus I want to be the first one through the door."

"Hard charger." He rose and limped toward her, naked. "That's my girl."

He leaned down and kissed the top of her head like a chaste uncle, then lifted her chin for a bristly peck on the cheek. Stepping back to meet her eyes, he let his gaze linger. What Lisa found there was strength, fondness, so much so she felt ashamed, and for an instant she imagined dropping all she was carrying, shrugging off her purse and briefcase, kicking off her shoes, dragging him back to bed. Wouldn't it be perfect, she thought, if life allowed for such a thing?

Suddenly he spun her toward the door, slapped her rump hard. Giddy-up. "Go show those weasels who they're up against."

⟨◇⟩◇⟨

Wanting to check in with Rayella, make sure she hadn't changed her mind about coming to court, Lisa raised her hand against the harsh morning light, the sun having crested the Santa Catalinas to the east, and pressed her ear to the door of the girl's room.

She caught a chattering murmur. ". . . westerly winds reaching thirty miles per—"

A gentle knock, hopefully loud enough to counter the radio. "Rayella? It's me."

A moment's wait, a peek from the edge of the curtain. Then the deadbolt slid free, the door cracked open. A slight wave of soap-scented warmth—dressed in the complimentary robe, Rayella stood beyond the tightened chain, toweling her hair, fresh from the shower. Her skin glowed with a sensual bloom, not just from a good hot scrub.

Right, Lisa thought. She said her boyfriend was coming. Was he already here? "I'm sorry, I just wanted to make double sure you didn't want to come to court."

Rayella stopped chafing her head with the towel and peered through the door crack like Lisa, her lawyer, might want a tip. "No."

From the foothills nearby, a waking band of coyotes barked hungrily. In the parking lot, a pickup's engine growled and sputtered then caught.

"Okay then." Lisa had to stop herself from saying, *Have fun.* "I'll check in with you later."

⊰◇◇◇⊱

Sprinklers hissed along the landscaped footpath, misting the poppy and pasque flower beds. In the lobby, morning sunlight flared through the window blinds, striating the rough-hewn wood and vibrant Mexican tile. Maybe, she thought, the day would have its grace notes.

Then she spotted the four strange men gathered at the desk—muscled like fighters but dressed casually, jeans and cargo pants and sports shirts, except for the footwear: boots, military-grade from the look of them, desert tan.

"Yessir," one of them said in a clipped and courteous drawl, a sandy-haired specimen with the wingspan of a power forward, arms spread out to either side as he leaned over the desk. "Vargas. Rayella Vargas. She's registered here as a guest."

123

The boyfriend, Lisa guessed. He wasn't up in Rayella's room after all. But why three others?

She ventured over, an edgy flutter in her chest.

"Hi." She held out her hand, offering a cordial smile. "I'm Lisa Balamaro, Rayella's lawyer. Can I help in some way?"

All four heads turned slowly toward her, like turrets on a dreadnought. Every single pair of eyes seemed prematurely old, emitting a charge of tamped-down horror.

The one who'd spoken had a kind of rough-hewn handsome strength, reminding her of a phrase Nico sometimes used—born outdoors, raised by strangers. But the face bore pronounced scarring on one side, a hand-sized blotch of red-rough skin, like an asphalt skid that had never quite healed. Except worse. Way worse. She doubted she'd ever again give her own scar a second thought.

The one behind him to the left looked Black Irish: rangy but athletically built and tall, with heavy-lidded eyes—which, despite the veiling, shone pure blue—plus that defining blend of creamy white skin and raven-black hair.

Behind to the right was a short, compact blond, freckles so red they resembled blood blisters. He had a prominent overbite that gave his face a horsey cast, except the soulless intensity of his eyes made him seem more like a feral Huck Finn.

Fourth and final was perhaps the largest, tallest African American she had ever seen up close, and that included LeBron, whom she'd met courtside once at a Warriors game.

He seemed possessed of a quiet calm that conveyed not gentleness or serenity but a laser focus. His shaved head glistened, and his crossed arms bulged.

The one with the scarred face stepped forward and took Lisa's hand. "Ma'am," he said, aging her instantly. "I'm Connor. Connor Trapnell. Pleased to make your acquaintance."

Before she could muster a response, a voice from behind said, "Rags?"

Not Rayella. Tuck.

The sound of his voice, the sight of him approaching from the doorway—they unsettled her in a way she couldn't quite place.

He came forward with a cautious smile—not for her—free hand out, the other gripping his cane, tapping its way across the sandstone pavers.

"I'm Tuck Mercer, the man Rayella's grandma hired to handle the letters. She mentioned you might be coming—Rayella, I mean, when I caught up with her by phone last night. Her grandma mentioned you too back when. Nice to put a face to the name."

An awkward handshake segued into a round of further introductions, conducted by the boyfriend, Connor, aka Rags.

The tall, blue-eyed lady-killer was Cody Brandt, nicknamed Chalky, or Chalkers. Huck Finn bore the wildly improbable name of Wander DeJesus—Rags rhymed it with "Hey, Zeus." Regardless, no nickname required. The shiny-domed giant was Cardale Shipman.

"But we call him BBK." This from the bucktooth blond, Wander.

A momentary, general, quizzical silence. In the background, the desk clerk stood at his post, smiling like a gargoyle.

"Black Buddha Killer," Wander explained. "Meanest Marine in Marja."

The man himself said nothing, just collected Lisa's hand, squeezed it vacantly.

Pushing back her jacket cuff to check her watch: "I need to get to court." She shook her sleeve back down, turned for the door. Stopped.

"By the way." She circled back to face the men. "I'm not saying this out of some prissy lawyerly squeamishness, okay? But I was expecting a boyfriend, not a security detail. Don't get me wrong, I'm glad to meet you, all of you, and I'm happy you're here. But I also know there might be some temptation, given what took place . . ."

She scanned the newcomers' faces, met their empty eyes.

"Please," she said. "Don't. It won't help. Quite the opposite, it'll make things worse, much worse." She adjusted the shoulder strap of her valise. "Trust me, we're going to get those letters back and fast, then punish the men who took them."

Said like she meant it, not just hoped.

Nothing at first, just the same unavailing stares.

Then Rags, the boyfriend, said, "No worries on that front, ma'am. We're good. Just safety in numbers, is all. More the merrier when it comes to moral support."

Tuck told the desk clerk, "It's all right," then turned to the four marines. "I'll take you on up. Room's this way." He pointed with the walking stick, his gift from Lisa, then offered her a parting wink, as though to say: I've got this handled, all good.

But it isn't, she thought, that's the problem. And his confidence, his uncanny knack for showing up at just the right moment and knowing so much. But not quite everything. Not quite enough.

⟞⟝◇⟞⟝

Rayella sensed his presence nearby even before he knocked, as though attuned to some subsonic vibration only he emitted. Just to be certain, she peeked out from behind the curtain, saw his handsome, half-ruined face with its sad-strong eyes, the bad-ass shoulders, the lanky boot-camp build. Behind him, down the walkway, three others and Tuck slipped into the next room down. Lisa the lawyer's room.

A combination of joy and panic turned her fingers into twigs as she fumbled with the deadbolt. Once the door cracked open, she threw it back, diving headlong into his arms then pressing herself so tight against his chest she feared for a moment neither of them would be able to breathe. But that would be fine. That would be wonderful.

Dragging him inside, she wiped at the tears streaming down her face. "I promised myself I wouldn't do this."

"It's okay." He wrapped her up again as the door clicked shut, pressing his cheek against her unruly hair.

Into his shirt, she whispered, "I missed you so much."

"It's all right. Everything's all right."

"I can't tell you how scared I've been." Wiping at her face once more, using the inside of her wrist, the back of her hand, sniffling. "I'm sorry, I know it's wrong, it's stupid, but I hate them so much —"

"You're not the one should be sorry," he said, rocking her gently back and forth. "Shush now. I'm here, it's all good, okay?"

She began to sob softly into his chest, trembling as he stroked her back and cooed reassurance.

"Know what's awful?" She pulled herself back from the closeness of his hold. "Yeah, I want the letters back, want them now, this minute. But that's not enough. I want those bastards to pay. Pay hard. To the point they beg for it to stop." Looking up into the brutal damaged miracle of his face, she whispered, "Does that make me a horrible person?"

~ 18 ~

THE parking garage for the courthouse was a low, two-storied, concrete bunker with slatted walls, through which jagged spears of sunlight offered the only relief from the dreary atmospherics. Great place to get kidnapped, Lisa thought as she pulled up to the ticket booth. Or killed.

A tiny Navajo woman wrapped in a fringed poncho took her money, handed back her change and a day pass to place on the dash, then returned to her folding chair to resume her knitting, surrounded by tottering stacks of dog-eared magazines.

The courthouse itself resembled a two-tone monument to architectural indifference, as though the government had hoped for something majestic, then settled for a postmodern fortress.

A dozen lawyers waited outside, gazing fixedly or jabbering like mad into phones as they stood around or milled back and forth beneath the high glass archway leading to the entrance. Lisa dreamed of her next jolt of coffee, picturing buckets of it—no, no, a caffeine shower, pelting her face, her shoulders, her breasts, and a beautiful shirtless man (Tuck perhaps, maybe not) waiting with a fluffy, immaculate towel . . .

Finally, at eight sharp, the marshals—blue blazers, white shirts, dark ties, gray faces—unlocked the doors, and Lisa headed the scrum toward security.

Echoes bounced forever off the smooth granite walls and the high glass-paneled ceiling as she surrendered her documents, purse, valise, and phone, passed through the scanner, then snatched her things off the conveyor belt and dashed straight across the shiny earth-tone tiles for the clerk's office.

Standing in the narrow vestibule, Lisa passed her documents and filing fee through a chrome slot in the bulletproof partition.

The clerk, a pretty and ample Latina wearing a turquoise blouse, read the caption on Lisa's complaint and stopped cold. A brief glance up, as though for a mental snapshot, followed by a wary smile, then back to work.

Lisa almost said something but, not wanting to interrupt the process, kept mum.

She'd named as defendant not just Littmann, a regional icon, but also Rankin, Giordano, the Whetstone Inn, plus the proprietor, who turned out to be named Phineas Honnicutt. And admittedly, the caption, worked out with Nico over the phone, was eye-catching:

Complaint for Injunctive Relief to Protect and Preserve Historic Writings; Conversion of Irreplaceable Historic Letters and Demand for Constructive Trust; Request for Damages for Personal Injury as a Result of Wrongful Assault, Battery and False Imprisonment; Request for Punitive Damages based on Malice, Oppression, and Fraud.

On top of her request for a TRO and an ex parte hearing for the next day to place the letters into an escrow account pending trial, she'd added a motion and proposed order that the proceedings be sealed, more as a gesture than a tactic. She didn't want to come off like a shakedown artist, using publicity as a pressure move. Besides, Tuck had specifically wanted the matter kept as private as possible.

The Latina failed to glance up again, except to negotiate the time of the emergency hearing—tomorrow morning eleven a.m.—and to hand back file-stamped copies of Lisa's documents. Her gaze held as she added, "You need to take the TRO and the ex parte application up to the judge." A matter-of-fact voice, muddied by the thick glass wall. "If she approves it, make sure you serve it on the defendants no less than twenty-five hours before the hearing. That only gives you," a glance at the wall clock, "a little over two hours."

———∞◇∞———

Lisa never got to meet the judge. Her clerk, a sprightly sixtyish dynamo in a well-worn cardigan, accepted the documents, asked for a brief rundown of the case, then disappeared with a promise to be back shortly, only to honor that promise with an alacrity that Lisa, given prior experience with the courts, considered almost spooky, like magic.

Maybe there's a little wind at my back after all, she thought, checking to make sure the TRO and ex parte order were both, indeed, signed.

Next stop, process server. She'd found him online—an outfit called Serving by Irving, first-rate testimonials from area lawyers despite the goofy name—and a man had phoned back that morning while she was in the shower, leaving a message that they could meet at the courthouse. He'd been called to testify about a witness dodging a subpoena, and would be waiting outside the courtroom.

True to his word, he stood there in the hallway, looking nothing like what she'd expected—tall, buff, bull-necked, with arms heftier than her thighs.

She stuck out her hand. "Hey. I'm Lisa Balamaro. You must be . . . Irving?"

His hand swallowed hers. "Mr. Subotnick retired. Bought the business from him two years ago." An affable shrug. "Name's too catchy not to keep. I'm Eric Boone. Call me Boonie. Got something for me?"

She dug the documents out of her briefcase and handed them over. He scanned the caption but, unlike the Latina clerk, offered no response, except to say, "Last known addresses in here?"

"At the back."

He thumbed through, found them, nodded. "Looks like we're set."

"I'm filing for emergency injunctive relief, so the hearing comes up quick. Late tomorrow morning, in fact. Time's tight. Do your best. If you can't get them served inside the deadline, I may need you to testify. I'm sorry."

"Not a problem." He spread his arms, as though to remind her why he was there. "There a local number in case I can't reach your cell?"

She dug a business card out of her wallet, wrote down the hotel info. He took the card, read it. "No offense, but you don't sound like someone from San Francisco."

"I grew up back east, Philadelphia." Interesting—she seldom got called on her accent. Unless she was talking too fast. Like now. "Only came out west a few years ago."

"You think San Francisco's the *West*?"

Yeah, she thought. Definitely not an Irving. "Well, it's west of the New Jersey Turnpike, how's that?"

That earned her a smile. "Got me there, Ms. . . . "

"Balamaro." Sparing him the agony of struggling through it. "Lisa's fine. And easier."

"Okay then." Once again, his hand devoured hers. "Take care of this for you pronto, Ms. Lisa."

———◆◇◆———

The elevator hummed like a walk-in freezer as she rode it back down to the first floor. Making way across the cavernous lobby, she spotted the Latina clerk from earlier waiting along the wall outside the court clerk's office.

Their eyes met. The woman gestured with a sideways nod toward the entrance, then eased away from the wall and sauntered outside, heading for the far end of the courtyard.

Lisa followed, glancing around to see if anyone might be watching or loitering a bit too intently. Satisfied they were alone and unobserved, she came up slowly beside the Latina, noticing the tightly crossed arms, the lowered chin.

"There are some things you need to know," she said, "about the men you named in your lawsuit."

~ 19 ~

OFFERING no further explanation except to introduce herself—her name, she said, was Asunción Ortiz—the woman walked briskly to a bus shelter up the block and on the opposite side of Congress Street. They sat side by side on the bench. The brittle fronds of a giant windmill palm chattered overhead in the breeze. Lisa felt grateful for its shade.

"The men you are suing," Asunción said. "One man in particular, Littmann. Be very careful."

A bus roared around the uphill corner and pulled to the shelter, stopped. A woman wearing a rumpled suit and a pained expression disembarked, turning instantly toward the courthouse. Lisa waved the driver on. The folding doors squealed shut, and the bus thundered off in a choking black plume.

Lisa said, "I'm not surprised by what you just told me," waving away the exhaust. "They've already—"

"They are killers," Asunción said. "They are animals." Her hands sat clasped tight in her lap. Her eyes glistened.

135

"This Littmann, this man who calls himself a judge but has no use for justice. He is the head of a group that patrols the border, hunting for people coming across. When they find them, they do not turn them over to La Migra, no. No. That would be too kind. Too . . . just."

Her chest began rising, falling with the effort of containing herself. The tears she could no longer blink away began winnowing down her cheeks.

Lisa said, "And . . . what?"

"They tie their hands and feet," Asunción said, wiping her face, "then hang them from gallows put up in the mountains. They loop signs around the necks of the bodies that read *No pasaran*. Do you know what this means?"

"Yes," Lisa said, registering the irony.

She'd had a special devotion for Latin American history as an undergrad at Georgetown. The phrase — it meant "They Shall Not Pass" — first became famous among the anti-fascist Republicans in the rebellion against Franco, then reappeared in Nicaragua in the war against Reagan's Contras. How perfectly broad-minded of an anti-immigrant lynch mob to bend the phrase to its anti-Hispanic purpose.

"Perhaps I'm mistaken," she said, "but I get the sense this is personal for you."

An absent nod. Thousand-yard-stare. "My sister." A ragged sigh. "My niece."

She dug into the pocket of her slacks, removed a folded slip of paper. "You should call this man. He can tell you more. Tell him I gave you his name."

———⊰◇⊱———

The name was Elan Wingfield, and he worked at the Public Defender's Office—at least, that's whose receptionist picked up the phone when Lisa called the number.

A brief hold and then he came on the line, and she explained herself, what she was doing, how she got his name, where she was calling from. The recitation earned her a painful silence, charged with apprehension she'd just blundered into a reckless mistake.

"Mister Wingfield?"

"Walk up Congress two blocks," he said finally, his voice lilting and deep and calm, an accent she couldn't place. "Cross over to Veinte de Agosto Park. Wait for me near the statue of Poncho Villa."

A public spot, Lisa thought. That bodes well. "How will I know you?" Another interminable silence.

"I will give you the secret sign of my ancient people." An acid chuckle, rumbling up from smoke-scarred lungs. "My office is nearby," he added. "I will not be long."

———⊰◇⊱———

Lisa walked up the four-lane boulevard to a small municipal park, surrounded by the county government complex, a shimmering office tower, a Catholic church.

Finding a shaded bench, she made herself comfortable, settling in for her wait. After a moment she lifted her eyes to the large bronze sculpture of the merry, murderous *generalissimo*, Poncho Villa, atop his steed. She wondered what Tuck would make of it.

That promptly brought to mind the worrisome four marines: Rags, Chalky, Wander, Black Buddha Killer—and what the hell was *that* about?

She gnawed at her lip. Moral support, yeah, right. Fire support, more likely. Please, dear God, please don't let them be stupid.

⚜

Rags watched from the passenger seat of the rental van as the one called Giordano left his office—nothing but a sign in a window otherwise sheeted by blinds, single unit in a Sierra Vista strip mall.

The man headed for a sandwich shop three doors down, went in.

Sitting at the wheel, Wander said, "Consultant, my ass." A throaty hiss—Clint Eastwood as Dirty Harry. "If that ain't a front, I'll eat my fingers."

Wander had earned good money in Helmand, typically over cards, taking side bets from fellow jarheads that he could impersonate any entertainer, politician, or talking head they could name.

"Go ahead," Rags said. "Pull across the road, park as close as you can."

As Wander waited for traffic to clear, Rags turned around in his seat to face the van's windowless storage bay— no seats, just space, and thick with heat.

He said, "You sure you're up for this?"

Rayella, sitting Indian-style on a flannel mat, dabbing away sweat, replied with a bloodshot smile. Behind her,

Chalky and BBK—one lean and long with opalescent skin, the other massive and solid, arms like mahogany—sat with their backs against the van's walls, knees up, feet flat, like paratroopers waiting out the drop. They'd stacked their duffels like cordwood against the windowless rear door, along with the weapons.

Wander pulled the van into the parking area and hitched to a stop near an exit, easy access back onto the street, twenty yards from the sandwich shop. He kept the motor idling as everyone but him and BBK got out.

"Bring me back a pickle," Wander said. Mel Gibson impression this time, vintage *Lethal Weapon*, that Aussie-inflected Angeleno thing. Again, pitch perfect. "Something crunchy."

Rags pulled a map from his back pocket. Once he got near the shop, he spread it out across the hood of a car, as though to study it. Chalky eased up alongside.

Rayella, meanwhile, headed in.

The place was called The Rye Smile—low ceilings and brash light, a sign in the window reading: *Life, Liberty, and the Prosciutto of Happiness.*

Inside it smelled like fresh bread, pickle brine, and something else, something vaguely foul, like one of the sandwich jockeys had dried his wet sneakers in the oven.

It being just a little past ten o'clock, there were only two customers, three if you counted Giordano. He had his back to the door, jingling change in a loose fist as he studied the breakfast sandwich menu, written in chalk on a wall-mounted blackboard, then leaned in to place his order with the counter girl.

Rayella waited near the door, trembling as she studied the back of the stocky man's neck. What I wouldn't give, she thought, to get him alone. Five minutes. Just that. Not ungrateful for Rags and the others, their gung-ho chivalry, their methodical devotion to making things right. Hardly. But remembering the punch to her face, the rest of the rough stuff, then the stench of his breath, feeling it on her skin, warm and wet as he whispered his filthy little monologue. Was it really only a couple of days ago that life had been okay?

Giordano's order came. He collected the small brown bag, turned to leave. After a few head-down steps, he finally glanced up. Stopped in his tracks.

Rayella traded stares with him. Gradually, he broke into a yellowish smile. A second check of the other customers to see if anyone got up or even paid him any mind — no one did. He turned back, eased toward her.

"Looky, looky."

"Can we talk?" She half-turned toward the door.

"What's wrong with right here." Not a question.

"Nothing. I just thought you'd want—"

He leaned in to whisper. "Trust me. You have no goddamn clue what I want." She could count the pores on his nose. He straightened back up, once again scanned the room. "What's there to talk about?"

"Look, I don't want trouble. I just want the letters back."

"Yeah? Good luck with that."

"Whatever's going on between Tuck Mercer and you people has nothing to do with me. My grandmother gave me those letters. They're a gift."

"Your lawyer know what you're doing here?" He checked out her blouse, as though looking for odd lumps, a wire.

"This doesn't concern my lawyer."

"Bet she sees it different. Let me see your hands."

Despite herself, Rayella shuddered. "Why?"

"Just show me."

She held up her hands, steadied them just above waist-level, as though preparing to conjure the dead.

Giordano's eyes never left hers. "You know, in ancient Egypt, when someone got caught at forgery, they cut off both their hands."

Rayella swallowed. "I haven't forged anything."

"You really don't know what's going on here, do you? Or who you're dealing with." He nudged her aside, pushed open the door, and left.

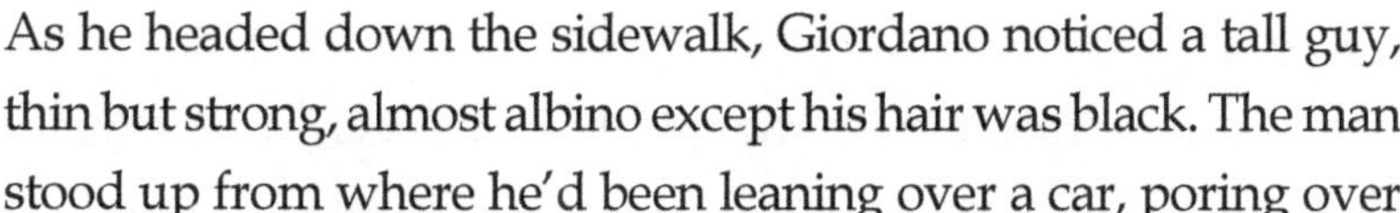

As he headed down the sidewalk, Giordano noticed a tall guy, thin but strong, almost albino except his hair was black. The man stood up from where he'd been leaning over a car, poring over a map with his buddy.

"Excuse me." Desert rat accent. Eyes like ice picks. "Could you show us the quickest route to Benson?"

Giordano never got an answer out. The second of the two

men—face a blur, just a flash of something rippled and red, a blotch, a birthmark, a burn—rose and spun and delivered a crippling kidney punch.

Just as Giordano's knees turned to muck, a van throttled up, screeched to a stop, the side door slid open fast. They bundled him in—the girl, Rayella, followed. The door slid shut. The van sped off.

They bound and gagged him with duct tape, working fast, then covered him with the flannel mat.

Rags watched from the passenger seat. Once they had Giordano securely bundled, BBK glanced toward the front, waiting for the go-ahead.

Rags nodded.

BBK lifted his thick dark arm, fist clenched, then brought it down so hard and fast Rayella cringed, even before impact.

From beneath the flannel mat, behind his duct tape gag, Giordano screamed as something, probably a bone, snapped dully.

BBK glanced up again. Rags waited, met Rayella's eyes.

Another nod. Another hammering blow. More muffled screams.

Break his ribs, Rayella thought, one by one. Not all of them, though. We need him to live. We need him to talk.

The beating went on as they drove up Highway 90 toward Huachuca City, where there was an abandoned house way out on Babacomari Road. Tuck had found it. He was waiting for them there.

Meanwhile, up front, Wander sang:

> *"'You can run on for a long time*
> *Run on for a long time*
> *Run on for a long time*
> *Sooner or later God'll cut you down*
> *Sooner or later God'll cut you down.'"*

Like Johnny Cash was right there in the van.

~ 20 ~

"Miss Balamaro?"

She hadn't noticed him approaching. True to his word, he'd gotten there quick. "I am Elan Wingfield."

He stood with the sun behind him, and she had to shade her eyes to make him out. A tall man, bit of a mid-life paunch, dressed like a hip professor: rumpled denim shirt beneath a tweed jacket, blue jeans with a hand-made silver buckle, scuffed boots. His black hair, parted in the middle and shoulder-length, worn loose, bore threads of gray, and she was wondering at his age—same as Tuck, perhaps, or a few years older—when his face at last came into focus, haloed by sunlight. It was broad and smooth, the color of mesquite, younger than his body. The nose of a Roman senator and the full lips of a matinee idol. A gentle courage warmed the eyes.

"Nice little park," she said, thinking: Was that lame enough?

144

"Last summer, it's wall-to-wall squatters, till the city kicks them out." He sat down heavily at the bench's far end. "Been a homeless camp for five years. Some still trickle back, time to time, sleep on the sidewalks, others have tents they call 'Dream Pods.'"

A smoky chuckle, like the one she'd heard over the phone.

She wondered at his using the present tense even to discuss the past. Maybe that's an Indian thing, she thought. Speaking of lame. Thank God you didn't say that out loud.

"Admiring our prize abomination, I see." He waved a listless hand at the statue of Poncho Villa.

"I have a friend named Tuck Mercer with, shall we say, a unique understanding of Western art. I was trying to imagine what he would think of it." She cocked her head, as though a different angle might improve the appraisal. "It's kind of Remington-esque," she said, "only not as, well, good." She turned back toward him quickly. "Oh God, I'm sorry if that seems—"

"I'm no judge of art." The man shrugged. "But I know the name Remington. He drew a sketch of the Skeleton Canyon Massacre for, you know, some magazine back east. Sixty of my people, the Yavapai, wiped out. But he didn't draw that part. Just showed the soldiers firing from behind rocks at, you know, the enemy. The savages." He turned back toward her. "You have any idea what I'm talking about?"

His glance seemed to slice right though her. "I'm afraid . . . no. I don't."

"Christmas morning, 1871. General Crook's men, led by his famous Apache scouts, who are actually Pima and Maricopa, our traditional enemies — but no one can tell us apart, or bothers to, and even 'Apache' is, you know, their word, not ours — they slaughter men and women and children hiding in a cave not that far from here." He gestured to the northwest. "A captured Yavapai boy, Hoomothya, guides them there against his will, and he watches as, you know, it happens. Right up until the death chants end. He writes about it much later. Interesting book. *All of My People Were Killed*."

Lisa felt a sudden shameful warmth, like a head-to-toe sunburn.

He returned his eyes to the statue. "As for Ol' Poncho here — Mexican government offers this thing as a gift to the people of Phoenix, or a suburb, can't remember which one. They refuse to take it." A wry smile brushed across his face. "Even here, people file lawsuits twice to keep it out. And after it finally goes up, there are protests for years, but the picket lines gradually dwindle away. So here it is."

Scratching an itch at the back of her memory, Lisa said, "Right. He crossed over the border, murdered some people."

"Fifteen civilians. Plus some soldiers."

"They chased him into Mexico, but . . . "

"Blackjack Pershing has no more luck catching Poncho Villa than General Crook before him, trying to find Cochise. And that continues to rankle some folks here. Like the man you and I have in common."

He turned back toward her, his expression strangely both warm and stern.

"Gideon Littmann," she said.

"Which judge was assigned to your case?"

"Let me check." She opened her valise, searched through the file-stamped pleadings. "Here it is." Handing him the complaint. "Celestina Numkena."

He smiled, taking the document from her. "Lucky draw."

"That's good?"

"She's a very impressive woman." He paged through the document. "I can't imagine her putting up too much with Littmann."

Lisa felt her shoulders ease down from her ears. "All I ask of a judge," she said, "is that she read my pleadings, listen to my arguments, and rule fairly."

"You're going to need a lot more than that." He set the complaint beside him on the bench, crossed his legs, lifted his eyes to the sky, and dug a cigarette pack from the inside pocket of his sport coat. "Make yourself comfortable. This is kinda, you know, involved."

⤐∞⤏

Rags tossed his flavorless wad of gum across the sun-cracked hardpan, standing in what passed for a front yard—ramshackle bungalow, long abandoned, out on a lonesome two-lane road. The buckling asphalt stretched east and west, dusted with windblown sand and marked by a single roadside sign: *Drive Hammered – Get Nailed!* It was peppered with bullet holes.

Nothing else around for nearly a click, and even then just a rusting caravan perched on blocks, an ancient VHF antenna pinning it in place, no vehicles parked outside.

Welcome to Crazy Acres, he thought.

Beyond that perimeter lay sagebrush desert and alkali flats spreading in all directions toward jagged eruptions of sky-island rock—Santa Rita range due west, Huachuca Mountains a little to the south, Whetstones to the northeast.

It was in the Huachucas that the renegade Chatto began his famous raid, the beginning of the end of the Apache wars, butchering every white man he came across for the sake of bullets and horses, then fleeing south over the border.

And it was in the Whetstones where Juh—husband of Geronimo's favorite sister, Ishton—sprang his trap and got revenge for the U.S. Army butchering a camp of peaceful Mescaleros.

Rags often likened the fight in Afghanistan to the Indian wars, and the more he read, the more apt the analogy felt. It was no coincidence the military likened the Taliban's tactics in the siege of Barge Matal to those of the Apache, or compared how the Durand Line bordering Pakistan provided the same strategic advantage to the Taliban that the Mexican border had for Victorio and Cochise and Geronimo.

But the similarities ran deeper, from the inventively cruel ferocity of the adversary to the constant political meddling in the rules of engagement. It wasn't hard, in either war, to gain a greater respect for the enemy than one's own chain of command, or the chicken-shit civilians you were supposedly fighting for.

It wasn't just that aspect of the history, though, that stirred his reflections.

The West had welcomed men like him, veterans of a godless Holy War that turned its soldiers into strangers and drifters and misfits. Nothing like miles and miles of rugged terrain to exorcise the devils of memory.

To Rags, though, the territory felt like home. He'd grown up not that far north in Winslow. Chalky came from a high desert small town, too—Barstow, across the California line—and like Rags had spent his boyhood buck hunting, fly fishing, camping alone in the mountain wild, nothing but fragrant pines and a star-dusted sky for company.

Wander and BBK were the city boys, Reno and Compton, respectively. Irregular warfare training in the desert at Twenty-Nine Palms cured them of their urban stupidities. If not, the Battle of Marja sure did.

But none of them had been involved in finding this hideaway. That was Tuck Mercer's doing—said it came up fast this morning on the Internet listings, properties for sale, ten grand or under, most unlivable, like this one, valuable solely for the dirt beneath the concrete slab.

Maybe all that was true. But Rags couldn't help thinking the old rodeo hand, the famous forger, was a little too eager to chip in, lend a hand, like he'd been planning all this for a little longer than any of them knew.

And the thought of getting dragged into another man's fight, after all they'd been through at the hands of the Karzais and their cronies in the Land of Bones . . .

Enough of that, he thought. Work to do. There was a fat Italian phony to question. While he still could manage to get out the words.

~ 21 ~

WIND rustled the leaves of the small park's shade trees as Elan Wingfield conducted the elaborate ritual of lighting up—poking a lazy finger inside the pack, fishing out a cigarette. The man possessed excruciating patience—Lisa had to restrain herself from reaching over, snatching the pack, and holding it ransom until he spoke.

"Various tribes," he said finally, "not just the Yavapai-Apache but the Chiricahua, Mescalero, Zuni, Hopi, several others—we all have the right to return to the Coronado National Forest and the Dragoon Mountains to forage for desert willow, yucca root, devil's claw. The shoots and seed pods are used to make burden baskets, parching trays." He tapped his unlit cigarette hard against the back of his hand once, twice, three times. "About a year-and-a-half ago, a group of Yavapai-Apache women—"

"I'm sorry," Lisa interrupted, thinking: Don't be testy. "You said you were Yavapai. So that's a sub-group, sub-tribe—I'm sorry I don't know the term—of Apache?"

"No. The Yavapai and Apache are distinct tribes, from completely different language groups: Yuman, Athabaskan. The government doesn't know the difference, so they mix us all together, call us one tribe. Because, you know, they can."

He lipped his cigarette, tugged a match from its matchbook, and struck it against the flint strip till a flame came to life in his cupped hand.

"I'm sorry," Lisa said again, surrendering at last to the man's expansive sense of time. "I didn't mean to butt in."

"It's fine." He waved out the match. "Where was I?"

"A group of women. The Dragoons."

"Right. So these women are foraging along the mountain ridges—just above where Littmann has his ranch, the Bristlecone—when a band of armed men drive up in a Range Rover. The women, they figure these guys for hunters. Folks still go up there looking for cougars, coyotes, whitetail. Anyway, the men get out and tell the women they gotta leave. Now."

No one else around for miles, Lisa thought, picturing it.

"The women protest, say this is public land, they have a legal right. That gets several rifles pointed their direction, one guy fires in the air—redneck punctuation—says something like, 'How's that for a legal right?'"

Lisa swallowed, a nervous reflex, wondering how much of this story was meant to serve as background, how much as prediction.

"The women come back to Camp Verde, tell the tribal elders, who pass it along to the Bureau of Indian Affairs in

Whiteriver, who pass it along to someone else who passes it along again. You get the idea."

"Pretty much. Yeah."

"A month later, another group heads off to forage, this time with some men, you know, just in case. I'm one of the men. Nobody drives us off this time."

A deep, contemplative drag, exhaling the smoke in a long curling plume.

Lisa ventured, "But . . . "

"We don't encounter any gunmen. We do find something, though. Along the central ridgeline, somewhere mid-range." He squinted slightly, as though sharpening his focus on the scene in his mind. "There aren't a lot of tall trees up there, even in the forest along the northern slope. All the pines and junipers and larger oaks, you know, get cut down and sent to sawmills during the Tombstone boom. Except for the protected areas around Cochise Stronghold, all that's left now is some mesquite, ironwood, emory oak. Scrub, basically. So if you want to hang someone, you need to put up your own scaffold. Or, in this case, three."

He tapped ash onto the sidewalk. Lisa pictured Golgotha.

"Simple structure, old-time gallows—no platform or drop door, just two four-by-fours, one planted deep in the dirt, some big rocks to prop it up and hold it straight, the other beam parallel to the ground, an angled brace between the two to handle the weight of the body."

Still staring into some imaginary distance. Another of his customary silences.

"The lack of a long drop," he said finally, "means the victim's neck won't break. Takes a long time to die."

From the opposite side of the park, a homeless woman—skin dark from cirrhosis, barefoot, shawled in a dirty blanket and wearing a feathered Homburg—shuffled toward them, trailed by two panting dogs. Glancing up, she spotted Elan and Lisa on their bench, then took an immediate detour, angling away beyond the statue. The two dogs followed.

Lisa said, "Asunción, the woman who gave me your name, she said her sister . . . "

"Yes. She's one of the three we find. Her daughter, too."

"How old?" she asked, almost hating to.

"Young," Elan said. "Eight or so, I think. A child."

He dropped his cigarette butt onto the sidewalk, crushed it with the toe of his boot. Then he picked it up, tossed it toward a nearby trash bin. Missed.

"We contact the sheriff for Cochise County, since that's where the Dragoons lie. He calls Border Patrol, and they fight over who has jurisdiction because, you know, neither wants it. Same old thing. The story makes the local news for a day but goes nowhere, just another bunch of *mojados* found dead after crossing the border, happens all the time. The fact they've been strung up like old-time horse thieves gets shrugged off, blamed on the *coyotes* who brought them across. Probably tried to shake down the *pollos* for more money mid-trip. They can't pay, so they get left as an example to others."

"But you don't believe that."

"Couple days later, Piper Cub flies along the border dropping leaflets. Thousands of them, from Douglas to the Huachucas, they end up both sides of the border. The leaflets have a picture of the three bodies we found hanging by the neck."

Lisa said, "I'll bet I can guess the caption."

No pasaran.

Giordano, stripped naked, his rippling pinkish fat exposed, stood tiptoe on the concrete slab, handcuffed to a rusty four-inch pipe that ran along the ceiling of the garage. No blood, they'd been careful. But the skin on his torso had erupted in florid bruising here and there from internal hemorrhaging.

Chalky had monitored the man's condition, checking the carotid artery for pulse, placing an ear to his chest to gauge heart rate, monitor the fluid building in the lungs.

Chalky had served as corpsman for their platoon over in Helmand, but he'd finally turned in his medical kit for a .50 cal sniper rifle after zipping one too many marines into a glad bag. He was doubly blessed in skill set, equally capable of stitching you up on a highback's tailgate or blowing out your eye at 300 yards.

Once Chalky nodded to assure them all the prisoner was fit, Rags drew close, raised the man's chin so their eyes met.

"I'm not the kind to run to lawyers," he said. "Where I come from, somebody steals something from you, you steal it back."

Giordano's head lolled on his neck. His eyes swam.

"Now you've got an opportunity to make up for what you did to my girl. Look at yourself. Same thing happening to you, you did to her. Know what that's called?"

Rayella, standing to the side, said, "It's called justice," answering for Giordano who, after all, couldn't speak. Duct tape still sealed his mouth shut.

"Let me be clear," Rags said. "Every man here's a trained killer—well, except for you. When it comes to pain, we know our business. All that stuff you hear about torture doesn't work? It's a lie. Torture works swell. Depends on how much time and ingenuity you're willing to put into it."

Chalky, Wander, and BBK all moved a little closer. Rayella stepped back.

"Now I know what you said to my girl after you popped her, knocked her down, tied her up. Don't pretend you don't remember. Started off something like, 'Not to worry, Skank. You're so damn ugly, I wouldn't rape you with some other guy's dick.' Words to that effect. Am I right? Now here's the thing—I'm gonna give you a chance to make it up to her. I'm gonna give you a chance to walk away clean. How's that sound?"

Rags jiggled Giordano's chin. Somewhere deep in the scared man's eyes, a bolt of hope flickered.

"Give me the layout of Littmann's house, down to the last room. I want to know ways in, ways out, where the outbuildings are. I want to know how many people work there, where they are any time of the day. And when Littmann comes and goes."

"Security system," Chalky said, taking out a notepad to write on. "Don't leave that out."

"I'm in no mood to hear 'I don't know,'" Rags said. "Thing is—and you really need to understand this—thing is, for men like us, everything we've been through, everything we've been asked to do, everything we've gone ahead and done, there's no doubt or hesitation once we know the answer to one simple question: Who's the enemy? Not a blot on our conscience once that's clear. And that's where we're at right now, with you—understand?"

The men edged still closer. Giordano nodded.

"Good man," Rags said. "Now you've already been through a lot. Nothing you didn't deserve, but still. You want to spare yourself more of the same, don't play dumb."

He began unraveling the duct tape wrapped tight around Giordano's head. The last few turns snagged hair and flesh. Giordano winced, jerking his head away.

Rags said, "Steady, steady. Almost there."

Once the tape was free, long and twisted like a shed snakeskin, Rags handed it to BBK who placed it inside a large black trash bag where they'd stuffed the man's clothes.

"All set?"

Wander stepped behind Rags, the better to watch Giordano as he told them what he knew—no surprise, he didn't even try to act tough. Between whimpers, ragged breaths, and sniveling pleas he explained not just the geography, which Chalky sketched out in his notepad, but the personnel, which told a more complicated story.

Littmann had his own security squad on site, usually four men, two at the gate, one in the house, one on patrol around the ranch's perimeter. But they were part of a larger group of volunteers spread out across the county, ready to answer any call. Because of them, the alarm system seldom got used, unless the house was empty, which it seldom was, since the wife was an invalid, half blind or something.

With every phrase, Wander repeated the words verbatim—not to memorize, but to mimic, get the inflection and tone just right, the accent, the rhythm.

At one point, mustering his last shred of pride, Giordano looked up and said, "What are you, a parrot?"

Everybody laughed. Then BBK delivered a thudding blow to the lower back. Giordano, finally able to cry out, let out a sharp keening bark of pain.

"We make the jokes, tubs." Wander talking, though it could have been Giordano himself. The man looked stunned, as though coming face to face with his own echo.

Wander said, "Now I know what you're thinking," same voice, eerie in its perfection. "I got a gift. Could be famous. Play Vegas, play Hooters, do the *Tonight Show*. Could be rich. Here's the thing—I *hate* the whole showbiz scene. Comedians, in particular. Met Seinfeld once, no lie. Backstage at the MGM in Reno. Total snooty boojwah shmuck. I swear—came *this close* to ripping him a new one."

He held up his forefinger and thumb a micrometer apart.

"And there's the irony, ya know? I'd be in prison for murder within six months, I tried to do this legit. Hollywood gasbags? Hecklers? Fuhgeddaboudit. Combat changes you, Guido. Just can't deal with phonies no more. Know what I mean? Guys like you."

The whole room seemed dazed. Chalky murmured, "Sweet Jesus . . . How do you *do* that?"

"I binge-watched *The Sopranos*," Wander said. "Like this pudge."

Giordano hung there, wincing with each rough breath. Even so, he managed finally to lift his head, meet Rags's eye, and whisper, "Mercer . . . The forger . . . "

Each man glanced at the other, then Rags leaned in. "What about him?"

"He's fucking you. Fucking everybody . . . "

Rags waited. "Care to elaborate?"

"I don't know — don't hit me, okay? No more. Please. But I don't know. Some old beef, him and Littmann . . . "

He closed his eyes, let his head hang as he shuddered against some sudden pain. Chalky moved in to check on him but with a glance Rags held him back.

"Beef as in what — he buy a fake painting?"

Giordano, unable to lift his head. "I don't know — honest, please. Enough — "

From the large black trash bag, BBK produced the pair of socks they'd stripped off the man, lodged one in Giordano's mouth and tied the other around his head to secure the first in place.

Rags said, "Lemme get back to you on that. Meantime, hang tight."

~ 22 ~

THE noontime lunch crowd began trickling from the nearby government buildings and bank tower. Lisa cleared her throat. "Mr. Wingfield—"

"It's okay." He was leaning forward thoughtfully, elbows on knees, hands tented. "Call me Elan."

"Elan." She winced from a sudden glare of sunlight lancing through the shade trees. "I appreciate your telling me about what you've learned. And seen. It's really shocking and awful and terrifying, and I get, I think, what you're trying to tell me. But I'm really only after a packet of letters. I wish I could help you in some way but . . ."

His gaze hardened ever so slightly. "You think I'm asking for help?"

"Please don't take offense. I didn't—"

"I'm trying to give you an idea of who and what you're up against."

"You're saying these men, the ones who drove off the women from your tribe, the ones who lynched the three immigrants—assuming they're one and the same—they're linked to Littmann?"

"To him and his family, his history."

"What does that mean?"

"Give me a moment," he said. "I'll explain."

Once again, the ceremony of the cigarette—tugging the pack from his pocket, probing for his smoke, tapping it hard against the back of his hand. Lisa snuck a glance at her watch. She'd wanted to spend the afternoon in the law library, doing additional research.

"There's a tradition down here," he said, "going back to when the whites first showed up. Freebooters, vigilantes, most with full support of the government. 'War to the knife and knife to the hilt'—that's how the territory charter reads."

Lisa wondered if there was any part of the region's history that wasn't depressing.

"A man named King Woolsey is notorious for lynching Apaches or luring them into phony parleys so his men can open fire. If that doesn't work, he poisons them by adding strychnine to *pinole*, corn meal mixed with mesquite beans, and giving it out as a peace offering. He calls it the Pinole Treaty."

"And this Woolsey, he's an ancestor of Littmann's?"

"Not directly," Elan said. "Ideologically, let's say. Littmann's bloodline—on one side anyway, or so he claims— goes back to a man named Judge Mike Gray, who helps organize and finance the Tombstone Rangers, a pack of amateur scalp hunters that, at one point, tries to wipe out the entire San Carlos Reservation. Ironically, from your viewpoint anyway, that particular contingent is led by a man named Milt

Joyce, who's better known as the sworn enemy of your friend Doc Holliday."

So that's the connection with Littmann, Lisa thought. Part of it anyway. Maybe.

"On the other side of the family," Elan continued, "you've got a man named Gus Littmann. He shows up sometime during the First World War, helps form the Citizens' Protective League to counter the mining strikes. Ever hear of the Bisbee Deportation?"

Lisa shook her head.

"Thirteen hundred miners, most with odd last names, you know? Get packed at gunpoint into cattle cars and shipped two hundred miles — sixteen hours through the desert in July, no water, no food — and dropped off in Tres Hermanas, New Mexico."

"I'm guessing that's the middle of nowhere."

"Pretty much. Anyway, like I said, that's the tradition. And with the hatred so strong around here for Washington these days, you know — not just them, any outsiders — the militia idea has come back strong."

"You're saying Judge Littmann is in charge of this group you've been describing, the ones you came across in the Dragoons."

"He's not that blatant. Word is he channels money to them and uses some of the members as security on his ranch. He's also written a couple articles and editorials that suggest he thinks they're not just legitimate, there's Constitutional justification."

Good God, Lisa thought, I should have seen this coming. Article One, Section Eight. "Letters of marque and reprisal."

Elan smiled appreciatively. "Give the young lady a prize."

They were designed to give the government the right to use privateers—pirates, basically—to plunder enemy ships. "Libertarians have been arguing they should be brought back to fund private armies—contractors, mercenaries—in the War on Terror."

"Or patrol the Mexican border. Even conduct raids onto Indian reservations, where, you know, they say smugglers operate freely. Like we're to blame."

"They're attacking you, too?"

"Not yet. But they don't just operate in the Dragoons. Around twenty bodies have been found so far, most down in the Peloncillos and Chiricahuas, closer to the border, but sometimes it's hard to know who killed who. Point is, they're a menace, a pack of weekend patriots armed to the teeth. Even if you get everything you want in court, and Littmann's ordered to hand back what he stole—who's going to make him comply? You think U.S. Marshals want to risk a bloodbath over a bunch of letters that, for all they know, might be fake?"

They're not fake, she thought, they're genuine. I've seen them, read them, touched them. And yet for some reason, at that particular moment, she couldn't bring herself to say that out loud.

"If you don't mind my asking," Elan said, "what possesses a nice young lady like you to get wrapped up with this kind of character in the first place?"

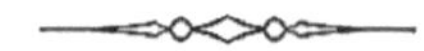

Rags and the other marines, Rayella in tow, filed out of the garage where they left Giordano hanging. The forger, Tuck, was waiting for them in what once had served as the living room. He was standing over a map he'd spread out on the bare slab floor, nothing else in the room except a litter box and scratch pad for a long-departed cat.

"While you all have been out there entertaining our guest," Tuck said, "I've been thinking about the best way onto the Littmann property."

"Have you now." Rags crouched down for a closer look at the map. His squaddies followed suit. Rayella drifted back toward the wall, chewing on a thumbnail.

"I grew up just over the ridge in Harshaw," Tuck said. "Used to hike and ride horseback all the time as a kid in the mountains around here." Pointing at the map with the tip of his cane. "Your best bet is go down Ironwood Road behind the Dragoons, head for the Cochise Stronghold but don't go all the way in. May be campers there—birders, hikers, it's a popular spot." He glanced man to man, as though to make sure they took his meaning. "Instead, take this turn on the forest road and head for Blacktail Hill, right here. There's an unmarked road beyond that. Drive uphill to about five thousand feet—there's a flat area near a stock tank where you can park. From there you'll hike up and over

Rockfellow Dome. Keep Mount Glenn to your right, Council Rocks to your left. Won't be easy, especially at night, even with the moon waxing full."

"We've got NVGs," Rags said. Night Vision Goggles.

"Yeah, well, there's mesquite and scrub oak thickets so dense they might as well be walls, not to mention open mine shafts you can fall into. Plus all the cactus, the rattlers."

"We're not new to the desert." Chalky the one interrupting this time. "Besides, still early in the year to worry about rattlesnakes, even at night."

"All right then." Tuck seemed to sense the tension but merely pointed again with the tip of his cane. "Once you get over the summit you'll hit a trailhead here, at the end of Stronghold Canyon West. Follow it down to this airstrip—really just a patch of dirt, but the slope from the top is easier, better to get planes in and out. Beats having to rappel down sheer rock. From there it's a short hike to the back end of the ranch." Tuck checked his watch. "You better get going if you want a good start before sundown."

Rags collected the map, folded it back into pocket shape, and put it away, nodding toward the garage. "Fat man says there's security. Four-man team, twenty-four-seven, but there's plenty more at the beck and call of this judge. All he has to do is send out word, they'll come running. Part of some kind of home reserve down here. You wouldn't happen to know anything about that, would you?"

All eyes turned toward Tuck. He shrugged, leaned on his cane. "Should I?"

"You tell me."

"Look, I realize there might be—"

"You're the one found this bent judge, am I right? Found the lame lawyer, too, one who just sat there and let Rayella get pounded and robbed."

"Lisa Ball-o-sorrow," Wander said.

"Seems to me," Rags said, "we got any cause to fault someone for making a bad call, it's you."

"I can understand," Tuck said, "why you'd think that, but if you'll just—"

"Now we learn there won't be any quick in-and-out, not with that much manpower in the neighborhood. Somebody's sure to get hurt."

A bellowing groan came from the garage. Nobody bothered to turn.

"On top of which, you find this house here lickety-split this morning, like it's at your fingertips, ya know? But that's not the punch line. Wanna hear the punch line?"

Tuck met his eye with an easy calm. Had to give the man credit for that, Rags thought, especially after dealing with Fatso.

"Mr. Giordano in there says this whole thing has nothing to do with Rayella or those letters. All comes down to bad blood between you and Littmann. Goes back years. Got anything to say on that?"

"Yeah," Tuck said. His gaze held steady. "It's a lie."

"Do tell," Chalky said.

"I don't know anything about the man. I found his name on a list of collectors at the auction house where I do some consulting. That's it."

Rags said, "You're sure about that."

"When I made my plea agreement, I had to list every known owner of one of my paintings. He wasn't on it. Maybe he was dumb enough to get suckered into buying one after my arrest, thinking it was genuine, and holds a grudge. I've got no clue."

"You're saying the bad blood's all on his side."

"Far as I know. Point is, I didn't see this coming. And yeah, I feel bad about that. It's why I'm trying to lend a hand here, make up for the mistakes."

From her spot near the wall, Rayella murmured, "The least you could do."

"And don't call Lisa lame," Tuck said. "She's working her tail end off to make up for what happened."

"Like it'll do any good." Wander again.

"Don't sell that girl short. She's a fighter, believe me. Now I agree with you all, even if she gets the court to lean her way, given what we know already about these people, it's unlikely they'll hand anything back."

"Not without more incentive than a piece of paper," Chalky said.

"Which is why," Tuck said, "I also agree that the best idea is just go on in, take the letters back, settle this like men. Truth be told, though, you couldn't ask for a better diversion than Lisa. She's the reason you don't need to worry about being outnumbered. Given the holy hell she's gonna raise in court, nobody'll expect to see you coming over that range. Nobody. You can bank on that."

He looked face to face as though to see how his words landed. Rags, momentarily lost in thought, rose from his crouch. In for a penny, he thought. Fortune favors the brave.

"Mr. Mercer, I'd like you to drive Rayella back to the hotel. Wait for our call."

"No," Rayella said, stepping forward. "I'm coming along. I've played my part so far. I've got a right. Those letters are mine."

"You let me take care of the letters," Rags said. "Even with surprise on our side, there's no telling what might happen at that house. Besides, we've got some business here to wrap up."

He didn't elaborate, just met her gaze. Her eyes grew large as his point sank in.

"No need for you to be part of that," he said.

———◈◇◈———

"There are two other names you have listed here I should tell you about." Elan gestured with his cigarette to the caption on her complaint. "The lawyer, Rankin. He and Littmann get together when the judge sits on the criminal bench in Cochise County. Rankin's a defense lawyer, drug cases mostly, and a total smokehound."

Lisa felt her cheeks warm. Been there, done that.

"He gets pulled over for a DUI, they toss his car, claim they got his permission first. You know how that goes."

Yes, Lisa thought. Unfortunately, I do.

"Guess what they find," he said.

Nothing, she thought, if he was lucky like me and already wolfed it all. "I'm guessing it's not so much a question of what as how much."

"Ten grams. There's no personal use allowance under Arizona law, not for crack, and the threshold for possession for sale is seven hundred fifty milligrams. So Rankin's way over the line. That's a Class Two felony, mandatory minimum three years in prison, max of ten. Throw in getting disbarred."

"I think I know where this is going."

"He wants a deal."

"Of course he does."

"Who does a defense lawyer have to hand up?"

She let out a dispirited sigh. "His clients."

"A lot of folks down here just shrug. Or cheer. Only the innocent deserve a right to counsel, way they see it. Even federal judges, if they criticize what's going on, seldom toss the evidence. Anyway, a beautiful friendship is formed, and Littmann, with Rankin as his snitch, gets a rep as tough on crime."

"What about the other guy, the clown, Giordano?"

Elan put out his cigarette, crushing it with his boot, but this time walked it over to the trash bin, collected the first butt as well, dropped both in. He came back spanking his hands clean, sat down, then said with a smile, "You must mean Robert Jordan."

Lisa barked out a helpless laugh. "I knew it."

"Born in Youngstown, Ohio. Comes out to Las Vegas about ten years ago. Wants to be connected so bad he changes his name. Joke that goes around about him? Only guy in the history of Vegas who ever *added* a vowel to the end of his name."

"How'd he end up here?"

"Nobody who's for real wants anything to do with him in Nevada, so he wanders down here, gets popped moving stolen traveler's checks, somehow connects with Rankin, and they put their heads together, work up a scheme. Rankin uses his connection to Littmann to sell it to the County Attorney. Giordano gets out of his jam by fronting up a sting, impersonates a made guy from back east looking for willing partners to launder his cash."

"You mean somebody actually fell for that act?"

"There's a lot of yokels down here, by which I mean prosecutors and politicians and people who want to move in on the action, who claim there's mob money or cartel money flowing through the Indian casinos. So they buy into Giordano's routine like he's Joe Pesci. Waltzes in to Cliff Castle, which is on our land, and Mazatzal, run by the Tonto Apache, says he wants to put an offer on the table, wink wink. Gets the bum's rush both places—we may be ignorant savages, but nobody's that dumb. Anyway, even when there's nothing to show for it, Rankin falls in love with Giordano's mustard. Littmann, too. And so Robert Jordan of Youngstown, Ohio, gets to keep on playing Willy Wiseguy."

~ 23 ~

GIORDANO'S eyes swelled, focusing on the ugly, ragged burn that covered half of Rags's face.

"Ever seen the backblast on a Russian Vampir RPG?" Rags lifted his hand, his thumb and index finger an inch apart. "I have. About this close."

He unclipped the scabbard on his belt, pulled out the KA-BAR knife—seven-inch double- edged blade, combat spec.

"Know what I said earlier, about a chance to walk away clean?" He tapped the flat of the blade against his palm. "I lied."

Giordano screamed through his gag as Rags pulled his head back, exposing the throat.

"Be honest. You brought this on yourself. Only one way you can make up for what you did—you've no idea how much I care about that girl. Now hold still. I'll make this quick."

But he didn't. Again, he lied, though not of his own accord.

Before Rags could put the blade to skin, BBK eased up behind Giordano and slipped the man's belt around his throat, pulled tight, tighter, crushing the gagged man's windpipe while Chalky ducked in and spread out another garbage bag beneath the man's feet to catch the inevitable discharge.

Rags took two steps back, surprised, as Chalky, looking up from where he crouched, said, "You're not alone in this, okay?"

Once the former corpsman confirmed no pulse remained, no sign of breathing, they unshackled the body from the overhead pipe and set him down on the soiled black bag—at which point they just stood there, staring, for what felt like an eternity.

Combat prepared you for many things. Ironically, cold-blooded murder wasn't one of them.

Wander was the first to say something. He used his own voice. "Okay then. Let's make this knucklehead disappear."

—◇◇◇—

They drove out to an even more remote spot in the open desert, dragged the body to a low knoll, where BBK took a hammer to the teeth, decimating the jaw for good measure, after which Wander doused the body with gasoline, focusing on the hands and feet.

They curled the body fetal-style around a dropkicked claymore mine that BBK once bargained off a grunt he knew from his previous life in the hood. The brother made his living now selling stolen ordinance to the Spook Town Compton Crips.

They dug the claymore's legs into the sand so the impact of the explosion would evaporate the chest and head and hands and set the rest of the body afire.

Yes, an ace forensics team might be able to piece together a fingerprint or an identifiable segment of jaw from the shards of flesh and bone not fully incinerated or blown to hell, but overall that seemed a worthwhile risk — better than any other option they'd managed to brainstorm in the limited time they'd had.

They primed the charge, pulled enough wire to gain a safe distance, popped the shipping plugs, and attached the clacker.

Wander, reverting to Giordano's voice, said to Rags, "Sergeant Trapnell, would you kindly do the honors and mist my ass?"

The explosion generated a pressure wave spitting dust and a coal-black cloud licked by flames. As Chalky ventured forward to see if anything recognizably human remained, Rags reeled in the undestroyed wire, while Wander said, "Praise cheeses."

BBK just stood there, watching the smoke disperse. Rags was about to tell him to snap to, they were pulling out, when the big man, silent all morning till now, said, "Comes my time? Worse ways to go out."

He seemed transfixed, immobile, a pillar of dark salt.

"That's deep," Rags said, not wanting to sound dismissive. One of the only godly things he knew was this man's silence, making his rare utterances all the more wondrous and strange. "But it's also a little premature, don't you think?"

The big man nodded but still didn't move. Black Buddha Killer, the Silent Giant—he murmured some kind of chant, then said, "To conquer our fear, we must first surrender hope."

⸺◇◇◇◇⸺

Having finished a lengthy recitation of additional facts and rumors Elan thought Lisa might find useful—which lawmen she could trust, which ones she couldn't, where to find a decent *chile relleno*—Elan wished Lisa good luck and turned to go.

She stopped him. "I'm wondering—when I called the number I was given for you, the receptionist said I'd reached the Public Defender's Office."

"That's my hangout," he said. "Technically I work for Tribal Social Services. But I kinda, you know, freelance around. Wherever I'm needed."

Another gust of wind whipped through the park. Lisa tugged a few wild strands of hair from her face. "What exactly do you . . . do?"

Again he offered that gentle, cagey smile. "I'm the guy they call when a young buck from one of the tribes, you know, goes off the reservation, ho ho. Scores some crank, hits a liquor store or two, walks off with the cash, and holes himself up somewhere with his girl. I try to talk him down. Before bad turns to worse."

Lisa's respect grew a bit more spine. "You're a hostage negotiator."

He shrugged. "Whatever it takes."

"You work for the police, then."

"Not always," he said. "Seldom, in fact. Depends on who calls first."

———◇———

A guy the size of a linebacker stood at the door to Giordano's office, ringing the bell. Rags studied him as they drove past, wondering who the hell he might be, what business he might have with the dead man, how hard he'd try to track him down.

Meanwhile, Wander took out a cell phone—Giordano's, taken from his jacket after they stripped him naked—and speed-dialed the most frequently called number of late: Rankin's.

He waited for the voicemail beep, then said, in perfect Giordanian: "Hey, it's me. Listen, something's come up. This keno girl I bagged in Bullhead City last year? Says she's preggers with my kid. Thinks I'm a slot machine. I'll deal with it, but it's gotta be in person. You know what I'm saying. Be back in twenty-four hours, forty-eight tops. Temporary digression, nuttin' serious. See ya soon."

The cell phone tower would ping the call from near the office, offering no lead back to the abandoned house or the scratch of desert where the man's piecemeal, incinerated remains lay scattered.

Wander thumbed off and handed the phone to Rags, who removed the battery and SIM card, wiped them down. When they'd traveled another couple blocks, he pitched them out the window into the back of a gravel hauler while Wander hit the CD player.

Isley Brothers: "Fight the Power" segueing into "Take Me to the Next Phase."

———⬦———

As Elan walked off toward the government complex, Lisa checked her watch and rose to go, instantly lightheaded. What I wouldn't give for a nap, she thought, steadying herself with the bench, and yet the fuzziness of mind felt tinged with foreboding.

You need to call the process server, she thought. Boonie. Tell him what you've learned. Warn him about the men working security, what they were capable of, the trigger-happy swagger, the lynchings in the mountains.

Before she could dig her phone from her purse, however, she heard Elan calling out. "One last thing?"

He sauntered back toward the bench, hands in his pockets, long hair swaying casually. No wonder he always talks in the present tense, she thought. If time were gravity, he'd be able to fly.

He gestured to her valise. "Your complaint. One of your causes of action is for conversion."

"It's the civil claim for theft," she said.

"I know. That's not my point. Littmann's wife, Meredith's her name, she's got this condition called hysterical blindness. Ever hear of it?"

Where in the world, she thought, is this going? "Sure. It's supposedly caused by emotional trauma. Some people think it's bogus—I mean, psychosomatic."

"Way I hear it, when she's sixteen, she's driving down

176

some country road, top speed, falls asleep maybe, goes off into the ditch. When she wakes up, it's in the hospital. And her vision is gone. Not totally but, you know, a lot."

Lisa clutched the bench for balance again as she marveled at the symmetry. Except when I woke up from my car wreck, she thought, I finally began to see.

"That's interesting," she managed to say, "but I'm not sure—"

"You're suing her husband for conversion. Know the technical term for hysterical blindness?"

"I don't believe I do, no."

"It's called a conversion disorder."

~ 24 ~

THE phone in the vestibule rang, meaning the guards at the Bristlecone's gate were trying to get in touch with Gideon. Meredith picked up on the fifth ring. "Yes?"

"Sorry to trouble you, Mrs. Littmann." It was Logan, head of the gaggle of roughnecks Gideon referred to as the security detail. "The judge isn't answering his cell."

Her husband was in the training arena at the far end of the south pasture, working with the trainer, some wranglers, and a small herd of yearlings, trying to drill some cow sense into the latest group of ponies they hoped to mold into cutters in time for next year's Fort Worth Futurity. He'd probably switched off his phone to avoid interruption.

"Is there a problem?"

"There's a paper hanger out here at the gate, ma'am."

"Excuse me?"

"Process server. We figured we'd keep him here till we spoke with the judge."

Interesting, she thought. Not quite mysterious but certainly odd. "Send him on up to the house."

"Ma'am?"

"I'm right to assume our visitor is, in fact, a man?"

"Yes'm. He is that." A deep breath, trailed by a sigh. "All right then. I'll send somebody with him, make sure he doesn't get lost."

Good old Logan, she thought, hanging up. Such a wit.

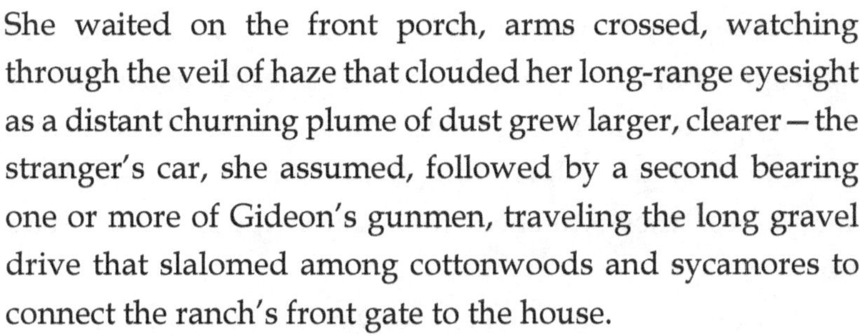

She waited on the front porch, arms crossed, watching through the veil of haze that clouded her long-range eyesight as a distant churning plume of dust grew larger, clearer — the stranger's car, she assumed, followed by a second bearing one or more of Gideon's gunmen, traveling the long gravel drive that slalomed among cottonwoods and sycamores to connect the ranch's front gate to the house.

Hearing footsteps behind her, she turned. "Everything all right, Mrs. Littmann?"

It was Seth Kirkendahl, the guard who normally watched the house. Meaning her. He was perhaps the most presentable of the roughnecks, changed his shirt more than twice a week, took the occasional crack at a crossword puzzle, face always bright with a fresh clean shave.

"Everything's lovely, young man. And how are you today?"

Despite knowing her well, having worked there almost a year, he blushed like a twelve-year-old. She'd learned to manage and even exploit this crush, to the point of letting him think of himself as a lovelorn protector, her knight.

"I'm fine, ma'am." He nodded toward the distant whorl of dust. "Who's this?"

"Someone bringing a bit of bother, apparently."

She could feel him stiffen beside her. "Want me to handle it?"

"I doubt that's an option, Seth. But thank you."

<hr>

The visitor's car pulled up to the concrete skirt of the porch. A very large and, from what she could tell, not unattractive man appeared from behind the wheel. Shortly the second car also stopped, and two guards whose names she couldn't place got out as well, crossing their arms as, through their sunglasses, they watched the visitor mount the broad stairway.

Seth gallantly took a step forward. Meredith, placing a gentle hand on his arm, drew him back.

Reaching the top, the process server said, "Afternoon, ma'am. I'm looking for Gideon Littmann?"

She had to tilt her head back to meet his eyes. Like talking to a bust on a plinth. "I'm his wife. Can I help you?"

"My name's Eric Boone. I have some legal papers for him."

"I'll accept them, if that's all right."

The big man nodded cordially, offering a smile. "Better if I serve him personally, Mrs. Littmann. Not to be a nuisance."

She could feel Seth growing heated beside her. At the foot of the stairway, the other two guards, eyes walled off behind their shades, stood with hands on their sidearms.

"My husband's unavailable at the moment. I can assure you, being that he's a retired judge, he's not one to dodge service or fail to appear if summoned. Whatever you need me to sign to validate service, I will."

The man nodded cordially, went back to his car, easing between the two armed men, then returned with a pro-forma affidavit titled "Acceptance of Service by Spouse." Holding it up close to her good eye, she read it through, signed under penalty of perjury.

"Thank you very much, Mrs. Littmann."

"You're more than welcome, Mr. Boone."

Seth's heat seemed to intensify. Oh grow up, she thought. We're not flirting. It's called being civil.

"I was wondering," Boone said, "if you might know where I could find Mr. Rankin. I tried his office, but—"

"I think you should go now," Seth said. "You got what you came for."

"Seth, it's all right. Please." She turned to Boone: "I'd try the Café Olé on Cherokee in Benson. They have a lovely young waitress there Don likes to annoy."

Boone bit back a smile and returned to his car. As he drove off, trailed once again by the two guards from the gate, Seth reached for the papers. "I can take those out to Judge Littmann if you'd like."

She turned away. "That won't be necessary, Seth."

———◁◇▷———

She fled to her room down the hallway lined with forgeries. Sitting on the edge of her narrow bed, she scoured the complaint and supporting affidavits—taking her time when she came to Tuck's, trying to hear his voice, tracing her fingers across the words—then continuing on to the end, increasingly furious at the Honorable Gideon Littmann with every turned page.

How dare he, she thought. To pretend he bought those letters, tracked them down with me in mind, a gift. To subject that poor woman to such cruelty, tie her up, take her prisoner.

Then again, where was the surprise in that? How better to describe their marriage? He comes from such a good family, her mother always said. Good stock.

Oh yes, the aptly named Grays. But they were mere background compared to the paternal grandfather. Gustav Littmann.

Good old Gus.

The man arrived in Arizona during the mining strikes of World War I. Shortly he found work with the infamous Sheriff Harry Wheeler.

Labor strife was harming the war effort, at least that's what the mining companies said, and so the strikers got tagged as German sympathizers, even saboteurs. Gus Littmann, to prove his patriotic bona fides, infiltrated the union, then testified before the kangaroo courts that convicted the members of treason, and thus gained his seat

182

at the table of power, courtesy of the Citizens' Protective League and Phelps Dodge Corporation.

Good family my lily-white ass.

And yet you married him. You caved. He was, admittedly, if nothing else, a relentless suitor.

And what did it matter? With real love impossible, hounded by your parents to end the silliness, make a good match, what difference did a sham wedding make?

Let him marry the rich girl who blinded herself in despair.

She pitched the documents across the room then went to her closet and pushed away a wall of blouses, exposing the safe where she'd tucked away the antique velvet parcel. Retrieving it, she returned to her bed, untied the old silk ribbon, and leafed through the powdery, brittle envelopes, pulling two out at random, suddenly more intrigued than ever at what the letters might say.

—◇◇◇—

July 6, 1877

My Dearest John Henry:

I have entrusted this letter to our cousin George, whom the family has chosen to travel west to where reportedly you now lay near death.

I have to confess that it requires great strain to keep my hand from trembling as I write. Absent explanation from you, I am left to imagine the quarrel that led to your being brought so close to the grave.

Did you fire first, or did your adversary, as they say, get the jump on you? And what sort of man was he — just another sore loser, which you indicate is the kind of moral defective most likely to take offense at your "abject savage" manner?

Forgive me if I seem callous or harsh. The thought of you so cavalierly dismissing the senseless risks of your way of life, only to end up mortally wounded, has made me both utterly furious and terribly afraid.

If you only knew the horrible nights I have spent racked with insomnia, pacing the floor in darkness when not kneeling in desperate prayer. If you only knew into how many pieces you have shattered my heart.

As I noted in my last letter, I had reached a point where I could no longer go back and forth wondering if my continuing devotion to you spoke to the nobler aspects of my heart, or were instead corrupted by vanity and deceit. With no response from you to guide me, I was obliged to face myself soberly, sternly, and honestly.

I came away with the sad conviction that I had misplaced my affections, and that you had chosen your westward path with no intention of circling back home. And so, with a grieving spirit, I closed that door of my heart to better widen the one devoted to God.

Then we received word of your being shot and in desperate need. My immediate, unguarded thought was: Go to him. He has won the battle of wills by placing himself on the altar of mortality. So be it. Admit the truth of what you feel and put aside your stubborn pride.

With all that in mind, I prepared myself to step forward and tell the family that I would go to Texas and nurse you, with the object of finally retrieving you home.

Secretly, I did not know if I would return. Why not abide his wish, I thought, and stay with him, make a life together far beyond the reach of scandalous rumors and small-minded gossip?

However, I shortly discovered the family had already chosen their caretaker. George had earned the right, so the argument went, through his able service when only a boy as a cadet in the defense of Savannah. He has no family obligations to restrain him from travel and time away, and he can capably take care of himself and you.

I can imagine you asking why I did not fight harder to take his place, or at the very least accompany him. The answer is threefold.

First, the logic of the decision seemed sound. I do, indeed, have many obligations here, concerning both family and my students, and though not irreplaceable, I suppose, I remain nonetheless much needed, the steadfast spinster upon whom so many rely.

Second, the issue of appearances could not be dismissed cavalierly. Rushing off to be by your side, regardless how needful and dire your condition, would arouse shameless talk. You know the world we live in.

Third, and most importantly, given a brake to my impetuous desire to flee to your side, I had time to think the matter through. When I did, I reflected on my previous confession to you of how, in darker moments, I felt responsible for the increasingly insidious turn of your mind.

Imagine how much more deeply my guilt afflicted me when you wrote back that, though you appreciated the family's protective concern and loyalty, you no longer could even consider a place among us as home. The stark and bitter loneliness of those words! I doubt I have ever felt more helpless before the utter wicked chaos of life.

And yet, despite these admissions of guilt on your part, you not only resumed your ways, but fell into even greater peril, to the point of getting yourself shot by some scoundrel. I could not help but wonder if, despite your obvious state of distress, you did not also possess some sly intention of luring me west, resorting to the extreme ploy of placing yourself before the door of death in order, at last, to summon me to your side.

Forgive me, but I could not convince myself that this might not be the truth. And so I surrendered to the general will within the family. Rather than going to you in person, I wrote this letter, handing it to George for personal delivery.

I await word from him and you as to how you are faring. I know that he will urge you, as I have, to come home. The family unanimously wishes this, for all are frantic with worry over your welfare.

None more so than I. And yet, given the tone of your last letter, I wonder if that matters to you at all.

You seemed to suggest there is nothing for you here. You discuss the family as though we were little more than a troop of specters, floating about the hazy edges of your memory. Worse, we seem to serve as mere reflections of your severe disappointment with yourself.

How wounded I was by those words. How could you say such things? You speak of being relentlessly alone, but are you so incapable of realizing that your isolation is purely a matter of choice? I love you with all my heart. Which is why I insist you must come home, you must.

Cicero speaks of the strangely tender love of family, and how it inspires and strengthens the courage for the duties of life. I beg *you, avail yourself of that courage, that tender love. Return to us. To me.*

You are not alone. I am with you every moment, every hour.

No, I did not come in the flesh, but open your heart and soul to my words here and you will feel me in the ineffable nearness of spirit. Let that embolden you to turn away from darkness and death and come home. I am waiting to greet you with every drop of love in my heart.

With unrestrained devotion,

Mattie

September 2, 1877

My Dearest Mattie:

First, let me assure you that I have managed to cheat death and am on the mend, owing in no small part to the care and concern of our good cousin George. I have told him more than once he would make a good nurse, or wife, and he has yet to strangle me, which no doubt counts as one more testament to the steadiness of his character.

As for the moral defective, to use your term – it is not inapt – who inflicted the wound, his name is Henry Kahn. He is now a fugitive, not merely for trying to murder me, I'm told, but also on charges of forgery.

As for our quarrel, it concerned his claim, made in public before several other men, that he had caught me skinning cards while dealing poker.

When a man who is an utter fraud accuses you of being a cheat, the affront feels especially insufferable.

I demanded he retract the accusation, which was baseless in every regard. He responded with an even more egregious lie — that I had played capper in a confidence scheme that had fleeced a traveler from Ohio of fifty dollars.

At that point I lifted my walking stick and caned the man right there in the street, demanding he admit the falsity of his statements. This drew a crowd, as you can imagine, and the mob attracted the police. In short order we were both taken into custody, charged, and released.

Sadly, that was not the end of the matter. Later that afternoon I came upon the wretch again, but before I could so much as offer a reproach he drew a pistol and fired.

The bullet entered my side, carving a nasty little track through my penetralia, if you will excuse the word play, and I drifted several feet before collapsing.

Meanwhile, the odious Mr. Kahn fled, being not just a liar and a fraud but a coward. He has been on the run ever since.

I drifted in and out of consciousness for several days, but managed to stay on this side of the veil until George arrived.

I have read your letter at least twice daily, often more frequently than that, ever since George presented it to me.

Do not worry. I have betrayed no confidences. Your reputation as "steadfast spinster" — speaking of words that can break a heart — remains unblemished.

That said, when I learned the family was sending someone, I cannot help but confess that I hoped, with all my heart, it would be you.

Poor George. If only you could have beheld the expression on his face when he noticed the disappointment in mine.

As for what you wrote, it pains me to reflect you would think me so shallow and calculating as to court mortal injury with the sole, insidious intention of luring you west.

Please know that while death hovered at my bedside, two things hardened into stone-like certainty: the desire to live, and my love for you.

Over and over, those two things inspired me to resist the urge to relent, surrender, and drop beneath the surface of the unending darkness I so frequently observed, like a sea of oblivion, stretched out before me.

However, as my strength returned, I came to realize that these two certainties, to live and to love, did not coalesce. On the contrary, they revealed a fundamental, even tragic contradiction.

If there is one thing I've gathered from experience, whether during the war or at Mother's sickbed or out here in the railheads and cow towns, it is that there is nothing to distinguish a good life from a bad life, there is just life, and it must be lived.

I cannot help at times but wonder if your Romanist faith is not a kind of armor against the terrible ambiguities of a life lived simply, fully, honestly, without pretense of nobility or purpose. When I lingered near death, and felt the immanent, infinite coldness entering my core, I found no solace whatsoever in pieties. Rather, what comfort came to me arrived solely through the relentless will to defy the odds and continue the meager reckless enterprise of my existence.

Incidentally, I cannot and do not take exception to the intemperance of tone in your letter. On the contrary, rather than finding it callous or harsh, I cherish the fire, the anger. I know well, and miss profoundly, the generous heart in which that rage is forged.

However, I also suspect that your anger offers evidence of a need to hack at the bonds that have lashed us together all these years, and to free yourself at last — from this unwholesome and vexing situation. From me.

You may argue against that interpretation, but the more I reflect on your remaining behind in Georgia, and your justifications for doing so, the more I realize that my lust for the raucous noise of bareknuckle life cannot be reconciled with what you consider the dutiful light of holiness and home.

Perhaps, then, the possibility of us must give way to the reality of you and me — individual, apart, alone. I can no longer resist the impression that, like separate planets, we circle in irreconcilable orbits around a common sun. I observe the light and feel the warmth as you do. If only that could draw us nearer.

I cannot end there. It sounds too small and defeatist, and you have always provoked me to a more expansive, honest, and manly disposition.

Let me simply repeat, then, that above and beyond everything else, the nearness of death reawakened my awareness of just how much I love you. Nor do I disregard or wish to minimize your generous admission that you love me as well, and with all your heart. How strangely odd and ill-fated, this longing, this beautiful and tender sorrow. Perhaps someday, somehow, one of us will find a way to make it count for more than words from afar.

With unrelenting devotion,
John Henry

PART III

Do not weep; do not wax indignant. Understand.

~ Baruch Spinoza

~ 25~

L ISA woke with the sensation of parchment sealed to her cheek.

She'd rushed from her meeting with Elan Wingfield to the county law library, only to doze off in the middle of her research—trying to anticipate the arguments Littmann and Rankin would throw at her, thinking through her counter-arguments. Apparently, the topmost page of the volume that had finally won the war of wakefulness had sealed itself to the side of her face, moistened by sweat.

Gingerly, she lifted her head. The thin, brittle page detached, peeling away inch by inch. Glancing around, she wondered who might have noticed, wondering as well if the ink had left an imprint, a blur of words across her cheek like a faded tattoo—worse, had she been snoring?

Only three other researchers occupied the vast, hushed room, planted at monitors, surrounded by books, and they seemed far too absorbed in typing and reading and massaging their temples to pay much mind to her plight.

Curiously, that realization prompted a sudden, childlike loneliness, as though she'd been exiled to some invisible corner of space, like some barely discernible planet circling a nameless sun.

The notion returned her to the final dreamlike images that had drifted through her mind just before snapping awake. She'd revisited her lovemaking with Tuck—late last night, early this morning, whenever it had taken place—throwing herself into it more willfully now in the safety of her mind, biting his shoulder, pounding her fists against his chest and arms, scraping his back with her bright red nails, weeping as her orgasm broke and she finally, gratefully surrendered to who he was, how she felt, and the thousand little disasters lurking in the shadows.

She dropped her face into the cooling softness of her hands, thinking: Oh get over yourself—at which point the image of three gallows on a mountain rose once again in her mind's eye.

She shook off the mood, chafing the drowsiness from her face with her palms.

Checking her phone, she discovered that neither Tuck nor Rayella had responded to any of the texts she'd sent throughout the afternoon. Where were they, what were they up to? What was so important that they couldn't answer back?

And what about Rags and his leatherneck legionnaires? Every time she tried to imagine why they were here, what they were up to, her pulse began a manic jig.

Maybe they'd just all gone out for Mexican—enchiladas and *pozole* and margaritas by the pitcher. Playing darts. Bitching about lawyers.

Sure. Or maybe they'd all sprouted wings and flown to Oz.

Opening her email app, she saw Nico had sent a message with an attachment—an affidavit from a filmmaker, one of Nico's clients, assessing the intangible value of the stolen letters.

The filmmaker placed their worth in pure conceptual terms, as the basis for a documentary or a miniseries or a feature film, at nothing less than $100,000 dollars, bare minimum—regardless of whether the letters were genuine or not.

The story alone, not just about Doc and his cousin but how the letters were presumably destroyed, then somehow reappeared—in the hands of a former slave who stayed with the family for decades despite being freed—then vanished once again in the Depression, only to pop up now by strange chance: It was just the kind of shaggy-dog history-tinged true-story soap opera that made Hollywood suits fall all over themselves in a froth of acquisitive glee.

This eliminated the problem of meeting the $75,000 threshold for bringing the lawsuit in federal court, the weakest element of her argument. Every muscle in her body softened just a little, bathed in a sunny wave of relief.

Leave it to Nico, she thought, smiling as she read though the affidavit again. And yet shortly that same odd loneliness descended. She found herself wishing once more, even more intensely, that he could join her in court tomorrow, sit beside her at the plaintiff's table, a friendly face, that rakish, heart-melting smile.

Someone in her corner, the invisible one at the edge of space.

—◦◇◦—

Tuck pulled up to the hotel with Rayella beside him, the two of them having exchanged scarcely a word or even a glance the entire drive. Tuck tried not to imagine what had happened to Giordano after they'd left, and figured the girl shared the same state of mind.

Lodging the car in park, he said, "You go on in. I've got a couple errands I need to see to." Rayella didn't move, not even to turn his way. Her backlit profile, small and soft and plain, reminded him just how young she was. "There some problem?"

"You tell me." She glanced down at her hands, flexing them open and closed in her lap.

"Not sure I understand."

"Oh, I think you do. I think you understand real well."

A couple appeared from the stone walkway leading back toward the hotel lobby—sweethearts, maybe even newlyweds, judging from their laughter, their locked arms, the absence of sunlight between their hips.

"I think I've explained myself," Tuck said. "Whatever you and your boyfriend may think is going on, behind the scenes or what-the-hell-ever, like I've got myself an agenda or somehow even planned this disaster, the truth is—"

"The *truth*?" She managed to spit out the word without raising her voice. "That's funny."

"Now listen—"

"Here's the truth, you wanna hear it. I ain't leaving your side. Not now, not later. Not till this thing is settled and done."

"What—you gonna share my bed?"

"If it comes to that. Slept in worse places."

Tuck couldn't help but laugh at that. "This your idea? Or—"

"Don't really see how that matters, do you?"

The amorous couple lurched toward their car, and Tuck felt sadly envious as the woman spun the man around, leaned him back against the trunk. Shortly that envy hardened into something else, a feeling on the dark side of hope.

Tuck returned his focus to Rayella. "So that's how this is gonna be?"

She let silence answer for her.

"All right then," he said, finger-drumming a taradiddle on the steering wheel. "Yeah, I want to head out to Littmann's ranch, the Bristlecone. I want to be nearby in the morning when Rags and them come down off the mountain. No telling what they might run into, and I'm not just talking about three or four boneheads working security."

She seemed to turn that over in her mind. "Like what? I mean—"

"That's just it, I don't know. But I want to be close in case anything, anything at all, comes up. Like I said, I grew up around here, I know these people, I know the terrain. And, given what's happened, I feel obligated."

She sat there perfectly still, barely even a sign she was breathing, the window beyond her hazed with late-day light.

"Here's the problem," he said. "Your lawyer's most likely gonna want you in that courtroom tomorrow. Her case gets ten times stronger with you there in person, tell the judge everything they did to you. Show that cut and bruise on your face."

She let out a ragged laugh. "If I cared even a little about what's gonna happen in court," she said, "I wouldn't have let Rags and them . . ." She let the rest trail away and glanced down into her hands again—open, closed, open. "Know what I mean?"

"Yeah," he said, remembering Giordano strung up and naked. "Guess I do."

"Kinda hard to just turn around now, take back what's happened."

"True enough."

"So what else is there to talk about?"

The newlyweds, sweethearts, whatever they were—they'd taken their public necking to the next phase, the woman straddling the man now, hiking herself up onto his hips, grinding herself against him as they kissed, her hands locked around his neck. Nothing says romance, Tuck thought, like a public dry hump at sunset.

"I'd planned to sleep in the car," he said. "If you want me to find you a motel—"

"Car suits me fine. Like I said, I slept in worse places."

Oh, I'll bet you've got some stories, he thought, studying the outline of her face — button nose, double chin, jaw locked tight. Tough little bird.

She's gonna need to be.

~ 26~

M EREDITH heard his footfalls thundering toward her as she sat in the sunroom, her back to the doorway, looking out the high plate-glass windows as the day's fading light warmed the harsh, striated face of the mountain range. Even blurred, the ancient massive wall of rock, less than a mile from the house, reassured her.

Coming to a stop behind her, he said, "I believe you have something of mine."

No matter how courtly his tone, she thought, he can't hide the needy, put-upon ego. "I'm not sure I know what you mean, Gideon."

He rested his hands on the back of her chair. She could feel the pressure.

"Oh, I think you do. You know — those documents you signed for without consulting me."

His breath smelled of coffee clouded with mint. "You weren't answering your phone. I thought — "

"You could have waited."

"It seemed important. And, from what I gather, that's true."

He tapped his left hand against the chair back, his wedding band striking the wood. "It's nothing, I assure you. Now once again, they're where?"

She fluttered a hand toward an end table across the room. He went and picked up the papers, dog-eared and battered from earlier, when she'd flung them against the wall.

He read as he sauntered back, then took up position in front of her chair, blocking her view. "Have you looked at this?"

"Some," she said. "Here and there. You know, just for the sake of discussion."

"Is there something to discuss?"

"You tell me. Have you turned on a TV or radio yet this afternoon?"

A flicker of trepidation slipped across his eyes. "How could I?"

"The lawyer who filed those papers asked that the proceeding be sealed, but someone apparently already leaked it to the media."

Some clerk at the courthouse, she imagined. So many were Hispanic or Indian, and they hated who he was, what he claimed to stand for. He'd explain that away, of course, by saying their kind always side with the losers.

His trepidation acquired a smile. "My money's on the lawyer. Old trick—ask for confidentiality then sneak word to the press and play innocent in court." He resumed glancing through the pleadings. "No worries. I'm sure Don was contacted for comment. He'll let them know this is just a shakedown."

"Oh, good. The children will be so relieved."

The smile withered. "You let me worry about that."

"I'm sure they'll wonder about these reports you were involved in beating a woman, tying her up, robbing her."

He held up the papers. "There's not one word of truth in this."

"Well, there's a comfort. Not one word. My."

"Which should be evident, given the involvement of your old friend."

Here it comes, she thought. At last. "Yes, wasn't that curious."

"You read what he says under oath. Under penalty of perjury."

"As I said, here and there."

"It's nothing but lies, front to back, the cat crawling out of his bag."

"Speaking of lies," she said, "I thought you found those letters, how did you put it, with me in mind. A gift. But that's not even close—"

"This is all an elaborate scam, planned and put into motion by Old Loverboy. Now why do you think he did that, Meredith? Why did he have that idiot lawyer contact me, of all people? Or think I was so damn thick I wouldn't figure it out."

She'd considered that possibility, ever since seeing Tuck's name in the pleadings, reading his words, wondering if maybe, possibly . . .

Her silence seemed to confirm something for him—he straightened back up, shook his head in disbelief. "After all I've done, tried to do."

"Oh, Gideon, don't be tiresome."

It was his turn, now, to pitch the documents against a wall. The staple broke, pages scattered everywhere. She refused to look.

After a moment, he said, "I'm sorry. Was that tiresome?"

"Getting back to the children. I already spoke to them, to prepare them. Get them ready for any questions they might have to face about their illustrious father."

"They won't believe any of that. Or you. They know better than anyone who you are."

She tried to hide the sting of that. "I wanted them ready."

"You wanted them poisoned. Against me. Because you know how they really feel about their mopey weakling of a mother."

"Like they can't see for themselves who *you*—"

"Woe is Mommy with her endless spells. Still pining for her rodeo bum—the cripple, the fraud. You think they don't *know*?"

"You're a great one to talk about—"

"All those years I defended you to them, stood up for you, explained away your little act. Because, for all your flaws, all the pain you caused—"

"Oh don't even start with—"

"But they knew, they're not stupid. You wanted them *ready*? Maybe you're the one who needs to brace yourself. Because whatever that bull did to Loverboy way back when is nothing compared to what he's got coming now."

She rose from her chair and took a step toward him, forcing him to meet her clouded eyes. "And you had the gall to ask—this morning, remember? Ask if I could think of you, our life together, as anything but a pathetic mistake."

His smile turned into a soft, chesty laugh. For the slightest moment, something like surrender softened his eyes.

He glanced right and left, spotted a canister near the door holding umbrellas and walking sticks. Selecting one of the latter, a sturdy one made of polished oak, he said, "This should do."

He suddenly hurried back through her rooms toward the hallway lined with Tuck's paintings. Before she could catch up he started swinging the cane like a madman with an ax—ripping the paintings off the walls, smashing them in godlike fury, gouging the canvases with hammering blows, tearing them to shreds, stomping the frames till they snapped and splintered.

Fearing, if she tried to stop him, he'd just turn his wrath on her—beat her unconscious, beat her to death, it was long overdue—she stayed just outside the doorway to her room, watching him perfect his massacre.

Finally, chest heaving from the effort, shoulders slack, he reached the far end of the hall and turned to survey the ruin. In the sudden stillness, the mania slowly drained from his face. He looked spent.

She said, "And you call me a weakling."

He tossed the cane on top of the wreckage. "I'm sorry. I forgot to ask. Which fake was your favorite?"

In the kitchen, Littmann poured himself a tumbler of ice water and drank it in halting sips, hoping to regain his calm. The track lights hummed faintly overhead. The dark granite countertops reflected the glow, soft pools of radiance.

He mopped his brow with a dishtowel, standing at the sink as his breathing slowed. I would kill that woman, he thought, strangle her with my own bare hands . . .

Perhaps it's the phony blindness that makes her immune to her own beauty. Makes her unaware of its effect, even after all these years. Especially after all these years, more of them behind than ahead.

What else but beauty can stand up to death?

His cell phone throbbed in his pocket, breaking the spell. It was Rankin. Littmann picked up. "Have you heard from Bobby?"

"Just a message," Rankin said. "He sounded kinda off his mark, to be honest."

"What are you telling me?"

"Something about a waitress in Bullhead City, says she's pregnant. He's gonna be gone a couple days."

Littmann took a second to consider the news. "You believe him?"

"What do you mean?"

"Do you think he's telling the truth or did he just decide to run?"

It was Rankin's turn to reflect for a moment. "Christ, I don't know. Run?"

"Don't act so shocked. I've never shared your high opinion of him. Besides, he's the one who actually put his hands on the girl."

"Yeah." Rankin drew out the vowel, as though dubious.

"Pack a bag and come pick me up. I'll book two rooms at the Miraval. We'll spend the night in Tucson, have a nice supper, prepare our response, get a decent night's sleep."

"Sure. Give me an hour."

"Has anyone from the media been in touch?"

"Some woman from KGUN, the ABC—"

"I know what it is. What did you say?"

"I denied each and every allegation, what do you think?"

"Call her back. Call the other network outlets, too."

"What—why?"

"Tell them all to have a camera crew on the courthouse steps tomorrow morning. We'll have a full statement, put matters in perspective. Let them know who the out-of-towners really are."

"Nice." Rankin chuckled. "You want to bring the letters? Little show-and-tell?"

"No. Too easy for the judge to order we just hand them back right there in court."

"Good point."

"I'll have Logan and a couple of his men come along as well. Speaking of show-and-tell. Like we're the ones that need protection."

"Put 'em in suits. Faces bright and shiny. Very professional."

"Exactly."

Littmann leaned back against the counter, letting the logic click into place. "We're going to let the world know just who Tuck Mercer is, cheating honest people, stealing their money, mocking their pride. We're going to wrap him tight around his little dago lawyer's neck and let them hang together."

~ 27 ~

FOLLOWING Tuck's directions, the Merry Band, as they'd called themselves ever since serving together in Afghanistan, headed for the Dragoons from the east along Ironwood Road.

In the day's last light, Rags got a glimpse of the granite formations near Cochise Stronghold—like a giant had stacked boulders to form a labyrinth of hideaways crowned by towering jigsaw columns, feathered with cypresses—before Wander turned north on the forest road, away from where they might be seen by campers, hikers.

After a little more than a mile, they turned again onto an unpaved track and started the slow, jerky climb up the barren mountainside.

Working by flashlight in the back, the beam sailing around as the van pitched into culverts and climbed over rocks, Chalky pulled coordinates from their map of the area, pinpointing various trails and landmarks they could use for navigation, then entered them as waypoints in his handheld GPS.

Not that the gizmo would spare them much grief. They'd still be hiking over an unknown mountain across rough terrain in all but total darkness, given moonrise wasn't scheduled till one a.m. Still, it might make it easier to find their way back.

The road leveled off after a while and Wander, pointing ahead through the windshield, said, "This must be the water tower he told us about."

It was an old, small structure—rusted metal, warped wood. Rags supposed it was intended, once upon a time, to serve livestock that had wandered far off the range, or been driven all the way up here for protection from monsoon flooding on the valley floor.

Wander pulled to the edge of the clearing, lodged the van in park, and killed the engine.

Silence enveloped them instantly, nothing but the rustling of sage and mesquite in the wind.

Rags cleared his throat. "Listen up."

He checked behind, to make sure Chalky and BBK had heard, then nodded to acknowledge Wander's attention.

"This has already taken kind of a wicked turn, given what happened to Fatso."

Subtle nods of affirmation from Chalky and BBK. From the driver's seat: "And the wicked shall be silent in darkness."

"Wander? Hear me out, okay? Don't interrupt."

"Yeah, sure. Sorry."

"I'm grateful for the fact you all answered the call. Stepped up. You know what I mean. Counts for a lot. Hard for me to say just how much. But we greased a civilian back there. Not saying he didn't deserve what he got."

"Let me repeat—"

"Wander, I asked once."

"Oops. Gotcha. Wilco."

"What I'm trying to say . . . " Rags looked out at the darkening mountainside, etched with steep ravines chocked with impenetrable scrub. "None of you owes me more. I've put you in a serious bind already. Seems like it could get way worse. This was just supposed to be about getting those letters back, do right by Rayella, but . . . " He took in a long, heavy breath, felt it slip from his lungs like lost heat. "I can handle it from here."

A sudden gust of wind raked the side of the van and the emptiness outside, giving everyone a moment to think. And what Rags thought about was a story his granddad, a Nam vet with the 7th Cav, once told him.

There was this guy named Keller, entire platoon got wiped out in the Cheu Pong Hills. He re-upped with the special forces and, once again, another ambush, everyone but him in his team wiped out. He hid in muddy grass beneath the body of another Green Beret as the VC came around with knives to make sure the kills were good, laughing as they stripped the bodies of weapons, boots, the prized green beenies. Having survived that, there was nowhere for Keller to go but the Lurps—Long Range Recon Patrol.

And that was the point—the man couldn't hack it at home, like the war had become a kind of second-rate angel, calling him back. Sometimes, during his short stays stateside, he'd sit on the roof of his apartment building with a six-pack and a hunting rifle, leading the cars and trucks that sped by on the freeway. Looking into his eyes, Grandad said, was like gazing into a badger hole.

Rags couldn't help but wonder, Is that us? Is that what we've become?

Finally, Chalky broke the silence. "You want us to wait here," he said, "while you hump in alone?"

"I'm asking you to stay behind, yeah. Here, down the mountain, wherever."

Chalky looked at Wander who glanced toward BBK. "Wouldn't bet on that happening," Chalky said. "Sweet Jesus, you serious?"

"Look—"

"You know why we're here." Chalky leaned forward, asserting himself as spokesman now. "Who got us out of the shit when we were pinned down with the askars outside Heroin Haji's compound?"

He was referring to a Taliban drug lord whose hilltop mansion—in the sense it was the biggest house in Marja—served as a guard post for his poppy plantation. Askar was their word for an Afghan soldier.

"There were seven wounded. BBK here had shrapnel in his hip. Wander had a pass-through in his hand. They had us outnumbered, bulletproof cover, sun at their backs. You coulda phoned in a Medevac with air support—"

"I did call it in. Called in smoke, too."

"But you knew the chopper wouldn't get there in time."

Rags shook his head. "I just—"

"You jumped in the Humvee, nobody in the turret to man the Mark Nineteen, give you some cover."

"That was my mistake, I shouldn't have sent you—"

"No. No. You did right, sent me ahead with the squad. So totally solo you plowed uphill through a shit-show of PK and RPG fire to get to us, pull those askars out, get everybody out—not once, not twice. You did that five times. Faced down the heat and charged on. Semper fi. Shoulda earned you a goddamn Silver Star. Instead . . ."

Chalky nodded toward the disfigured flesh on Rags's face. In his final trip up the rutted, rock-strewn lane carving its path through the poppy-field hillside, he'd stopped and jumped out amid nonstop gunfire to heft a gut-shot marine into the Humvee. That accomplished, he'd scrambled back to retake the wheel, only to have a Talib RPG whiz right past. The missile missed him by inches. But not the tail flame. Half his face scalded, all but blinded in one eye, he nonetheless somehow found it in himself to climb back into the driver's seat, finish the mission, get that last marine to safety.

"And you think," Chalky said, "we're gonna hang to the rear while you head in alone to deal with . . . Christ, I dunno, you tell me. No offense, brother, but screw that."

"I second that emotion." Wander, raising his hand, the one still bearing the scar from his wound, as though to testify. "One for all, all for whatnot."

Once again Rags stared out the windshield at the darkening sky, like God had wiped his hands on the clouds, leaving behind smears of violet, crimson, gold.

"Assume," he said, "sake of argument, all that is true. Let's say I saved your lives. Why then would I want you to throw them away on a snipe hunt?"

"We're answering the goddamn call of justice," Wander said.

"It doesn't really concern you," Rags replied.

Chalky said, "That's a hell of a thing to say to us."

Rags said, "Know what Captain Mayhew told me right before that mission you're talking about, the one where I was supposedly so damn heroic? Told me, 'You do anything stupid and get a marine killed today, I will personally cave in your skull.' I tried to live up to that at Heroin Haji's, I'm trying to live up to it now. I owe it to you not to do something stupid."

Finally, it was BBK's turn to speak. He did so, as always, without words.

Unsnapping one of the duffels, he dug out a rucksack and filled it with boxes of cartridges and extra magazines, his pistol — a matte black .45 Combat Commander — his knife, some rope, duct tape, NVG goggles, an extra pair of socks, leather gloves, and his boonie hat.

From the second duffel, he took out a machete in a leather scabbard and the fully auto Belgian FAL with mounted scope he'd bought off a deserter from the Mexican special forces. He slammed in a magazine, chambered a round, then slid open the van's side door, and stepped out into the windblown scrub.

He stood there, mute as a rock, waiting for someone to follow.

Chalky said, "In revenge there is life."

It was something the Taliban judges used to say right before an execution.

~ 28 ~

ARMED and equipped, the four ex-marines passed around the Adderall tabs, the better to focus, then started walking west, following the rubbled track uphill, figuring that was the best way to avoid rattler burrows and abandoned mineshafts.

After an altitude gain of a thousand feet, the road first began to bend, then turned into a series of zigzagging switchbacks, littered with fist-sized rocks, and they followed that trail to the main ridge.

By then, without any more road to follow, darkness prevented further advance without the NVGs. They slipped them on, and the world transformed into a murky, spectral green.

The going from there went slow. The first major hilltop crested at 6,720 feet, where they angled south, dropping into a saddle walled with rock. They humped up and over the slope, then kept climbing, hilltop to hilltop, the going brushy and steep.

At about 7,000 feet, the scrub and mesquite and ironwood closed in, even more thick and nested, and BBK had to take the lead, hacking with the machete. Even then, paths that seemed promising became anything but, and they had to backtrack over and over, searching for another way up.

The last 400 vertical feet became a brutal bushwhack, and at times they had to drop to all fours, crawling through the overgrowth like sappers cutting a path through concertina wire.

About 100 feet below the top, they encountered another cliff band, this one rimmed with evergreen. Gratefully, the climb was short, and the bracing scent of pine encouraged them.

One option, veering right, looked like a hopeless scramble through overgrowth, but nothing else looked viable. They took a moment to wipe away sweat, then ascended to the top, walking a ridgeline with the mountain's jagged crest to the north.

As the trail began to flatten out and they continued east, Rags thought about the debt he would owe the other three men once this was over, measuring it against the debt that had launched the whole endeavor, the one he owed to Rayella.

When his face got wasted, and he was shipped to Landstuhl—treatment, rehab, waiting for his decom orders—he felt that peculiarly unrewarding form of luck that comes when you realize, as bad as your disfigurement is, it could be worse.

He befriended grunts who would never walk again, never grip another man's hand. Met men whose faces or whole bodies looked like badly molded plastic.

Yes, they could do skin grafts, and surgery of that sort might well lie in his future, but the laws of decency and triage dictated that he surrender his number to someone who needed it more.

Back in the States, he found himself avoiding mirrors or even shiny surfaces, anything that could hold a reflection. What woman would want to wake up in the morning and face a face like that?

Turned out, Rayella did. Not only did she find him not repellant, she loved him, said so, openly and often. She had no problems walking on his arm, holding him close, even kissing him in public. My God, imagine it. And every time he blushed, turning the scalded redness an even brighter hue, she smiled up at him and told him just how happy he made her feel.

The fact that RPG didn't take him out wasn't the miracle. She was. You want happy? Happiness was getting the chance to show her at last just how deep and strong his gratitude ran.

⸺◃◇▹⸺

Right on schedule at one a.m., the moon nudged up from the horizon line and rose radiant and full, claiming its place among the vast spray of stars. Its light to Rags seemed overly stark, like sun-bleached bone, but that was the problem with desert moons. They reminded you too vividly that all those seas—Sea of Tranquility, Sea of Cleverness, Sea of Crises—were nothing but cratered dust.

They pulled up on a low rise to rest, lifting off their NVGs to enjoy for a moment the milky light and the things it brought into focus.

For the first time since leaving the forest road, they caught signs of other humans: water bottles, paper bags, cellophane, wads of soiled tissue, other trash, some of it clinging to mesquite and manzanita branches, the rest of it hastily buried or tangled in the sage and bear grass.

The anthropology of litter, Rags thought. The Dragoons and the other regional mountain chains served as a kind of over-ground railroad, lending a refuge as migrants shuttled north from the border toward waypoints and safe houses spread across this entire corner of the state.

The mountain passes offered daylight shelter and a first-rate hiding place, just as they had for the Apache a century and a half before.

Returning his eyes skyward and gazing into the canopy of stars, he shortly caught himself humming quietly, and smiled once he recognized the tune: "The Night Has a Thousand Eyes."

Wander, restless as always, ventured ahead, scouting out the next leg of the trek. He disappeared over a shallow knoll spiked with scrawny pinyon pine and century plants, the long thin stalks of the latter rising like ostrich necks.

Shortly, they heard him calling, "Rags, Chalky, BBK! Check this out."

They followed the direction of his voice, scrambling over the low hill. It opened onto a wide meadow walled by rock and bedded with tall grass rustling in a stiff wind coming from the west.

Wander pointed to three makeshift gallows in a clearing, arranged around a fire pit. Bodies hung from two of them, or rather the remains of bodies. The legs had been chewed away by a pack of coyotes who'd retreated to the distant edge of the clearing.

A chorus of whimpering snarls emanated from the yellow-eyed shadows where they circled and massed, meaning to scare off the intruders and get back to their feed.

To no one in particular, Wander said, "So whaddya think — this the work of that potshot judge and his posse we heard about?"

His voice had a keening edge, like he'd seen a ghost. There were those who believed Cochise himself wandered around up here. Maybe the coyotes themselves embodied the souls of slain braves.

Rags ventured into the clearing, training his weapon, a Benelli semi-auto shotgun, at the alpha coyote who'd also inched forward, blood clotting the fur on its snout, lips snarling back to expose the fangs.

If he'd had his Mossberg, he could've racked it, using the deep scraping crack of the slide to scare off the animal, but probably not even that would've worked. The pack was here to finish the job, and a mere four men weren't going to keep that from happening.

Rags didn't want to risk exposing their position by actually firing off rounds, but the animals didn't know that, so as he edged toward the nearest scaffold he trained the shotgun on the alpha male then scanned the barrel this way and that toward the gray-brown shapes behind as they slithered back and forth beyond the rim of scrub thickets.

The closer he got to the swaying remains of the nearest corpse, the worse the stench and the more agitated the coyotes became, not just snarling now but letting out their distinctive, eerie yips and howls. When they edged forward, BBK and the others did as well, hissing as they advanced, and the hunching animals inched back again.

Rags, gagging from the smell, ran his hand along the coarse, splintered wood of the scaffold's shaft, tested it with a nudge—no give, no sway. The thing was solid, meant to be used. Meant to work.

And so it had. The dead man's eyes stared blankly down—a Mexican, maybe in his twenties, the skin of his broad empty face gray from the loss of blood.

Wander said, "Puts a whole new meaning to hanging judge." His voice edged toward shrill. He wiped at his face with his sleeve. "This here seems like some kinda message, ya ask me."

The dead man's tattered plaid shirt fluttered in the breeze, nothing but dangling scraps of flesh and exposed bone where his legs and viscera used to be. Blood darkened the ground, littered with scraps of denim and flesh, splinters of bone, some small, some large. The larger pieces were pitted from where the coyotes had gnawed away.

A single sheet of shiny white cardboard—like you find inside a store-bought shirt—hung crookedly around the young man's neck, attached by a loop of twine. In bright red magic marker, the words: *No pasaran.*

All guilt and regret over Giordano's death melted away. Whoever does something like this, Rags thought, orders it, condones it, turns a blind eye, deserves what he gets.

He said, "I'd call this more than a message."

LISA lay awake with a song echoing faintly in the background of her thoughts: Richard Thompson, "Dad's Gonna Kill Me."

From sheer exhaustion, she'd fallen asleep twice, once when she'd returned to her room after supper and once again after suffering through the late-night news.

From the local broadcast, she'd learned not only that someone, despite her motion to seal the proceedings, had tipped off the media, but that Rankin, playing spokesman for the defense, lustily denied everything he and Littmann and the others had done.

Worse, a senior member of the Holliday clan, the great-granddaughter of a female cousin to both Doc and Mattie, categorically reaffirmed the family's position that the original letters had been destroyed. If any had supposedly surfaced, they had to be fake.

Go ahead and say it, Lisa had thought, they're worse than worthless. She tried to take heart from Nico's affidavit, the one from the Hollywood producer placing the letters' intangible value at $100,000 minimum. How much weight would that carry? Would even the Honorable Celestina Numkena, judge of the U.S. District Court, find that value a bit *too* intangible.

She'd switched off the TV at that point and, despite the uptick in anxiety, or perhaps because of it, once again crashed. Now, two and a half hours later, her whole body shimmered with wakefulness. It felt not a little like terror.

She checked her phone. Finally, an email:

Sorry to be out of touch all day. Everybody was restless and on edge, so I took Rayella and the fellas down to the Chiricahuas for a hike in Cave Canyon, then a drive up through the oaks and pines to Massai Point to check out the hoodoos. We all scrambled around the rocks for a while — even me, imagine that, though admittedly only a bit — then drove down to Douglas for supper. Everybody had too much to drink for a safe drive back, so we're hunkered down at a local hotel, down for the count. I'm about to turn in, too, but I've finally got Internet and wanted to let you know we're all safe, nothing to worry about.

Good luck tomorrow. Sorry we won't be there to cheer you on, but we all know you'll do great. Show those bastards what you're made of, lady. Knock 'em dead. ~ Tuck

She read it through twice, face brightened by the glow of her phone. With each pass, the same two words snagged on the door of her mind: *imagine that.*

Struck by a sudden wave of nausea, she decided to catch some air.

Rising from the bed, she shouldered into her robe—she'd bought pajamas late that afternoon, so she'd no longer be naked underneath as she ventured about—and slipped out barefoot onto the second-floor walkway.

The air felt cool and smelled of windblown sage. Still queasy and a little lightheaded, she told herself to take slow deep breaths, and that did the trick for a moment. Then, as though thunderstruck, she found herself gripping the handrail, trying not to keel over.

She stood there, like a seasick stowaway fighting the heaves. Finally, she gathered the strength to look up and became aware of the moon.

It had ascended plump and white above the Santa Catalinas, the random markings across its surface so like the wrinkles and freckles of a big fat jolly face. How like Mr. Moon, she thought, to greet you with such radiant mockery.

And that returned her to the memory that had darted along the edges of her mind all day, and in shards of surreal abstraction had bled into her dreams.

—◆—

Just before sunset, the day of the senior prom.

Her gown was floor-length with a sweetheart neckline and keyhole back, made from chiffon lace with a patterned tule overlay and corseted piping.

She'd stolen the retro hairstyle from Zooey Deschanel, using a boar bristle brush—volume up top, a tucked-under chignon, pins here and there to hold it all in place.

One last glance in the full-length mirror, a final spin to enjoy the swooshing fullness of her skirt—time to show Father.

He was out on the tennis court behind the house, one last game before dark, playing against her younger sister, Phoebe—the youngest, the whiz kid, the beauty.

Even from a distance, Lisa caught the triumphant glisten of sweat on their skin, heard in every screech of their sneakers against the clay and every grunt as their rackets slammed the ball the utter joy of competition, the family obsession.

Lisa was lousy at tennis, of course. Lousy at sports in general, crummy at puzzles, worthless at cards. Middle child. Middling in every respect.

She stepped onto the porch. When, even after what felt like hours, she'd failed to get their attention, she waved—tentatively at first, then bit by bit more grandly, her whole arm sailing back and forth over her head, until finally she caught their eye—Phoebe first, for she was facing this way, then her father, who followed the direction of his favorite daughter's gaze.

Come look, Lisa thought, wanting to say it out loud. Shout it. The words caught in her throat.

I've never looked lovelier. Please.

Standing together at the net, her father and sister returned her wave, offering smiles. Then her father dribbled the ball with his racket as he walked back into position to resume his serve.

I'm invisible, she thought. Like Old Lodge Skins in *Little Big Man*. The magic fool. Maybe not so magic.

When her date arrived—Gabriel Kinzleman, her male BFF, incredible artist, hopelessly gay—her mother was upstairs on the phone, talking to Jonathan, oldest of the children and the only son, calling from Cambridge. And so it was Thuy, the housekeeper, who helped Gabe pin the corsage on Lisa's gown.

Once at the event, they parted ways, Gabe to find his real date, Donny Blackwell, Lisa merely the beard.

Within minutes, she was halfway to hammered, sharing a flask of rum with Monica Sloan, Nicky Lancelotti's fiancée— Nicky, the nephew of Michael Lancelotti, the infamous Mikey Lance, underboss to Handsome Stevie Mazzone, suspected triggerman in the hit on Joseph "Joey Chang" Ciancaglini.

It was virtually impossible in Philadelphia, once you'd risen to a certain social and economic plateau, or attended certain schools, not to find yourself, in whatever peripheral way, connected to the so-called connected.

Shortly, Nicky sidled up, two of his friends in tow, wearing their liquor reasonably well and, judging from the aroma, a blunt or two.

Nicky lifted the flask from Monica's hand, threw back a swig, passed it on to his nearest pal, then glanced around the ballroom, grimacing. "This thing blows."

"We were just saying," Monica lied, nodding to Lisa for affirmation.

"Definitely." Lisa, always the trooper.

At the sound of her voice, Nicky turned, checked her out top to bottom. "Holy goddamn. You are a stone cold fox."

She smiled, her skin tingly and hot all over, thinking: There. Is that so hard?

He turned to his buddies. "Boyle, Ferry. Check out Balamaro."

The two eyed her up and down like they had pulleys attached to their necks.

"Cha-didda-cha," Boyle said, wiggling his hand, Ferry adding, "Lisa All-a-Smokeshow."

"We got a suite at the Rittenhouse," Nicky said. "Private party. None of this," gesturing with the flask around the room, the scrolls of bunting, the clustered balloons. As though on cue, the DJ segued from Mr. C's "Cha Cha Slide" to Clapton's "Wonderful Tonight."

In unison, Boyle and Ferry groaned, rolling their eyes. "Somebody wake up Grandpa."

"I'm serious," Nicky said, leaning closer toward Lisa, looking a little possessed. "Bar's fully stocked. Party hearty. We can flag down a cab."

"Couple cabs," Monica said. "There's, like, five of us now."

"Whatever." Nicky's eyes like switchblades. "Come on, Smokeshow. It'll be fun."

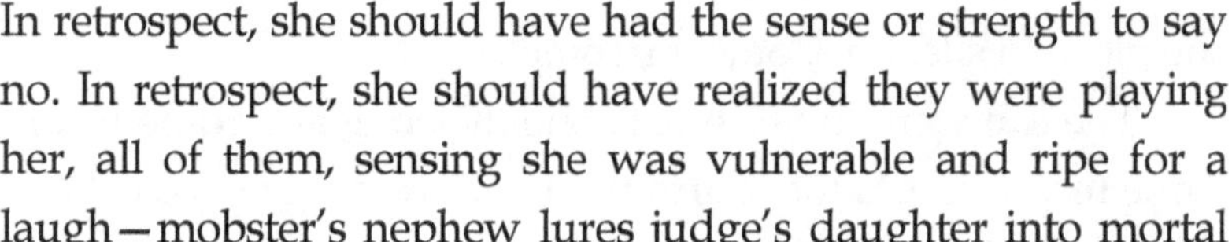

In retrospect, she should have had the sense or strength to say no. In retrospect, she should have realized they were playing her, all of them, sensing she was vulnerable and ripe for a laugh—mobster's nephew lures judge's daughter into mortal sin.

Not just any judge. The Honorable Jerome Balamaro, U.S. Third Circuit, constitutional scholar, routinely short-listed for the Supreme Court, just as routinely not chosen (too candid, too smart, too hard to predict and thus control).

In retrospect . . .

That was the problem with looking back. From the vantage point of the immaculate future, everything looked grim—her life a shambles, punctuated here and there with glimmers of promise and poise, sudden flashes in the dark, like fireflies in a graveyard.

And so she went, she saw, she surrendered. In the guilty haze of memory: kissing, fondling, clothes coming off. No talking. Why bother? The answer was yes.

When she woke, she was naked, her gown across the room with somebody's puke caked across the front—hers? Did it matter?

While everyone else slept on, she pushed through her merciless hangover and washed out the discolored tulle and lace in the bathroom sink, then tracked down her purse, dug out her phone. What cash she'd had was gone—she'd let them talk her into paying for both cabs.

It meant she had to call home for a ride.

Her only hope: Phoebe. She dialed her sister's cell. Pick up, she pleaded silently. Come on, come on . . .

The call went to voicemail. She dialed again. Same result. Same response. On the fourth try, finally, a groggy voice. "Are you nuts? What the—"

"Phoebe," she whispered. "Look. I'm in a jam. Don't tell Mom and Dad. Okay? Please. I need a favor."

She gave her sister directions, hung up, and searched for her underthings, her shoes, then slithered back into the rank, sopping gown.

The elevator to the lobby felt like a descending coffin—the silence, the smell. Outside on the curb, she sat down on a bench to wait. A half hour passed before the familiar Subaru appeared.

She almost ran, only noticing once she opened the door that Phoebe wasn't behind the wheel.

Her father was.

Dad's gonna kill me . . .

And there you have it, she thought. Your friends played you for a sucker, and your sister snitched you out.

Her father said nothing the whole ride home. In fact, he never said much of anything to her ever again, even when she graduated summa cum laude from Georgetown, or earned her JD from Fordham. He returned his attention to his other two children, the ones who understood who they were, where they came from.

And so, Lisa thought, staring up into the night sky—dressed in her spanking new PJs, silently howling at the moon—there's the million-dollar question.

Who am I?

October 11, 1878

Dear John Henry:

I am in receipt of your most recent letter, the one mailed from Kansas. No need to apologize for the tardiness in your writing. I understand how time can slip through one's fingers. So many daily commitments, so little time for probing thought. Forgive me, though, if I permit myself a wry smile at the ironic aptness of the town's name: Dodge City. Indeed.

I will confess to growing concerned, since your last letter arrived so shortly after your convalescence in the wake of being shot, when you lay so near death.

How pleasant, though, to hear from you at last, even if your news is largely offhand. How doubly rewarding to see that you are in such cheerful spirits, relative to the more bitter, cynical frame of mind you yourself admit characterized so many of your previous letters.

I am in particular touched by the fact that, contrary to your previous admission to living by necessity in a state of abject, even savage solitude, you now find yourself almost swarmed with friends.

Can I rightly assume that most prominent in that circle of camaraderie is the woman you call your bride?

Let me see if I have my facts right.

Her name is Katherine or Katrina or Kate, and she claims a noble heritage somewhere in Europe — Germany, perhaps, or Hungary.

You have registered as man and wife at a boarding house owned by a man named Deacon Cox. There is, however, also some scurrilous gossip that she once worked as a nymph du pave.

Now, I can imagine you wondering how I came by this information.

I believe that at some point during your sojourn in Texas you made the acquaintance of a buffalo hunter named Bob Fambro, who harkens from southern Georgia. Apparently, his family received word from him about your present circumstances, and they shared it with Uncle John and Aunt Permelia.

As you and I have both kept secret the more intimate feelings between us, they saw nothing untoward in alerting me to your marriage. Admittedly, I had to dig a little to learn the more salacious details, but I am nothing if not persistent, would you not agree?

Although the more salient question at this juncture is this: Why did you not see fit to inform me of these matters yourself?

You can imagine the devastating effect of the news, not simply because I am, at last, rejected for another. The fact that you could write to me and speak at length with such an air of contentment about friends and settling down, while saying nothing whatsoever about this change of affection, made me feel more than shunned. I felt as though I no longer truly understood who you are, who I am. It seemed we both had ceased to exist.

Have you so little regard for me, or your own dignity, as to act with such cavalier dishonesty?

Have you lost any sense of the man you are, the man I know you to be?

I do not begrudge your choice of happiness, but I also cannot resist the suspicion that the other half of that happiness, the dark half, is that you have come to believe I am nothing more than a pitiless moral scold, a sanctimonious shrew.

How unfair. And yet if our roles are chosen, let us play them in full measure. For my part I will do so with utter candor, the virtue you elected to withhold from me.

Do not think me possessed of that peculiar blindness that renders one incapable of reading between the lines. I commend your embrace of human fellowship, but it also remains clear that the devil on your shoulder has lost no command of his voice, regardless how subtle his whisperings. And there is the tragedy.

Of all the men in the world, you remain the dearest in my heart, but you also are the one most suited to greatness. You possess a keenness of mind, a delicacy of feeling, a fineness of spirit that I cannot help but believe you yourself neglect.

Don't misunderstand. I am happy that you have put aside the restlessness that characterized your prior life. A man wanders because he is lost.

If your newfound circle of friends and this woman with whom you have joined your life permit you at long last to claim a sense of home, I am happy for you. But do not deceive yourself into thinking it all is as simple as that.

There is also a weakness in your nature, a powerful doubt in your own worth, that continues to put your very soul at risk.

Perhaps the blame is mine, in that I should have loved you more wisely, with much less thought of myself.

In my own defense, I have tried to counsel you as best I know how, reminding you as often and in as many ways as I can that you possess a singular dignity, and are worthy of love. Perhaps, in the end, I should take comfort that you have, at least to some degree, heeded my words, and now feel at home in your new environs. If so, I am glad.

Regardless, I cannot nurse my wrath against you, despite the pain you have caused.

True, the swains do not beat a path to my door. Despite the innumerable consolations of family, loneliness has become my most faithful companion.

However, as Uncle John often remarks in his kind attempts to console his spinster niece, husbands are like painted fruit, and marriage nothing more than a cage for many women.

I turn to Our Lord for guidance, and He offers what solace I deserve. May He do so also for you. Do not neglect Him, even in your current state of contentment. Were you to allow that to happen, it would truly and forever break my heart.

With fond concern, always:
Mattie

$$\sim 30 \sim$$

Reaching the courthouse well before eight, Lisa turned into the bunker-like garage, lowered her window as she reached the ticket booth, and handed her money to the small Navajo woman in her fringed serape. With a business-day queue of cars stretched out behind her, Lisa dropped her ticket and change into her lap and promptly pulled ahead, while the tiny woman, rather than returning to her knitting and nest of magazines as she had the day before, remained at her post, waiting for the next exchange.

Pulling into a slot on the second tier, Lisa held up her hand against a spear of light flaring through one of the tall narrow openings in the wall. As she killed the ignition, her cell started humming inside her purse. Popping the snap, she dug the phone from her clutter of stuff, thumbed in her code, and opened her TM app. A message from Nico.

> *Wish I was with you. There in spirit.*
> *Remember: shoot to kill.*

She pictured him again in sweatpants and T-shirt, hair disheveled, waiting for the coffeemaker's felicitous beep as he thumbed those words into his phone. The image left a vapor trail of loneliness across the empty sky of her mind.

She wondered if he'd slept with one of his beautiful enigmas the night before—a Slovenian poet, perhaps, or some other variety of slutty artiste. Maybe she was standing there beside him right now, twirling his hair in her fingers, wearing one of his shirts, the classic feminine move, a claim of morning-after possession. Maybe she wasn't even wearing that much.

Indulging a moment of resentful envy, she wondered: Why are all the good men gay, taken, or playing hard-to-get?

Checking for other messages, she found nothing more from Tuck, nothing from Rayella. No surprise in that, she supposed, given the text from last night. Still, it would have been nice, something, anything.

She shooed off the self-pity, grabbed her briefcase, and left the car.

⊰◇◇◇⊱

"I think I see them," Tuck said, squinting into his field glasses. "Along the ridge line."

He passed the binoculars to Rayella who lifted them to her eyes. "Where?"

He popped several mints into his mouth, kill the morning breath. They'd spent the night in the car, him the front seat, her the back, blankets bought from a trading post outside Benson. She'd looked almost angelic in her sleep, eyes closed, hands open.

"All the way at the top," he said, nodding to suggest the direction. "Little to the right."

"I don't see anything."

"They may have already dropped onto the trail heading down toward the airstrip. It's pretty overgrown." He passed her the tin of mints, shook them for emphasis when she didn't take them right away. "And a pretty fair distance."

They'd parked as close to the Bristlecone as they dared, just off the Tombstone road, half a mile from the gate. The sun had yet to crest the mountain range, so the whole valley floor remained carpeted in shadow, fragrant with pine and sage.

Rayella finally lowered the field glasses and took the mints, slipped several one-by-one between her lips, staring through the windshield. "So what now?"

"We wait."

"For what?"

"Give them time to get down off the mountain, reach the house."

"And then?"

Tuck smiled thoughtfully. "That depends."

"I'm gonna try calling."

Tuck stretched out a hand, stopped her. "Not just yet."

Her eyes flared. "Why?"

"You don't know what kind of equipment they have at that ranch. Some kind of interceptor or monitoring device, pluck your signal right out of the air."

It was largely bullshit, but not so entirely out of the question he couldn't sell it. He'd spent a good portion of his life spinning nonsense far more bizarre.

Her gaze tracked back and forth, trying to read whatever she could from his eyes.

"Besides," he said, drawing back his hand, "it's no picnic coming down off that mountain. Trail's steep and wicked with switchbacks, and you've got cactus and thorn bushes all the way down. Then they've gotta scramble across the pediment at the bottom, which'll be tricky with the downslope and the rocks, then hack their way through scrub till they hit the ranch. Let's not distract them."

"So we drove all this way and slept in this car just to sit here?"

"Only till they've had time to reach the bottom, maybe an hour or so. Be patient, okay? Besides, there's something I need to walk you through."

He told her to open the glovebox, and when she did, discovering the two pistols he'd hidden there—both Smith & Wesson, a .45 for him, a smaller snub nose for her—he said, "You ever used one before?"

She didn't reach for either weapon, just stared. "Some. Not much."

"Well, here's hoping it's not an issue today. But if it comes to that, you're gonna need to feel comfortable with it. The smaller one's got a nice long trigger pull so it won't go off unless you mean it to."

She nodded, more to acknowledge than agree. "Where did you get these?"

"Private dealer. No names, no record, strictly cash exchange."

"When?"

"That's not the issue." He waited for her to look up, meet his eyes. "Look, I heard you. I get it. You didn't come out here to sit. You want to chip in, take part. Do your share." He reached over for the larger of the two guns. "Good for you. So do I."

Even before she turned the corner, Lisa heard the thrum of the generators for the TV satellite vans. A throng of cameramen and reporters stood before a sprawling crowd, circled around a quartet of clean-cut men perched atop the courthouse steps. Behind them, the building's giant glass entrance flared from the morning sun, its reflection like a blinding white god.

Edging closer until she found a spot of shadow, she saw that it was Gideon Littmann at center stage, his voice amplified for the sake of the crowd. The lawyer, Rankin, stood two steps behind, flanked by two well-groomed bodyguards. Like they expect to get mugged, she thought. By me.

Giordano and Phin? Nowhere to be seen.

She felt her heart crawl into her throat, followed by an almost volcanic fury surging up from somewhere. You miserable gas bag, she thought. You insufferable coward.

Seemingly carried away by the swells of his own oration, Littmann did not seem to notice her as she melted farther into the crowd from the back.

"...simple fraud, nothing more, nothing less, masterminded by a convicted felon named Tuck Mercer—a *forger*. He has the unmitigated gall to give a declaration under penalty of perjury that's nothing but lies beginning to end—that's the level of farce we're talking about here. Behold the man behind the scheme, if you will. A man who spent a decade in prison after cheating hundreds of people out of millions of dollars, ruining lives, bankrupting innocent gallery owners."

That's not entirely true, Lisa thought. Even unspoken, the defense felt meager.

"And let's not forget the other notorious fraud at the center of this, because it all comes together in one neat picture." He folded his hands to demonstrate the image materializing, taking shape before their eyes. "Who's the star in all this? Doc Holliday, the most notorious cheat, drunk, bunko man, and back-shooter in the history of the West. Sure, some say different, put him on a pedestal, but folks down our way know better."

Little knots of nervous laughter. Heads nodded. Knowing smiles.

"The scheme would be scandalous if it weren't so transparent. Well, we refused to fall for it. And we refused to let them scurry away so they could dupe some other unsuspecting party. We felt that was our duty. What law-abiding person wouldn't?"

Lisa scanned the crowd again, studying them a bit more closely. Plain Janes, Ordinary Joes. Mortimers and Whitneys, America's backbone—plus some lawyers with time to kill in the mix. Appraising the span of expressions, she couldn't determine just how many were buying in, as opposed to simply passing the time.

None of which would matter inside, before the judge. But that, of course, was the point.

When you don't stand much chance before the law, rally the pikes and torches. They'll be your defense when you defy the court's order, refuse to perform. Because that's what this is about—isn't it, Mr. Littman? You're going to hang on to those letters until someone puts a gun to your head.

What in the name of God have I gotten myself into?

"And of course the nasty little lawyer behind the whole scam takes her phony case to the feds. She knows the locals would laugh her out of court."

Despite herself, Lisa felt the heat rising in her cheeks. Had he spotted her out here? How soon until he pointed her out?

"Ever since the territory's first days, we've been fending off the arrogant stupidity and conniving greed of Washington and its shills and sympathizers. Looking down their snooty little noses, telling us how to live and who's boss, telling us how to deal with the Indians, the unions, the borders, not a clue as to what's right or wise or even common sense. They just sit there on high, loaded with lofty nonsense, because they know best."

This seemed to gain some traction with the crowd, men especially.

"This here is beautiful country, filled with honest people. And yet listen how beauty and honesty gets shouted down—by vulgar resentment, laziness, envy. By arrogant spite. Listen to the smug comedians on late-night TV, mocking decent people. Watch the coastal elites turn their backs on anybody who believes in work and responsibility and a fair shake. Well, guess what? We're tired of it. This is the West, not Washington, and thank God for that. We know who we are, and we won't let outsiders, no matter where they come from or what they think they know, play us for fools."

This garnered real applause, with calls of "Damn right!" and "Lock 'em up!"

Lisa began edging away when she backed into something solid. A man. "Oh my God, I'm so sorry . . ."

It took a second for the face to register, not merely because of the cryptic warmth of its smile. Elan Wingfield, wearing a fresh shirt but the same jeans and boots and tweed jacket as the day before, greeted her with a curt nod, then returned his gaze to the courthouse steps.

"Enjoying the show?" He reached inside his jacket, withdrew the inevitable pack of cigarettes. "To every tribe its truth. And its trouble."

Lisa checked the time. "I should probably head in."

With his usual command of the enigmatic, he said, "How well do you know your bible, Ms. Balamaro?"

He worried a single smoke from the pack, snagged his lighter from its pocket.

"As well as any other recovering Catholic, I guess."

"Do you remember the story of the Manasseh?"

Just what I need right now, she thought. A pop quiz. "Off the top of my head?"

"They're one of the tribes of Judah. They come into the central highlands of Canaan where they encounter, you know, the indigenous people." He lit his cigarette, then tucked his lighter back in its pocket. "In particular, a group called the Midianites. This is all in Judges, by the way, you want to look it up. A group of a mere three hundred from the tribe of Manasseh, hand-picked by Yahweh from over thirty thousand warriors, take on the Midianite 'raiders,' as they get called—you know, same word they used to describe the Apache—and drive them off. Care to guess the name of the Manasseh leader?"

Lisa obligingly racked her memory: Joshua, Aaron, Samuel, Saul . . . Finally, the name drifted up, and not from an expected place.

"Gideon," she said.

He exhaled a sideways plume of smoke. "The Catholic has apparently recovered."

"You are a veritable font of fascinating minutiae, Mr. Wingfield."

"There's some dispute as to what Littmann means. Most experts agree the name traces back through Germanized Slavic, but it's unclear whether the name's origin lies in the word for 'grim, fierce, ferocious, wild,' or the word for 'dear, beloved.'" He tapped ash onto the pavement. "Turns out the two words are quite similar, despite meaning nearly opposite things."

In such paradoxes, Lisa thought, lies the heart of the human story. "You've really made a point of studying this man."

He shrugged. "Like I said yesterday, we've seen his breed before. And we'll see them again. But yeah, you're right. I've taken a special interest in the judge."

Finally, she understood what he'd been getting at, not just today but yesterday, and felt ashamed for having misjudged him. They were all fighting for the same thing. A packet of letters, a way of life. The Promised Land.

"Thank you," she said, extending her hand to say goodbye. "For everything."

His grip felt warm and strong. "I wish I could join you, lend some moral support, but there's a situation at the county jail that apparently needs my . . . attention."

I can only imagine, she thought. "Good luck."

"To you as well." He glanced toward the courthouse steps. Littmann had begun his grand peroration. "He's an impressive talker. And he fights dirty. But he's not invincible. No one is."

With that and a smile, he walked off. As he wove a path through the crowd, she found herself sensing once again that lonesome trail of vapor.

~ 31 ~

WHIPTAIL lizards scurried across the dusty rocks in the deep morning shade as Rags and the others made way down the steep, narrow trail toward the landing strip at the mountain's base.

Trying their best not to lose traction as the jagged gravel and powdery dust gave way underfoot, they also had to dodge a variety of cacti, only to have snarling branches of thorny ironwood and desert hackberry snag at their trousers and shirtsleeves. The brush provided cover, though, especially in the spare light, making them all but invisible as they made their descent.

Halfway down, they spotted a circle of dark-skinned women in ponchos, black hair braided in long pigtails, digging up mescal plants in a sheltered gully about fifty yards off the trail. The women did not look up from their task, and the four men silently, respectfully continued down.

Once they reached the valley floor, they passed from the stony hardpack of the seldom-used airstrip onto the sprawling bajada carpeted in red chuparosa and yellow brittlebush. Here and there, Mexican buckeye with its desiccated seedpods rattled in the morning wind.

They advanced to within a hundred yards of the nearest corral and took cover in the scrub, watching as the Bristlecone's wranglers, waving their hats as they whooped their commands, ran a herd of ponies from their stable stalls to a pasture somewhere to the south. As the thunder of hooves grew faint and the dust began to settle, the ranch hands climbed into their Jeeps and pickups, cranked the engines, and followed the horses out.

The patrol car had already made its pass along the base of the mountain. This was their window. Rags rose and signaled the others to follow as he headed for the ranch house another quarter mile due east.

The plan had always relied on stealth and surprise, with a little dumb luck thrown in.

First and foremost: Avoid a frontal assault, since the gate, out closer to the road and several hundred yards from the house, was where at least two if not three of the guards hung out most of the time.

Instead, come up from the rear, pretend to be hunters if anyone notices, play dumb, act nice, then neutralize the in-house guard and the woman, tie them up good and tight so they don't get free before, voila, the letters. Then hightail out and scramble back over the mountain, using the same overgrowth along the trail for cover.

The car that patrolled the perimeter did so every two hours like a drone, same exact circuit, same exact speed. Just before dawn, as he'd looked out from on high across the lowlands, he'd watched the monotonous headlights and timed its route, doing so again as they'd snuck down the trail, lying still in the brush when the driver had any chance of spotting them.

Forty-two minutes on the dot to make its rounds, and it'd cross their entrance and exit route just once in those two hours, making it relatively easy not to get spotted if all went well.

As plans went, it was not particularly spectacular. It relied on timing, sure, and a certain level of skill, speed, and daring, but it also assumed the guards were victims of their routine—days and days of empty habit, seeing what they've always seen instead of paying attention, failing to notice what's actually happening in front of them. Easy to get the slip on men like that, which was why you constantly goaded men in combat to keep alert, stay frosty.

If the whole thing went sideways, well, they'd hijack one of the vehicles on the property, take off on one of the dirt roads snaking along the base of the mountain, head for the Middle Pass, and hope for the best.

If anybody gave chase, so be it. Wander would be manning the wheel, and he wasn't one to let anybody catch up, especially with the other three laying down cover fire.

⎯⊰◇⊱⎯

A line of Indian laurel trees grown in columns provided a visual barrier along the edge of the back garden. Peering through the thick hedge, Rags spotted a manicured landscape of chaparral sage, plus a variety of fragrant wildflowers: cowparsnip, beeblossom, catclaw. The house sat quiet beyond. Easing his way toward the side yard, he was gesturing for the others to follow when his cell phone thrummed in his pocket.

Digging it out—the caller ID read: Rayella. Rags answered, a whisper. "Not a good time."

"Don't be mad," Rayella said, the words etched with static. "But I'm not far away. Right outside the ranch, in fact, near the front gate."

A pause, as though she were waiting for Rags to say something. Words failed him.

"Tuck's here with me. We wanted to be here when you came down off—"

"And why is that?" What's so hard, Rags thought, about sticking to the plan?

"I've got a right to be here." Sounding like a teenager. Making a point. "And it just felt wrong leaving it all to you. It's not fair."

By now the others had gathered around, crouching behind the laurel hedge to remain unseen.

Rags could feel his carotid artery throbbing in his neck.

He said, "Not sure I understand what fair's got to do with it."

"Here. Tuck wants to say something."

Like that'll make a goddamn difference, Rags thought.

"Hey. This is Tuck. Listen, I realize you probably think we crossed a line, showing up out of the blue."

Welcome to the realm of understatement, Rags thought. "Yeah?"

"But seems to me the weak link has always been the gate up front. No guarantee they won't get tipped off somehow—the guy inside the house, if you don't get the jump on him. Mrs. Littmann. And if they get word—"

"You're not telling me anything I don't already know."

"Okay, fine. But hear me out. We coordinate it right, I think there's a workaround that'll solve the problem."

Meredith heard a voice calling to her from the end of the hallway outside her room—Seth, her private guard with the hopeless crush. Tightening the belt of her robe, she peeked out, still somewhat shocked to see the walls bare except for French cleats and picture hooks, the floor littered with wreckage—the mutilated canvases, the splintered frames.

"Yes, Seth. Is something the matter?"

He made a face that seemed to say, How can you ask that? "You want me to clean all this up, m'am?"

"Not at all. I believe Judge Littmann—this is his handiwork, in case you were unclear on that point—prefers it be kept just the way it is. Incidentally, is there coffee made?"

His expression seemed to compress, as though she'd spoken in some unknown language. "Not recent, m'am. I can make fresh."

"Don't bother, it's fine. I'll come on out make some for both of us."

She hiked up the pant legs on her pajamas and began making way along the wall, aiming each step for a bare spot on the floor. Here and there, a portion of one savaged painting or another, peeking through the torn canvas, met her glance, and for just a moment that glimpse of familiar form and color broke her heart.

⎯⎯∞◇∞⎯⎯

As Tuck and Rayella approached the Bristlecone's gatehouse, gravel rumbled beneath the tires and pinged against the undercarriage. A churning cloud of coarse white dust ballooned in the car's wake.

Tuck said, "I know you're scared. Try turning scared into angry, okay? Remember what these assholes did to you. Time to get even. Better than even."

Rayella said, "I don't need a pep talk, Pops. Okay?"

It wasn't entirely true. She glanced down at the heavily creased map sprawled across her thighs and knees. The .38 snub nose lay underneath, nestled against her thigh

She said, "This is the same damn trick Rags and Chalky pulled on Giordano outside the sandwich shop. More or less."

"If it ain't broke," Tuck replied. "Okay, here we go."

One of the guards, wearing jeans and a western shirt with the sleeves rolled up, no uniform, exited the gatehouse, palm raised. He had a shortstop's trim build, short-cropped beard, shades perched in his hair, smeary tats on each forearm. Easy gait, cautious eyes, a holstered pistol at his hip.

Tuck turned hard left and pulled to a stop so the guard stood on the passenger side. Rayella lowered her window then returned her hand beneath the map.

The trim, bearded guard leaned down. "Can I help you folks?"

That was Tuck's cue. He opened his door, got out as though in pain. "Damn leg cramp," he said sheepishly and made as though walking it off, up toward the front of the car, then across.

The guard's gaze followed him, but then came back to Rayella when she said, "I think we took a wrong turn somewhere." She flashed a girly smile and lifted the map with her left hand as though to help him see, while her right hand secured its grip on her pistol. "Could you point out where we are?"

Tuck, exaggerating his limp like he had a burr in his boot, made way toward the gatehouse. The guard sitting there hadn't even bothered as yet to glance up at what was happening, seemingly preoccupied, some handheld gizmo, likely his phone.

The first guard leaned in at her window for a better look. Rayella grabbed his shirt with her left hand, pulled him down as the pistol came up from beneath the map, and she jammed the barrel hard into his throat.

"Don't move or say a fucking word or I'll blow your neck to shit. Show me your goddamn hands. Now!"

Tuck reached the gatehouse door and collected the .45 from beneath the shirttail at the small of his back. He offered a beaming smile to the second guard, this one hefty and baby-faced. "That one of the new Androids?"

"No, no, it's an old—"

Tuck rushed him, slammed his soft face down onto the desktop. "Drop the damn phone, Chuckles, hands where I can see 'em." He grabbed the man by the scruff, yanked him hard like a stubborn cow, lifting him with his gushing nosebleed out of the chair.

"Outside. Now. Move!"

⊸०<>०⊶

Seth's cell phone rang as Mrs. Littmann, across the kitchen at the counter, poured coffee carefully into their mugs, leaning close the better to see. As she tucked a strand of hair behind her ear, the thought of her dressed only in pajamas under her robe created an uneasy inner heat. He'd already caught himself staring at her bare ankles more than once.

His phone began vibrating, a welcome distraction. Caller ID read simply: Billingham. "Ray. What's up?"

The man—ex-military, two tours in Iraq—walked point for the judge's bushrangers, and worked security here at the Bristlecone weekends.

"Yo, Seth. Yeah. Hey. Listen. Got a problem I was hoping you could rectify."

Meredith delivered his mug, now filled and steaming, then sat down across the island from him, hiking herself onto a stool. Glancing down blearily at an open magazine, she stirred her coffee with one hand while the other drifted up into her hair, mindlessly twirling a strand.

Seth wondered what it was with older women. Even the simplest things screamed sex.

Returning his attention to Billingham, he said, "Yeah. Sure. Shoot."

"My sister-in-law's getting married this Saturday and Maribeth is just hammering at me, 'You can't skip this, numbnuts, this is family,' on and on. Anyway, cut to the chase—I was wondering if we could trade shifts, like, maybe—"

The doorbell rang—a thundering carillon three-chime *bong*. Seth couldn't remember the last time he'd heard it. This wasn't the kind of place to attract visitors, let alone welcome them.

In unison, he and Meredith traded puzzled expressions.

"Ray? Gimme a minute, okay? Somebody just showed up at the door."

Seth slipped off his stool, eased toward the entry, Meredith trailing behind. He gestured for her to stay back, but she ignored him, her robe fluttering open slightly as she walked.

First, he checked the panes of rippled, frosted glass to either side of the door. Two men, one tall, one not, nothing distinguishable beyond that given the distortion.

Through the peephole, he saw they both wore cammies, the tall one black-haired and pale, the shorter one a freckled, bucktooth redhead. Another distortion, the fisheye curvature of the lens, prevented any further verdict.

The tall one pushed the doorbell button again. That strange, loud, demanding toll.

Seth lifted his phone. "Ray? Call you back." He thumbed off and considered the shotgun in the closet to the right. At Meredith's specific request, he no longer carried a sidearm.

She eased forward, gently nudging Seth aside, placing her better eye to the peephole. "They look like hunters."

"Can't jump to conclusions, m'am."

"Shall we open the door like civilized people and find out?"

Nothing like this had ever come up. What you are, he thought, what you've always been, is a babysitter.

"I need to get you into the panic room, m'am."

She cocked her head. "My God. We have a panic room?" A feathery laugh. "Let me guess, it's in Gideon's half of the house."

"They're likely armed, m'am. Please."

He grabbed her hand, clutched it tight, and began to drag her away from the door.

She broke free. "I won't be stowed away like a crazy aunt."

"M'am, please, I—"

She turned and headed straight for the door, opening it before he could stop her. He turned to the closet, opened it fast, grabbed the pump gun from its vertical rack and, discreetly as possible, racked a shell into the chamber.

———◦◇◦———

Meredith said, "May I help you gentlemen?"

The tall one had powder-white skin and devastating eyes of a glacial blue. The shorter one resembled a ventriloquist's dummy, one who spent a lot of time at the gym.

Blue Eyes spoke, offering an embarrassed smile. "Sorry to be a bother, ma'am. We were hoping to tag some bobcats or ki-yotes up in the hills, but our car broke down about a mile east of here, along the range bottom. Can't get a cell signal on either of our phones—we were wondering if we might use your landline?"

Seth appeared at her side. It wasn't until she caught the change in expression of the two visitors that she turned and noticed the shotgun. Seth held it barrel-down, along his leg, as though trying to pretend it wasn't really there, his expression vivid with fright.

He said, "Back away from the door. Both of you. Now!"

Neither of the strangers moved. Blues Eyes, calm as can be, said, "There a problem?"

In the distance, a lone car—unaccompanied by the security detail, which seemed odd—rumbled down the curving gravel lane from the front gate, spewing dust as it passed between the cottonwoods and sycamores.

"I'm not playing games." Seth edged forward, lifting the shotgun, gripping it in both hands now.

"Whoa there, partner." Blue Eyes raised a cautioning hand. "No need for that. We're not here to stir up trouble."

"Then back the fuck up!"

"What's your name, brother?"

"Don't call me that."

Finally, the smaller one spoke, barking out his words. "Let's call him Hoo the Hell-nose. Hangdog Tidyboots. Chairman Meow."

If he was hoping to get under Seth's skin, it worked. Edging out farther from the door, Seth tried to back the strangers away, shotgun now tucked against his shoulder.

What happened next occurred so quickly Meredith felt an almost dreamish disbelief.

Two men appeared, one from each side—on the left a tall boy-scout type with a terribly burned face, on the right a mountainous Negro—both pointing rifles of ominous appearance.

The Big Black Mountain pressed the barrel of his gun to Seth's head, while the other reached for Seth's weapon and gently lowered the barrel.

Little Barker said, "Don't make the big man angry, Hangdog. He'll pull that trigger in a heartbeat, just so he can brag to his sister about it."

The one with the burned face spoke next—softly, calmly. "We're not here to hurt anybody. Just came to collect something that belongs to a friend. Then we'll go."

The letters, Meredith thought. Of course.

After a few encouraging but gentle tugs on the shotgun barrel by Mr. Burn, plus an almost inaudible exhalation from the black man, as though he was readying to shoot, Seth relinquished the weapon. At almost the same moment, the strange car pulled up to the porch skirt in a breezy swirl of dust.

A sudden, clearly coordinated flurry of action: Two figures emerged from the car's front seat, one on either side, both bearing pistols. The passenger seemed to be a smallish, tan-skinned woman with wild hair, the driver an older man, vaguely familiar, not so much from appearance, which remained hazy, but a nagging intuition.

They opened the back doors of the car, and the two guards from the gatehouse emerged, hands atop their heads. They were led to the porch steps and forced to lie face-down. Seth joined them shortly, marched down the steps at gunpoint by the black man and the little loudmouth.

Mr. Burn glanced at his watch then told Blue Eyes, "Ten minutes till the patrol car returns to the gatehouse. That's the fourth guard. Better get to it."

Without a word, Blue Eyes hustled down the steps, rifle in hand. As he did, he passed the driver of the car, who favored one leg as he ascended the steps. It seemed to take a very long while before he made it all the way to the top. Once he did, he crossed the porch and, in a voice from behind the last locked door of her memory, said gently, "Hello, Meredith."

March 10, 1879

My Dearest Mattie:

A very long while has passed since either of us has written. Your last letter, so deservedly harsh in its tone, created within me a paralyzing reluctance. Perhaps you were serious, I thought, and no longer wished to communicate, no longer wished even to know of my existence. I would not blame you if that were the case.

However, as time has passed, I have found the silence between us increasingly unbearable, to the point I have come to feel like a man who gradually discovers that his shadow has mysteriously vanished.

I apologize for not being entirely honest and open with you about Kate. My intentions were not in any way mendacious, nor did I mean to play you for a fool. Never, ever has such a thought entered my mind.

Rather, I simply wished to spare you needless distress. It has been my experience that those who conduct themselves all according-to-Hoyle in matters of personal candor, confessing to things that can only bring pain to their listener, all too often simply mean to veil their spite in rectitude.

I am not like that. And you deserve better treatment than to be subjected to such hypocrisy. As for your reference to Kate as my "wife," let me dispel that illusion at once.

We are not, nor have we ever been, married. Rumors to the contrary are largely her doing, and the presumptuousness of that has driven a wedge between us, a wedge that has only widened over time.

As regards her occupation, Kate by and large gave up the role of "nymph du pave," as you so delicately put it, in 1877, when she and I became reacquainted in Texas.

I say "reacquainted" because we first met during the winter and spring of 1872, when I joined one of my dental college classmates in St. Louis, hoping to gain some experience in his practice. A theater lay not far from his office, where Kate worked as a dancer. I learned she came from a colony of Hungarian immigrants in Davenport, Iowa, but left home after her parents' death, finding work where she could.

Since your last letter affirmed your expertise in reading between lines, I will not spell out the matter more specifically. As I have already noted, I do not wish to make a weapon out of excessive honesty.

I realize that my failure to confess to this relationship, in its earliest manifestation and then again in its recent reappearance, reveals not one but two sins of omission. You no doubt wonder how many more deceptions lie in wait, with each new secret bearing an additional dose of betrayal.

I can offer nothing in self-defense to mitigate such reproach. Like every sinner, I am reduced to begging for a mercy I in no way deserve.

But let me, at least, in as clear and straightforward a manner as possible, describe the basic framework of Kate's and my understanding.

We share a strange and barren tenderness, and it is nothing to envy. Even at its most agreeable, our connection more resembles a contract of convenience than anything that might be mistaken for an intimate bond.

By the time we met up again, my physical condition had reached the point where I often despaired of my body. I recognized the symptoms from Mother's decline: Throat ulcers so bad I could barely eat or talk above a whisper. Racking coughs, almost constant, mitigated only by liquor. And the phlegm that emerged looked all too familiar, clitchy and green with yellow streaks, laced with blood. I certainly sought no comfort that would require Kate to ply her previous trade.

Instead, we agreed that, when my condition deteriorated, as it so often did during the colder months, she would serve as my nurse and companion.

In return, I agreed to care for her financially, obviating the need for her to work. I became, as the saying goes, her meal ticket, and as long as my winnings exceeded my losses by sufficient degree, I proved capable of supporting what she considered a suitably respectable lifestyle.

I also, perhaps alone among men, can withstand her dramatic distempers, to which she is exceedingly prone. The woman's rage, especially when primed with drink, can reduce a barn to cinders.

Mind you, I am only too aware of how often I have rightly stood accused of a similar disposition. Perhaps that is why and how she and I found each other, to withstand the gale-like fury of each other's whiskey hate.

All of which brings me to the ultimate point.

I would have no need of Kate, nor any other woman, if not for your absence. Had you joined me it would be your care I relied upon, your affection I gratefully cherished and returned. Do not for a moment think otherwise.

Let me share, in that regard, an observation very much on my mind of late. As it turns out, it comes from another consumptive — Spinoza, the great stoic Jew.

He argues that we are only free with respect to objects that we moderately desire, because that want can easily be controlled by the thought of something else. However, we are by no means free with respect to what we seek with violent emotion, for our longing cannot then be allayed with the remembrance of anything else.

As I said at the outset, the silence between us has withered my soul. I have never sought freedom from you or your memory. Nor do I now seek such liberty. You remain the one and only person in my life whose image I cannot blot out with remembrance of someone or something else.

Regardless of all I have admitted here, that truth, my bondage to the violent emotion I feel for you, remains certain, fixed, and absolute. Never doubt that. Never.

With all the love I possess,
John Henry

~ 32 ~

L ISA stepped off the elevator, turned into the hallway, and spotted Boonie, the process server, waiting down the corridor outside her assigned courtroom, clutching a sheaf of papers.

"Top of the morning," he said with a smile, Lisa hearing, *Stop all your moaning.*

"Nice to see a friendly face," she said. "Got something for me?"

He handed over his documents. "Proofs of service all signed. The hotel owner—Phin, Phineas Honnicutt, out at the Whetstone—ran me off with a rifle, called me every kind of so-and-so you can think of. Wrote that up in my supporting affidavit."

He offered Lisa a game wink. It conjured an unexpected warmth.

"Never could find the Giordano fella. Went to his office and condo, back and forth, several times." A big hapless shrug, arms crossed. "Zip. Nada. Nobody home."

"I appreciate all the work, the effort, the . . . "

"It's my reason for being."

"Diligence," she said, finally managing to pinpoint the word.

"You gonna need me for anything here on out?"

It was like a hole opened up in the floor. "I honestly don't know. I hope not."

"I've gotta make tracks, unfortunately. Business is off the hook—which is good, of course. You need me, though, just hit my cell. I can hightail it back here, no problem. Or testify by phone if the judge'll allow it."

Let's not hope for too much, she thought, at the same time wondering why every man wishing her the best this morning couldn't stick around.

"Thank you. For everything." She held out her hand. "You're a wonder."

⟨—∞◇∞—⟩

The courtroom was high-ceilinged but small, about the size of a hospital chapel, its walls paneled in a kind of industrial corduroy, its color a sedate beige. Except for the Court Security Officer, the courtroom sat empty. How long, Lisa wondered, did Littmann intend to stay out there on the courthouse steps, wailing away at the cameras and crowd?

As she passed through the modest spectator's section toward the counsels' tables, the CSO, dressed like a marshal's deputy—blue blazer, gray slacks, striped tie— put down the print-out he'd been studying, pocketed his reading glasses, and rose from his perch atop a stool in the left-hand corner behind the judge's bench.

"I'm Lisa Balamaro," she said as he approached, "the plaintiff's lawyer." She nodded toward the jury box. "I assume you'd like me on the usual side?"

He offered a cordial nod—classic jaw, lawman eyes, brushed gray hair—and extended his arm to the table on her right. "I believe her honor would prefer that." His voice was a gentle baritone, just a hint of twang. "Judge Numkena's no stickler, but she does like her routines."

Lisa went to the table and began laying out her documents, the complaint, the supporting affidavits, the motion and proposed order for preliminary injunction, the signed restraining order to preserve the letters, the various proofs of service and supporting documents provided just now by Boonie. Last, the now largely irrelevant motion to seal the proceedings.

The simple task of arranging the papers across the tabletop helped calm her, for now that she was here, inside the arena of battle, only moments away from the fight, her heart had started hammering against her ribcage like it was hoping to break out and run.

The doors behind her banged open. Despite herself, she turned. Littmann and Rankin strode forward, the two bodyguards trailing behind. A scrum of thugs. The bullyboys.

Littmann didn't meet her gaze, but simply marched to the defendants' table and took a seat. Rankin pulled what looked like a small-town phone book out of his briefcase and slammed it down in front of her, scattering the documents she'd so painstakingly arranged.

"Oops," he said. "There's our Verified Answer to that legally incoherent farce you submitted, plus a counterclaim for harassment—blame that moron you hired as a process server. Get ready for sanctions. The scene he caused at the restaurant where I was eating lunch? Pathetic. You're apparently as lame a judge of character as you are a lawyer."

He began to turn away then stopped, noticing the empty seats beside her. "Where's your skank client? Afraid if she showed up, she'd end up in jail?"

"Listen—"

"Or good old Tuck Forger."

"Where's your buddy the would-be wise guy? Where's—"

"We're going to assert our right to cross-examine," Rankin said, brushing her off. "But you knew that. It's why those two weasels aren't here. Because those affidavits you filed?" He shook his head, laughing, like it was just too rich. "You must be such a goddamn embarrassment to your old man."

"Do you honestly think," she said, clenching her hand to hide its trembling, "that you can scare me with this kind of—"

He'd already turned away, sauntering over to the defense table where he pulled up a chair beside Littmann and sat.

Shortly the CSO approached. Directing his words at both tables, the man said, "Recording devices of any kind are forbidden in the courtroom. This means as well that all cell phones get switched off." He glanced face to face. "Not later, folks. Now. I need to see you power them down."

He waited as Lisa, Littmann, and Rankin complied then directed his gaze at the pair of bodyguards. "That means you fellas, too."

They took out their phones, thumbed them off.

"Very good. If I see a phone turned back on, I will have no choice but to confiscate it for the duration of the proceeding. Thank you for your cooperation. The judge will be out shortly."

⋯◇⋯

Lisa tidied her documents back into order while, behind her, the courtroom door began swinging open and shut, each time with a creak and a muted hush.

Glancing over her shoulder, she vaguely recognized some of the faces from the scene outside. Littmann supporters, perhaps — oh how lovely, the home-team crowd. She wondered if some had been hired. And how many more were waiting in the hall?

A few looked like reporters, and she'd already had a taste of how this was playing in the local press. Their being here hammered one more nail in the closed-proceedings coffin, making her wonder if she should even bother submitting that motion. Regardless, how would this group manage with only ancient technology — pen and paper — for notes?

Sure enough, only a moment later, the no-nonsense CSO ambled back into the spectator section and in that soft, handsome, gray-haired voice offered the same admonition on cell phones and such, then waited as everyone performed as ordered.

Lisa took her seat and began paging through Rankin's Answer. Shortly she wondered if it was meant to be serious — he'd asserted virtually every imaginable equitable defense under the sun, over eighty total. Talk about throwing everything you could think of against the wall.

Several of the arguments were obvious enough, if a bit of a reach:

Unclean Hands. (Could see that one coming a mile away. Oh yeah. We're the bad guys.) Unjust Enrichment. (How about just return the letters, hotshot.)

Assumption of Risk. (Like we should have known we'd get robbed. Right.)

Even Force Majeure and good old Laches, can't forget them. Okay, fair enough, raise it or waive it, blah-blah whatever. But a handful of the other defenses weren't just speculative or irrelevant, they were frankly nuts:

Restraint of Trade. (An anti-trust argument — really?)

Innocent Infringement. (And how exactly does copyright figure into this?)

It was as though he'd found a list of every defense imaginable and added the whole bag of cats, regardless of whether any given thing applied or even made sense. Did he actually expect the judge to read all this, let alone consider it?

Okay, she thought. You say I'm lame, call my pleadings legally incoherent. Have at it, big fella. But you just walked into a trap.

If only that bravado could have lasted. As she read on, page by dispiriting page, she realized that Rankin and Littmann weren't just aiming for some kind of elaborate distraction. They were lying through their teeth. And were brilliantly shrewd about it.

<h1 style="text-align:center">~ 33~</h1>

<hr>

ALL four guards at the ranch had been collected — the last, the one patrolling in his car, getting jumped by Chalky at the guardhouse upon return from his most recent circuit of the property. They now lay on their sides on the dining room floor, trussed up hand and foot with duct tape, gagged for good measure.

Wander watched over them from his backward perch on a high-back chair, dragged from the nearby table. He wasn't sure what to make of them. One was a certified blubber butt, another so clean-cut he looked like he combed his hair to suit his mother. The other two had that scruffy, badgered, hollow-eyed look that Wander knew only too well. Maybe they'd served, he thought. Then again, looks can fool you. Just as likely they were wannabes, tinhorn patriots, pogues, same as the first two.

He glanced at his hunting watch — the laminated hands seemed to be moving backwards. What the hell was taking so long? They were supposed to be in-and-out, grab the letters and go. What was there to discuss?

⸺◦◇◦⸺

Beyond the French doors, in the living room, Rags felt his frustration mounting as he leaned over the lady of the house, the woman Tuck called Meredith. What was that about? Apparently, they knew each other — since when? One more thing about the folksy forger that didn't quite add up.

She was barefoot, dressed in nothing but pajamas and a robe, a somewhat slight but attractive, fortyish woman with dark, shoulder-length hair, sitting on a raft-sized sofa.

"Ma'am? I don't know how else to say this, so I'll just back up and repeat what I've already gone over. Those letters do not belong to you. Or your husband. Or anyone else except my friend here."

He nodded in Rayella's direction. She sat swallowed up in an armchair that matched the sofa. A little gamey from lack of a shower like the rest of them, her hair a misshapen thicket of wiry tufts, she glared at the older woman with an expression that hovered somewhere between abject fury and stunned disbelief.

"We didn't come here to hurt you or your men or cause any harm whatsoever."

The woman responded with a soft, barking, irritated laugh. "A little late for that."

"All things considered, ma'am, I'd say we've been pretty thoughtful in that regard."

"Oh, come on. You've taken over my home by force. I'm sitting here this moment at gunpoint."

"No one's pointing a gun at you, ma'am. I'm not, he's not." Rags nodded at Tuck. "She's not." Ditto Rayella.

Chalky was outside watching the front of the house, BBK the back.

"Oh, stop playing innocent. I'm being held against my will. And ownership of the letters, as I understand it, is currently at issue. That's why my husband and that young lady's lawyer are in court this morning."

From the depth of her voluminous chair, in a voice that could slice tin, Rayella said, "How about we do to her what they did to me? Then let's talk about being held against your goddamn will."

"The *point*," Meredith responded, rising to Rayella's pitch, "as I have already explained more than once, is that the letters lie inside my safe. You can't get them without my agreeing to open said safe. *Capiche?* So far, I've heard nothing whatsoever to convince me I should."

It was like a hook holding Rayella in place had snapped. She lunged up from the big soft chair, shoved Rags aside, and if not for Tuck grabbing her around the waist just in time she'd have backhanded the woman across the face so hard they finally would have seen some blood.

"Whoa, whoa, whoa—" Tuck held the girl up off the floor. She kicked to get free. "Okay. I get it, I understand. You're right. Absolutely." He spoke in an urgent hush, as though trying to calm a colt. "How about you give me a chance here?"

He eased up on his grip, and the girl tumbled a step backward, colliding with Rags, who circled an arm around her, as much to control as to comfort.

Tuck turned back, knelt down before the woman like a suitor, and spoke softly. "Okay, listen. I know this is messed up. Whole damn thing is. But I can explain a lot of it. If you're willing to listen."

The woman said nothing, just stared back glassily. Gradually, a sly grin appeared. "Why yes, Mr. Mercer," she said, like this was the thing she'd been waiting for all along. "I would be most grateful for an explanation of these most vexing circumstances."

"All right then." Tuck glanced over his shoulder at the others, nodded. Turning back: "So—where can we talk?"

She extended her hand, palm down. Ladylike. "Mr. Mercer, would you please accompany me to my *boudoir*?"

⸻◈◇◈⸻

As Meredith led him arm-in-arm into the long corridor leading to her half of the residence, Tuck stopped dead-still, like a man barely recognizing himself in a mirror.

"Don't mind the mess," she said, fluttering a hand at the wreckage. "Gideon took exception to my artistic taste. Can't imagine why."

Tuck knelt down at the edge of the first ruined painting and lifted it gingerly to get a look at the other side of the canvas. It was the variation on Blakelock's *The Captive*.

"That was always my favorite," she admitted, lowering her voice to just above a whisper. "I identified with it, as you

271

might imagine. And I thought it was rather daring—forging a Blakelock, I mean—since rumor has it fakes outnumber originals two-to-one. Or maybe it's three-to-one. Four? I can't recall. Regardless, it's some outlandish number."

"Most of the fakes are pretty obvious." Tuck spread the canvas out, fingering tenderly the edges of a six-inch gash. "They never get that sensation of light emerging from within the painting itself. You have to layer the pale greens and silver just right."

Leaning down closer so she could peer over his shoulder, see what he saw, she whispered, "Tell me more. How did you go about it?"

He ran his fingertips across the textured layers of paint. "I used bituminous washes for the dark areas, created the shapes with scumbled colors thinned with Blakelock's own varnish—copal resin with a few drops of cold-pressed linseed oil."

"How long did it take you to get it right?"

"My God, months. This is maybe the fiftieth version of this painting alone. Took me forever to make it look the way I wanted. The way it needed to be."

"To fool people?"

He glanced over his shoulder. "To please you."

She felt her cheeks color. She rested her hand on his arm.

Turning back to the painting, he went on, "Every time the surface seemed over-glazed, or remained gummy, you know, from the wet-on-wet way he applied the paint, I'd dab here and there with a rag, or go at it with pumice stone. That tended to texture the ground, intensify the silver tones. Here and there you can see where I used the brush handle or even the tip of a meat skewer, the way he did, to outline the figures or remove paint. That's how you get that distinctive shimmer, reveal the silver glow from underneath."

He turned back toward her, their mouths close enough for the kiss they'd waited more than two decades to share.

Tuck saw in her face the same girl he'd loved, to which the years had added both the softening of maturity and yet a strange, almost hungry luminescence as well.

"I knew you were the one who bought up all these paintings."

"I didn't make much of a secret about it."

"Not even to your husband?"

"I wasn't aware until last night he realized who the real artist was."

"Pretty sly on your part," he said. "I guess."

"And are those letters inside my safe," she said with a nod toward her room, "also a bit of your handiwork?"

"You mean did I forge them?"

She nodded.

He said, "Have you read them?"

"A few." A flinching smile. "Most. Yes."

"Do you really think, with my education, I could word myself like that?"

The smile flattened as one eyebrow cocked upward. "You may be rough around the edges, Henry Mercer, but you're nowhere near ignorant."

"Think I could take on two distinct personas, like some Hollywood actor, create two distinct handwriting styles, age the ink and paper—"

"You did it with these." She pointed toward the scattered wreckage, the beautiful ruins. "You took on more than just two personas. Dozens just here: Farny, Bierstadt, Dixon—"

"It's a different kind of talent altogether, trust me."

She stood up straight, crossed her arms with a whisper of silk from her robe. "So this wasn't all just some elaborate scheme to get here. Be with me. Like this."

"I didn't say that." He rose to full height as well, tugged her hand gently from under her arm and laced his fingers in hers. "When those letters fell into my lap, I knew enough about Gideon Littmann to understand he'd never be able to resist them. Phony or bona fide, no matter. I'd done my homework. On him."

"So you were already scoping this out." Her finger traced an orbit, back and forth, between them. "This thing here. You and me."

"Been scoping this out a lot longer than that."

"How flattering. I suppose. Should I be flattered?"

"Yeah. And once those letters were in this house . . . "

The intensity of the desire to let that thought linger, hang there incomplete, nothing but promise, the thing left unsaid—it surprised him.

She seemed to be waiting for his eyes to return to hers. As though to prompt him, she said, "Once they were in this house—the letters—you intended to . . . what?"

He shrugged. "Not exactly sure, to be honest. Maybe begin sending letters of my own, quote the originals here and there, like hints, let you know I was behind the whole thing. Let you know I was out there, trying to get in touch. Pretty damn romantic in places, those letters. Never in the world thought it would get this, I dunno, complicated."

"So this sweet little visit we're having here," she said, "wasn't what you had in mind?"

Squaring himself, like a sophomore asking a senior to dance: "What I had in mind, I guess, was you packing a bag, nothing more than you need for a trip to San Francisco, getting in that car out there and riding away with me. You don't need that man's money, I've got plenty. Enough, any rate. We can live comfortable. Better than comfortable. We can have back what got stolen from us."

She offered him a bemused expression—neither yes nor no. Neither now nor never. "I have two children," she said.

"They're grown, I heard."

"Not quite. Away at college."

"There's nothing keeping you from them. Not on my end."

"I've made a life for myself here," she said, "after a fashion."

"You can make another with me." He gripped her hand more tightly. "But first thing we gotta do? Get those letters outta that safe, hand them over to these people, and let them leave."

She worked her hand free of his grip. "But that would mean surrendering my power." Turning away, she began stepping through the wreckage toward her room. The light from overhead shimmered in her dark tousled hair. "And to tell you the truth, I've rather enjoyed having power. It's been a while."

She glanced over her shoulder with a mischievous smile.

"But let me think about it. I'm not averse. It's just, this thing, what's going on between us right now—I don't want it to end. It's so incredibly . . ."

She looked to the side, as though the words were right there, just out of reach, fluttering across the naked wall.

" . . . so incredibly like it used to be, you know? Impossible, delicious. Wrong."

~ 34 ~

"**A**LL rise!"

The Honorable Celestina Numkena made her entrance—a petite woman with an ascetic air, pace steady but brisk, almost birdlike, mounting the bench in her swishing robe, coal-black hair fastened by a silver barrette and pulled back away from her lean, tawny, thickly browed face. Prominent cheeks tapering into a V at the chin, flat nose, prim mouth. A member of the Hopi tribe, per Elan Wingfield, first Native American woman appointed to the federal bench.

She seemed surprisingly young—maybe a decade older than me, Lisa guessed, wondering if that somehow tipped the odds, and if so, which way?

"Good morning, everyone." A Sunday voice, cheery and flat.

"Good morning, Your Honor."

"Please take a seat."

She shuffled through the papers before her as though from ritual, not necessity. "I have defendants'. . . extensive . . . answer to plaintiffs' complaint."

Lisa detected a whiff of sarcasm—or was that just her own wishful thinking?

"I assume you intend to argue against the ex parte application orally, Mr. —?"

"Rankin." He stood, smoothing his tie. "Yes, Your Honor."

"Ms. Balamaro, does plaintiff wish to submit any additional documents?"

"Your Honor, we have an affidavit from an expert, a Hollywood producer that my law partner, Nico Barragan, has worked with on several major film projects. It concerns the intrinsic value of the letters, placing that value at a minimum of one hundred thousand dollars."

A ripple of whispered interest from the spectators behind. The judge said, "Let's see it. You can traverse the well, hand it to my clerk if you would."

Lisa stepped from behind her table, dropped a copy off with Rankin without a glance, then marched forward, handed a second copy to the judge's clerk. As she returned to her seat, Rankin rose like a Memorial Day flag.

"We're going to object to this affidavit, Your Honor."

The judge glanced up. "Grounds?"

"Lack of foundation." Rankin shrugged as though it were obvious. "Relevance, depending. On what the thing says."

Old trick, Lisa thought.

"Noted," the judge said. "For now, though, overruled." She began to read.

Rankin coughed into his fist. "Your Honor, if I might—"

The judge cut him off with another glance, this one less accommodating. And yet, after only a second, she offered a quizzical smile. "Feeling a need to stretch your legs, Mr. Rankin?"

He winced peevishly. "I was simply hoping—"

"I suggest you take your seat."

Savor the little victories, Lisa thought. Rankin did as he was told, then began scanning the affidavit, passing it to Littmann once he was done like it was a handbill from a leper.

The judge, finished with her own review, said almost gaily, "Right. Anything else before we move on?"

Time to spring the trap, Lisa decided. She rose to her feet. "Plaintiff also wishes to reserve the right to file a demurrer to defendants' Answer to the Complaint."

Rankin dragged himself up from his chair once more. "Your Honor—"

"On what grounds, Ms. Balamaro?"

"It lists over eighty affirmative defenses, at least forty of which are pure boilerplate and have no relevance whatsoever to the matter at hand."

'*Slow down*,' an inner voice said. Nico's voice. Her Philly accent was creeping back. What-so-iveh. Madder-a-hand.

"Rule Eleven," she continued after a deep breath, "Federal Rules of Civil Procedure, grants us the right not only to file the demurrer but to seek sanctions. The defense has asserted defenses with no basis in relevant law, no facts to support them, and without a credible good faith belief in their basis."

"Mr. Rankin?"

"First, let me commend Ms. Ballyhoo—"

The judge shot forward. "Mr. Rankin!" Gone was the Sunday voice. "Don't. Not in my courtroom."

He nodded an apology. "Your Honor."

"Proceed."

"I admire . . . plaintiff's counsel's . . . presumed ability to read minds, asserting knowledge as to what our beliefs are, or whether they're in good faith. Perhaps she missed the class in first year law school where they teach—"

"Mr. Rankin, you've been warned."

"Yes. Your Honor." The words seemed to be getting more difficult to say. "It's hornbook law. Assert the defense or risk waiving it."

The judge perched her chin on her thumbs. "There are perhaps fourteen viable affirmative defenses to conversion, Mr. Rankin. Twenty tops. Throw in ten to fifteen for the other causes of action. I'm being generous. That's thirty-five. Let's give you forty. You're still asserting over forty more than make reasonable sense."

"We'd like to be given the chance to argue their merits, Your Honor."

"You will. In response to plaintiff's demurrer. Anything else?"

His color was reddening ever so subtly. "We would like to request a continuance. Mr. Honnicutt could not attend because, given such short notice and being a sole proprietor, he could find no one to mind his hotel. There's no way he could just abandon his guests."

Lisa resisted rolling her eyes. Guests? Mr. and Mrs. Tumbleweed, I trust you slept well.

"Also, we have been unable to reach Mr. Giordano, and given the outrageous falsehoods submitted by plaintiff in her affidavit—"

"Objection." It was Lisa's turn, once again, to stand. "Mischaracterizes the evidence."

"Sustained. Get to your point, Mr. Rankin."

"We particularly find it prejudicial that plaintiff herself is not here to face cross-examination on the fatuous claim she was in any way mistreated, let alone manhandled as her affidavit falsely suggests. This puts us at a distinct disadvantage."

"Your Honor," Lisa said, "if I may."

"I wasn't finished, Your Honor."

"Then wrap it up, Mr. Rankin. You want a continuance. And?"

Rankin stood there for a moment, an expression of put-upon disdain. "Nothing further, Your Honor."

"Ms. Balamaro?"

"I could make the same complaint about Mr. Giordano's absence that Mr. Rankin is making concerning my client. She's not here today because she was traumatized by what happened two days ago and wanted no part of once again being in the same room with her assailants."

"Your Honor—"

"But the truth is, the scope of this hearing is limited. All we request today is that the letters be placed in an escrow account for safekeeping. There's no need for all the parties to be present for that to be adjudicated."

"Mr. Rankin—care to respond?"

"As we note in our Answer, Your Honor—I can't recall the exact cite, but it's from the American Law Reports."

"I'm sure we can excavate it, Mr. Rankin, given the time."

"My point—the cite makes clear there can be no claim of conversion for counterfeit goods."

"Your Honor, there is no evidence that the letters are anything but genuine."

"Oh, come on—the Holliday family went on record last night saying the letters couldn't possibly be legit."

"On record where—the evening news? The point, Your Honor, is that all of this is irrelevant. The issue at hand—"

"If you don't have a claim for conversion, you have no case at all, meaning there is no reason to place those letters anywhere but where they sit right now."

"We have a claim for assault, battery, false imprisonment."

"Not based in fact. Or anything close. And speaking of irrelevant—"

"Counsel—both of you—quiet." The judge leaned forward, the better to peer down from on high. She then added, as though to a pair of overactive spaniels, "Sit!"

Lisa and Rankin took their chairs.

"Request for a continuance is denied. What objection does the defense have, Mr. Rankin, to a simple escrow arrangement pending trial?"

"The same objection we have to the whole proceedings, Your Honor. It's based on pernicious fantasy. There was no 'theft' of the letters. We asked if we could have them for the purpose of assessing their real worth. Plaintiff agreed. Simple as that."

"First, Your Honor, we clearly contend that claim is false."

"I wasn't *finished*."

"Second, again, it's irrelevant to the issue before us."

"I agree," the judge said. "Anything further, Mr. Rankin?"

He'd begun softly jackhammering the tip of his pen against the tabletop. "Plaintiff brought her action in the wrong venue, Your Honor. We shouldn't even be here. We should be in state court."

"Which part of her argument do you find lacking, Mr. Rankin? Diversity jurisdiction seems rather clear to me."

"The value she places on the letters, Your Honor. It's utter nonsense. The letters are a hoax. They're valueless. Not worth the paper they're written on. And absent a credible showing that their value exceeds seventy-five thousand dollars we should all go home. Or to Cochise County Superior Court."

"I submitted an affidavit from Mr. Mercer—"

"And there you have it!" Rankin, arms outstretched, his voice just shy of a bellow. "Her case relies on the perjurious testimony of a convicted felon, a forger. The man behind this whole scheme to pass off fake letters as genuine."

"First," Lisa countered, "character doesn't prove conduct, speaking of hornbook law. No matter what he's done in the past, it proves nothing concerning his actions in the present. Second, he owes no apologies on his character. As his affidavit makes clear and I can personally attest, since his release from prison Mr. Mercer has not only led an exemplary life, he has proved invaluable to a number of collectors, galleries, law enforcement agencies—"

"You just contradicted yourself," Rankin said. "Either his conduct matters or it doesn't."

"It's relevant as to *credibility*."

"Exactly." Rankin laughed sharply. "He's not credible."

"Mr. Rankin," the judge interjected, "you're dancing in circles. I'm the trier of fact, and Mr. Mercer's credibility or lack of it is for me to decide. Besides, Ms. Balamaro submitted a second affidavit just now that seems to make Mr. Mercer's moot, at least for the time being."

"We again cannot accept it at face value, Your Honor. My client has a right to cross- examine."

"If that argument fails on matters of fact," Lisa said, "it fails even worse as to expert opinion. The affiant is a Hollywood A-list producer offering his best assessment of the intangible commercial value of the letters. Your Honor, if I may, I'd like to walk you through the story of these letters.

I think, once you hear it in its entirety, you'll agree with the affiant that this is something with 'real legs,' as they say in show biz."

"Make it brief, Ms. Balamaro."

"Oh good God. Your Honor—"

"Mister *Rankin!*" The judge shot him a glance to snap bone. "I am wearying of your antics." She paused for that to sink in—four seconds, five seconds—then turned back to Lisa. "Proceed."

Lisa recounted how the letters came to be, their presumed destruction, their puzzling reappearance in the hands of the Holliday family's former slave, Sophie Walton Murphy, the chain of custody from Sophie to a safe deposit box at the failed Freedman's Fidelity Savings & Trust in Brooklyn to the U.S. Comptroller of the Currency in Washington, DC, to Savannah Murphy Royster in Oakland, California, who contacted Tuck for his advice on their worth, who passed them on to Savannah's granddaughter, the plaintiff, Rayella Vargas.

"When you add the events of the past few days," Lisa said, shooting an acid glance toward the defense table, "I think you can see that the letters have intrinsic commercial value, above and beyond their historical value."

"All of which presumes," Rankin said, no longer bothering to rise from his chair, "the letters are genuine, which they are not."

"As the affidavit makes clear," Lisa said, "the fact that the letters might not, in fact, be genuine, in no way diminishes the value of *the story*. Some of the most intriguing episodes in the history of art concern forgeries—look at Han Van Meegeren, whose fake Vermeers, especially given their role in the Nazi art thefts, make for a far more fascinating story than the originals." Another deep breath. "Sad as that may seem to lovers of Vermeer. My point: *that* is the issue here, the intrinsic commercial value of the story *behind* the letters. That value is what justifies this court as the proper venue for this dispute."

"Your Honor." Rankin fluttered his hand beside his head, as though that might help conjure his thought. "The chain of custody for the letters plaintiff just elaborated—it raises another problem. How do we know plaintiff is the proper owner of the letters? We'd like the time to contact the executor of the estate of this grandmother, Savannah Whoever—"

"Ownership is not the issue," Lisa countered. "All we need to establish is rightful *possession*. We've done that. If the estate has any issues concerning ownership, the proper venue is probate court back in California."

For once, Rankin made no effort to contradict her, just sat there with a look on his face like he'd swallowed rancid mayonnaise.

The judge, sensing the opportunity his silence presented, chose to step in. Leaning forward on her elbows, chafing her palms together thoughtfully, she said, "Mr. Rankin, I have an analogy I think you should consider. I'm sure you've heard of Heloise and Abelard."

She checked to see if the names registered. He offered only a diffident shrug, as though to say: Maybe I do. So?

"Twelfth century. Probably the most famous lovers of the pre-modern era. He was her tutor, hired by her uncle, a canon in Paris. When the uncle found out about their liaison—she got pregnant—he had Abelard castrated, and both he and Heloise then entered religious orders. He became a monk and a renowned if unorthodox scholar—he got condemned twice for heresy—while she entered a convent and, in time, became its abbess. Despite the forced separation they corresponded, and their letters are some of the most famous in history. I read them in a class on medievalism as an undergrad at U of A. Following me so far?"

Rankin blinked, like the kid in class unsure he's actually been called upon. Beside him, Littmann sat impassively.

"For the most part, those letters are reasonably staid and proper, especially the ones from Abelard, who was a bit of a whiny stick-in-the-mud, to be blunt. Heloise, on the other hand, knew her own mind, like when she told Abelard she'd rather be his whore than an empress. Still with me?"

"Your Honor, I—"

"Around 1980, over one hundred previously unknown letters were found—anonymous, and recopied by a scribe three centuries after Heloise and Abelard died—but at least two well-known, reputable scholars believe they're legitimate. One published his findings in a book titled *The Lost Love Letters of Heloise and Abelard.*"

Lisa suppressed a smile. Through some strange grace or pure dumb luck she'd drawn the perfect judge.

"Where the previously known letters are fascinating here and there, the newly discovered ones are, well, just plain juicy—on both their parts. Honest to God love letters, unguarded—"

"Your Honor," Rankin interjected, "I'm not sure I see—"

"Now, as you can imagine, not everyone agrees these more recently discovered letters are genuine. The tone is so different from the others it's hard to tell. And yet they clearly have immeasurable value—for historians, if no one else. Plus a novelist has taken a whack at the story with these new letters in hand, a filmmaker's written an updated biography—catch my drift? Who are Doc and Mattie Holliday if not the Old West's Abelard and Heloise? Now, given that parallel, tell me again why you think the letters in your client's possession are valueless. In particular, why go to the trouble of agreeing to consider their purchase if—"

"I can answer that, Your Honor, if I may."

It was Littmann, not Rankin. Apparently, he'd decided his lawyer's esteem in the judge's eyes had plummeted enough. He rose from his chair with senatorial self-assurance, buttoning his suit jacket, a whistle-stop smile.

The judge checked her copy of the moving papers. "Mr. Littmann?"

"Judge Littmann," he said. Asserting rank. "Retired."

With a wary glance, she replied, "All right."

"You see, when I was contacted by Ms. Balamaro concerning the letters, she made no mention whatsoever of this Tuck Mercer's involvement. That alone should arouse the court's suspicions."

He punctuated this with a dismissive wave of his hand in Lisa's direction, his expression agreeably venomous.

"I thought the letters would make an interesting gift for my wife. The story behind the actual correspondence is, admittedly, quite romantic. And though I knew the letters on offer were unlikely to be the real deal—I mean, let's be adults about this—there were at least two possibilities that made a potential purchase still worth considering."

He clasped his hands behind his back, rocking a little back and forth, as he related the two possible theories Rankin had outlined during their meeting at the Whetstone Inn: that Doc's cousin's wife, Mary Cowperthwaite Fulton Holliday, had possibly forged the letters with her son-in-law, the Swedish novelist Carl Olson; or that Margaret Mitchell, author of *Gone With the Wind*, had mocked them up with her copy editor husband when they were desperate for money.

When he was finished, Lisa rose. "Your Honor, the defendant has just admitted the letters have potential real value, not just intrinsic commercial value, even if forged."

"I'm admitting no such thing. I'm saying that's why I agreed to meet."

"You agreed to meet," the judge interjected, "in order to obtain something you considered worthy of interest. And money. Yes?"

"Your Honor, as I already stated, Ms. Balamaro made no mention of the involvement of this man, Tuck Mercer, a convicted felon and forger. We only learned this after the meeting at the Whetstone Inn, which—contrary to plaintiff's absurd accusations—went quite smoothly and peaceably. As Mr. Rankin noted, we asked for temporary possession of the letters for the sake of verification of their authenticity. Ms. Balamaro gladly agreed."

"That's a bald-faced lie," Lisa said. "It doesn't even make sense. Why would I—"

He raised his palm to her, as though walling her off. "It was only after taking possession of the letters, Your Honor, that we had a chance to perform our due diligence. Better late than never, as it turns out. We discovered Ms. Balamaro represented Mr. Mercer in several matters over the past few years, and could only conclude we were being played for fools."

"Except we're not," Rankin added. "Fools, I mean. And don't intend to be treated like we are."

Lisa stood there slack-jawed, amazed and yet also impressed at the sheer audacity. Behind her, murmurs and whispers purred among the spectators, prompting the handsome CSO once again to rise from his stool in the corner, step forward and raise a cautioning hand, accompanied by a government-issue stare.

The courtroom fell silent once more.

"Your Honor," Lisa said. "Even if all we've just heard from Judge Littmann is true—and I think I've made it clear, we contend it is not—that doesn't make it relevant." She held out her hands, palms facing each other, only an inch apart. "Again, the issue here is quite narrow. We want the letters placed in escrow so they're protected. Simple. Straightforward."

"But unfortunately," Littmann said, "highly unlikely."

This got everyone's attention. Even Rankin looked a little at a loss. The whispers and murmurs returned, louder this time, prompting the judge to call out from the bench, "I will clear this courtroom if I have to." Once the hubbub subsided, she returned her focus to Littmann. "You'd better explain that to me."

"It's simple, Your Honor. Straightforward. To borrow a phrase." He smiled with galling nonchalance. "I brought the letters home, showed them to my wife. Upon learning of Tuck Mercer's involvement in this, however, she felt an understandable . . . revulsion."

"Go on."

"When my wife was a teenager, Mr. Mercer stalked her relentlessly. She was a lovely girl from a prosperous family. He was an aimless rodeo mutt. She tried to be polite but he simply refused to get the message. One night he was following her in his pickup, basically chasing her down this empty road. Trying to escape, she took a turn too fast and—" He paused, the entire courtroom in his thrall. "The accident sent her to the hospital for nearly a month, and permanently impaired her eyesight. Even with that, her family had to go to great lengths thereafter to keep Tuck Mercer away from their daughter."

"When, exactly, do you intend to get to your point, Judge Littmann?"

"I wish I could describe for you accurately the look on my wife's face when she learned that somehow this man had weaseled his way back into her life. Hoping to get one more crack at her, I suppose. Or her money. She did what any one of us here in this courtroom would do."

"Are you saying—"

"The letters have been destroyed, Your Honor."

Audible moans and gasps erupted throughout the courtroom. Lisa sat stunned.

From the bench, the judge said, "I issued a Temporary Restraining Order. You violated it?"

"Not at all. That order didn't reach us till late yesterday morning. The letters were long gone by then. It happened the night before. In the fire pit behind our house."

Good God, Lisa thought, wondering how she was going to explain this to Rayella.

The judge said, "And you sat there this whole time, knowing the letters no longer even existed?"

"Your Honor, I wasn't hiding anything. And please don't blame Mr. Rankin, I haven't had time to tell him this yet. We've all been rather preoccupied. Plaintiff asserted several other causes of action, rather gaudy ones to be blunt, that we've all been scrambling to address. I at no time disrespected you or this court." An innocent shrug. "As for the letters, I frankly fail to see the problem. People burn trash every day."

~ 35 ~

A quick rapping knock at the door—Tuck and Meredith both glanced up, seated side by side on the bed, hands clasped. Rags stood in the doorway, Rayella behind him.

"What seems to be taking so long?"

Tuck unlocked his fingers, rose to his feet. "We were just—"

"Holding up the show?" Rayella pushed past Rags. "Little bump-bump kiss-kiss?"

"We should've been gone by now." Rags followed her in, hands restless at his sides, voice tight. "More time, more danger. For everybody."

"I understand," Tuck said.

"That so?" Rayella strode up like she wanted to knee him. "You're sure as hell not acting like it."

"I suppose I'm the problem," Meredith said, waving from the bed like it was a parade float. "I just wanted a little visit. Old times."

"Yeah?" That quick, Rayella was done with Tuck. "Well, there's time for that after we leave, lady. You two lovebirds can go at it all you want once we're gone. Now open that goddamn safe, get out those letters. *My* letters."

Tuck said, "Look, there's no need to—"

A rough hand gripped his arm and spun him around. Rags stepped in close. "I don't know what you're up to, cowboy, but it's time you came clean."

From Tuck's pocket, a sudden whirring buzz—his cell. He lifted one hand, like a flag of ceasefire, while the other reached slowly for the phone.

Tuck read the display. "It's Lisa." He looked face to face to confirm it was okay to answer.

He thumbed speakerphone. "Hey. What's up?"

"Where are you?" The words were burred with static.

"Somewhere between Douglas and Tucson. Thereabouts."

A pause, as though she was trying to make sense of that. "I've been calling, texting—"

"Yeah, I know. Finally got service. Lotta dead zones out this way. How'd it go in court?" A flurry of white noise, like an active hive.

" . . . not going to believe this. Littmann says his wife destroyed the letters."

Stunned glances caromed around the bedroom, eventually landing as one on Meredith. Wide-eyed, she shook her head no, pointing like a silent movie actress toward her closet, mouthing the words: *In the safe.*

Tuck returned his attention to the phone. "Littmann said that?"

"You should've seen the judge's face. Like he'd just set fire to her favorite aunt."

"He actually testified that—"

"I need to speak with Rayella, she's not picking up her phone, either. From here on out this is about money, nothing else, which to be honest—"

"Just to be perfectly clear," Tuck said. "Littmann said he ash-canned the letters."

Again, Meredith shook her head no, even more demonstrably than before.

"Not him, his wife. Is Rayella there?"

Tuck clicked through the options, sensing an unforeseen opportunity. A chance at justice.

Everyone stared.

"Gimme a couple minutes. I'll make sure she hits you back."

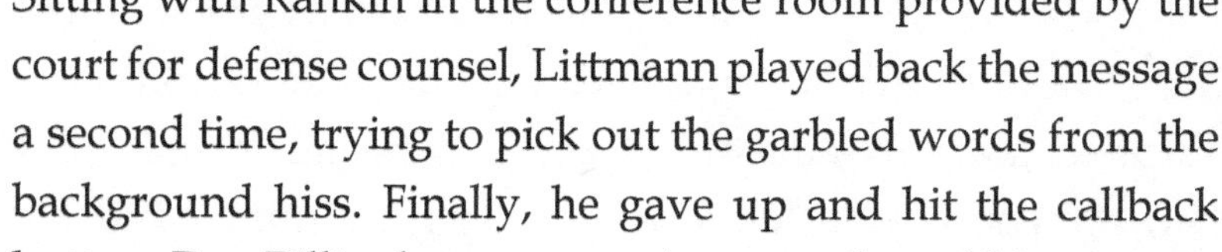

Sitting with Rankin in the conference room provided by the court for defense counsel, Littmann played back the message a second time, trying to pick out the garbled words from the background hiss. Finally, he gave up and hit the callback button. Ray Billingham, a part-time member of his security team, picked up on the second ring.

"Judge Littmann?"

"What's going on?"

"That's the problem, judge. I'm not real sure."

"Explain."

"I called a little earlier, to get in touch with Seth, talk to him about trading shifts, sister-in- law's wedding."

"The point, Ray."

"Somebody'd just shown up at the door. At the house, I mean. Seth seemed a little combobulated. I know, he's always that way, but this seemed, I dunno, different. He signed off quick, said he'd call me back. But he didn't. Hasn't. Not answering his phone now, neither. Make matters worse, can't rustle up no one else on the dee-tail. No one's picking up at the ranch, not Luke, not Sneezy, not Blaine. Tried to reach Logan then realized he's there with you. So . . . "

His voice trailed away, as though to invite Littmann to offer a suggestion, figure the thing out. Littmann was trying to do just that—mind darkening with implications, grip tightening on the phone.

"Judge? Tell me what you want me to do."

⊸◈⊷

Back inside the courtroom, Lisa sat at the plaintiff's table, staring at her phone, still trying to digest what she'd just heard. From Rayella. And Tuck. About their sneaky little surprise. Make that major sneaky. And big surprise. Behind her, the courtroom doors banged open. Littmann and his entourage strode forward—glowering expressions, menacing gait, worse than before.

Littmann was the first to reach her. "What the hell have you done?"

Lisa swallowed nervously. "I'm not—"

"Don't play coy with me." His finger in her face, eyes veined with fury. "So help me God, you think this has been rough so far? Get ready, you conniving little cunt. You're getting disbarred. For starters. After that, I'll have you flayed and quartered. Put the video up on YouTube for your daddy to—"

"Counselors?"

It was the ever-reliable CSO, gorgeous as ever. More so. To the rescue. He approached with a disarmingly offhand composure, though his eyes never strayed from the quartet of men.

"Problem here?"

Littmann seethed. Rankin said, "We're not allowed to talk?"

The CSO chuckled. "Oh, you guys." His glance trailed down to Lisa in her chair. "How about you—everything good?"

She smiled with relief, offered a peace sign. "Groovy like a movie."

"Judge is ready to see you in chambers."

Rankin's head jerked back and forth. "What's going on?"

"Don't worry. You're all invited." The CSO turned his stare toward the pair of hulking bodyguards and raised a naysaying hand. "Check that. Not you two."

The judge's chambers possessed the usual somber elegance— plump leather chairs, wall-length bookshelves packed with texts, a massive desk of polished mahogany stacked with tidy files.

The sole oddity: in the corner, an eye-grabbing display of Hopi ceremonial masks.

One resembled a tasseled tin bucket with slits for eyes, like a Teutonic helmet that had sprouted fronds. Another suggested a tiny-headed bird with a pointed, saber-like beak and long stringy locks made of tangled wire. Most impressive of all, a feather-headed wolf-man with an intricately beaded face, dark gray hawk wings for ears, a coiled gold snake for a mouth.

Judge Numkena sat in her swivel chair, spoon in one hand, carton of yogurt in the other. She wore a pleated, cream-colored, bishop-sleeved blouse and a charcoal herringbone skirt. Her robe hung empty on a hook near the door.

As though to signal where she stood, a copy of Joseph Sax's *Playing Darts with a Rembrandt* sat prominently on her desk, turned so her visitors could read the title on the cover. Lisa knew the book well—it argued against an individual's right to destroy artifacts of great cultural significance—like letters written by one of the most notorious figures of the Old West.

"I understand," the judge said, glancing briefly at Lisa before returning her attention to the carton, probing it with her spoon, "that you have some new revelation?"

Lisa sat down in one of the voluptuous wingback chairs, the softness of the leather like a giant, welcoming glove. It helped, just a little, with her nausea.

"I just learned of this a few minutes ago. I'm still a little floored, to be honest, for a number of reasons. Anyway, a witness wishes to come forward."

"What is this?" Rankin had yet to take a seat, nor had Littmann, as though they weren't yet certain they intended to stay. "If this is testimony or evidence, we want it on the record."

"We shall see," the judge said. "But I believe that Ms. Balamaro is trying to do you a favor. Why not take a seat, gentlemen? Take a load off, as they say." She waited for the men to obey, then: "All right, Ms. Balamaro. Your show."

Lisa hit the speed-dial button on her phone. "I'm going to use FaceTime," she said, setting the phone on the judge's desk, perching it up against *Playing Darts with a Rembrandt*. "Like you did, Judge Littmann, remember? At the hotel. When you wanted to show me how you'd taken care of my client."

Rankin shot out of his chair. "We object. This is—"

"Sit back down, Mr. Rankin." The judge tapped her spoon on the carton's edge. "Or leave."

Shortly the phone's display flickered to life. Littmann audibly sucked in a breath as the image of his wife appeared. She wore a simple plaid shirt. Her hair was combed.

"Hello?"

"Mrs. Littmann? This is Judge Numkena. I doubt you can see me."

"All I can see is bookshelves."

"Yes, well, I'm here with Ms. Lisa Balamaro, attorney for a woman named Rayella Vargas. Also, Mr. Rankin, whom I understand you know. And, of course, your husband."

Silence.

"I understand you have something you'd like to say."

"Yes," Meredith began. "Apparently, my husband testified this morning that I destroyed the letters he took from Ms. Vargas, the ones supposedly written by Doc Holliday and—"

"He didn't *take* them," Rankin said.

"Oh," Meredith said. "That sounds like Donald."

"It wasn't testimony," Littmann murmured. "I wasn't placed under oath."

"Hello, Gideon. I heard that."

"Go on, Mrs. Littmann."

"Yes, well, the letters were not destroyed. I have them right here."

She lifted the dusty velvet bag, so it was visible onscreen, then undid the fragile ribbon, removed one of the old brittle envelopes from inside.

Littmann seemed to give off heat, gripping the arms of his chair.

"Here. This one is from May 1873. The postmark's a bit faded, hard to see. It's one of the earliest ones, though." She held it up. "Look closely, you'll see it's addressed to John Henry Holliday in Dallas, Texas. Would you like me to read it out loud?"

"As delightful as that might be," Judge Numkena said, "it won't be necessary, thank you."

"Who else is there with you?" Littmann spoke through his teeth. "You're not alone. Come clean. Who's there?"

Lisa reached for her phone. "Unless you'd like to hear more, Your Honor?"

"This is a miserable, deceitful trick." Littmann rose from his chair, pointing at the phone. "Someone else is in that house. Tuck Mercer probably. He's holding her against her will. The security guards aren't responding to my calls. Something is very, very wrong and—"

"No one has forced me to do anything," Meredith said.

Lisa had yet to hit the off button.

"As for the security guards, they're skulking around here somewhere. Aren't they always?"

"Mrs. Littmann," Judge Numkena interjected. "I wonder if you could do me a favor. I have the names of some escrow companies in your area. I'd like you to deliver those letters to one of them. Keep a receipt. Let us know when you've done that. If not, I can send out marshals to take control of them."

"Why don't I just give them to Ms. Vargas?"

"Mrs. Littmann—"

"She's right here."

The view from the other end of the call pivoted. Rayella stood against a bare wall studded with picture mountings, ghosted with the outlines of absent paintings.

"And over here is Tuck Mercer."

The picture pivoted again, finally coming to rest in a selfie of Meredith and Tuck—heads touching, her arm wrapped fondly around his shoulder. He stared into the camera as though pinned in place. "We're very, very old friends. Dear friends." She pulled the phone closer. In a stage whisper: "In fact, when I was just a wisp of a thing, he was my *lover*."

Littmann dropped back into his chair with a muffled thud, murder in his eyes. Lisa, for once, could sympathize. Old friends, she thought, lovers, her mind returning to two nights before, his lips on her neck as he entered her . . .

"Mrs. Littmann, I'd still like you to place those letters with an escrow holder for safekeeping."

"I think I should let you know, Your Honor, that the fact my husband lied in your courtroom this morning comes as no surprise. He's always had a somewhat self-serving relationship with the truth. It's been a hallmark of our marriage—which, I am happy to announce, is at last, as of this day, this moment . . . over."

"Mrs. Littmann—"

The screen flickered, then darkened, then went black.

Littmann launched from his chair. "I want the marshals called. This woman—" He pointed to Lisa. "—used this court as a subterfuge while her gutter-tramp client and that liar, that criminal, Tuck Mercer, and God knows who else pulled a home invasion at my ranch. I can't reach my guards, they've most likely been taken hostage. You want battery, assault, false imprisonment?"

His face had turned scarlet. He looked ready to reach out and take Lisa's neck in his hands.

She looked up at him helplessly. "Think what you want," she told him. "But up until about ten minutes ago, I was told they were off on a hike in the hills. And I'm as stunned as you are by what I just—"

"You miserable, pathetic little—"

"Remember where you are." From behind her desk, Judge Numkena fixed Littmann with her stare. "Conduct yourself accordingly."

His eyes flashed with contempt as he wrestled with the button of his suit coat. "I'm the innocent party here! And by God, I'll get justice."

He stormed out. Rankin wordlessly trailed behind.

The judge watched them go, stirring her yogurt. Once the door slammed shut and she and Lisa were safely alone, she said, "Well, isn't this a perfectly awkward mess." She placed the carton down, wiped her lips with a napkin. "Don't presume, Ms. Balamaro, that you're off the hook. That man may be an utter pain, but he has a point. You still have plenty to answer for."

~ 36 ~

No sooner did Meredith sign off on Tuck's cell phone than Wander appeared in the doorway at the far end of the hall. A soft bucktooth whistle to get everyone's attention.

"Sarge, heads up. You need to scope this out."

He led them out onto the front porch, calling up to Chalky in position on the roof. "Tell him what you see."

"We've got company," Chalky called out. "Four vehicles so far, all showed up at once. Gathered at the front gate now."

Down below, Wander added, "BBK says he sees the same at the back, except they're up on the ridge."

Rags said, "How many?"

"Can't tell. I mean it's damn near a click away but—"

"It's the high ground," Rags said. Nothing but open terrain below.

Wander said, "No way we make it back across on foot."

"Roger that."

"Time for Plan B?"

Sure, Rags thought. Got one in mind?

As though on cue, the faraway crack of a single rifle shot echoed from the ridgeline down across the vast bajada behind the house. Then a splintering crumble of shattered plaster up top.

From above in back, the normally silent BBK: "Incoming!" He and Chalky lay exposed on the roof.

Rags shouted upward from the porch, "Find cover!"

"Roof's flat as a goddamn driveway." Chalky, shouting. "Just a couple chimneys."

"Get there!"

Through the ceiling, they heard the two men scramble for safety.

Then another sound, a rattling whirring rumble from the dining room. Wander went in to check—all four of the security guards' cell phones were vibrating atop the dining room table, two flashing, two spinning in circles like tiny dodgem cars. After a moment, one by one, they fell silent again. That's when the landline in the vestibule rang.

Everyone stared—like a miniature time machine had materialized on the narrow table. The small plastic mechanism jangled—twice, three times. Rags nodded his assent. Meredith picked up.

"Mrs. Littmann?"

"Who is this?"

"Ray Billingham, ma'am. I work security most weekends."

"Of course. Ray. How are you?"

A gust of wind from the west scraped the front porch. "You okay in there, ma'am?"

"Everything's utterly ducky. Why do you ask?" She could practically hear the man thinking.

"I'd like to come up to the house, Mrs. Littmann."

"Oh, Ray, I couldn't really advise that. There's really no need to do anything. So many problems in the world these days are caused by everybody feeling this obnoxious need to *do something*."

"Mrs. Littmann?"

"Just sit tight, Ray, this will all work out. I understand your sister-in-law is getting married. How nice for her. I bet she's feeling a bit overwhelmed." Rags gave her the cut-off sign, finger wagging at his throat.

"Oh, dear, they're telling me I'm being needlessly long-winded."

"Who, exactly, is 'they,' ma'am?"

"I'll let you know if anything changes but for now just sit tight, okay? This will all turn out peachy, I promise. Bye-bye."

She set the receiver back in its cradle, then turned toward Rags and Rayella and Tuck, hands on hips, still wearing her pajama bottoms despite the plaid shirt.

"I wonder how much those letters are truly worth. Whatever it is, I should get a cut, don't you think?"

From the dining room—sounds of a struggle, a strangled howl.

⎯⎯◆◆◆⎯⎯

One of the guards, the who'd met them at the door with a shotgun, had somehow worked himself free. Duct tape still clung to his shirt cuffs, his trousers, as he stood at the far end of the dining room table, gripping a bloodied carving knife taken from a drawer in a nearby cabinet.

Wander, blood bubbling from a wound in his neck, lay on the floor, kicking, whimpering.

You do anything stupid and get a marine killed today, I will personally cave in your skull . . .

Rags pulled his sidearm from its holster, raised it to shoulder height, left hand bracing the right as he aimed, and emptied three rounds into the young guard's chest.

Behind him, only a matter of feet, Meredith screamed, but she may as well have been miles away, or underwater.

Rags hurried to Wander's side, saw blood gushing through trembling fingers pressed hard against the wound — teeth clenched against the pain, eyes flaring with rage, one leg still kicking, as though to get something off.

"Keep that pressure on, press hard," Rags said, rising to his feet. He turned to Tuck and in a voice of calm authority said, "Holler up to Chalky, get him down here. Tell him Wander's down. Do it. Now!"

After another brief glance at Wander struggling to stay alive, Rags turned back to the dining room, advanced toward the three guards still lying there, bound hand and foot, and emptied a single round into each man's heart, ignoring the muffled screams, the pleading eyes.

Because that is who I am, he thought. The Devil Dog turned gunslinger. The Lurp on the roof. Turning back around, he saw the Littmann woman kneeling next to the guard who'd broken free. She seemed to be trying to figure out where to place her hands, but the would-be hero was already dead. Seth, he thought. That was what she'd called him.

Glancing up, hate in her eyes: "You had no right. He was hardly more than a boy."

"Boys can kill. Trust me on that."

Chalky burst in, found Wander on the floor, and rushed over to kneel down beside him.

"Take your hand away," Chalky said, "let me see. Okay. Good. I'm not gonna lie, that's nasty, but it looks like he missed the artery. I want you to press your finger here, right here where I've got mine. That's the pressure point, it'll slow down the blood flow. Now stay put while I get some pillows. I wanna prop you up, get the wound above the heart."

Rags walked over to Rayella, who stood in the doorway leading back into the living room, clutching the velvet parcel of letters. Tuck stood nearby, staring past the long white table at the Littmann woman, who was on her feet now, standing there, no expression, hands held out to either side like a plaster saint.

Rags told Rayella, "Once Chalky gets Wander stabilized, we're going to pile into that rental car and make a break south for the Middle Pass, head back over the mountain."

"You'll never make it," Tuck said. "Those men on the ridge, don't kid yourself, they know their business. You won't get five hundred yards before—"

"I wasn't talking to you." Rags kept his eyes on Rayella, hoping to melt the terror in her gaze. "Besides, cowboy, you're staying behind. With that bat-shit old flame of yours."

Arms crossed, head down, Lisa let her shoulder-slung briefcase bang against her hip as she trudged through the courthouse parking garage. Her footsteps echoed like hammer strikes against the concrete as she made way down the dim, narrow, low-ceilinged aisle for her car.

God only knows, she thought, where this nightmare's headed now. Assuming Meredith Littmann really does hand off the letters to Rayella, where does that get her? Where will she go, who will pay for the damn things now? If they weren't worthless before, they sure are now.

And talk about waving red at a bull—did they really think a man like Littmann would just let this go?

But that wasn't the worst of it. Not for her. She kept flashing back and forth, two distinct images: first, Tuck and his long-lost sweetheart with their heads pressed together in the cell phone's tiny screen; second, lying with him naked on the hotel bed, Tuck running his rough hands gently across her skin, whispering, "You are so damn lovely . . . "

Such a needy little pigeon—you moron, you fool—how could anyone be so blind?

A sudden desire to see Nico—talk to him, sit with him, hear him tell her she was better than that, smarter, tougher, prettier, sexier—swept through her with piercing neediness as, seemingly from nowhere, Littmann's two bodyguards appeared. They materialized from either side of a black SUV. Sensing the danger too late, she only completed half a turn, the first step of trying to run, before the little fanged weapon jammed into her neck.

Like her guardian angel had cut the lifeline—she not only dropped, she convulsed, limbs an agonizing blur of tremors, a seizure.

The awareness of being dragged, then lifted, thrown into the back of the vehicle, head striking metal. The airtight thud of a cargo door slammed shut.

PART IV

Therefore, those who believe that they speak or keep silent or act in any way from the free decision of their mind, do but dream with their eyes open.

~ *Baruch Spinoza*

August 22, 1881

My Dearest Mattie,

I apologize in advance for what I expect will prove a troubling letter. Knowing that word may reach Georgia concerning matters I discuss here, I want to tell you the truth, so you will not be misled by the endless flow of falsehood generated by a certain faction here.

By here, I mean Tombstone, in the Arizona Territory. I will not bother with details of how I got here or what calamities prompted the journey, only to say that it did not provide the escape from misfortune I hoped it would.

I can only imagine that you find tiresome my claims of innocence. You may even believe that, far from keeping my distance from trouble, I in fact pursue it at every turn, or it pursues me. The truth, however, is both subtler and more insidious. Trouble is the atmosphere we inhabit out here. It is as inescapable as the air we breathe — and, as you can imagine, a man with lungs as ravaged as mine comes to be a kind of savant on the metaphysics of air.

From almost the moment I arrived in town, I sensed an insidious tension, and shortly learned the rancor had been brewing for quite some time.

The chief problem lies with a group of freebooting rustlers the people here refer to simply as the Cowboys. They include characters with names like Pony Deal, Rattlesnake Bill Johnson, and John Ringo, a feckless brooder who fashions himself both a killer and a learned man.

The ringleader goes by the moniker Curly Bill, a man I happen to know from my time in Texas, that state I so despise. I considered him a scurrilous ape even then. Earlier this year, among other antics, he blustered into a church service and, at gunpoint, forced the preacher to dance.

I trust I'm providing a bit of the local color.

The Cowboys chiefly concern themselves with cattle theft. They strike against ranchers down in Sonora and have killed no small number of vaqueros in their raids.

Of late, however, their thievery has extended to cattlemen and teamsters on this side of the border as well, and not even the mules of the U.S. cavalry are safe from plunder.

When hate or greed turn their depredations in a particularly violent direction, they spread the rumor that Apaches have broken out of the San Carlos Reservation, and blame their own carnage on the renegades. At that point vigilantes assemble, pack up and head out, crying "Vengeance!" Nothing comes of such charades, of course, nor is meant to.

Most, like their leader, hail from Texas, others from elsewhere in the South, and remain sympathetic to the Confederacy and the Democrat party. I have to admit that with their vagabond swagger, they remind me at times of the free grazers we encountered when Major moved the family to Cat Creek to escape Sherman's savagery.

I can admire the hunger for freedom in such men. It's when liberty curdles into lawlessness, and then nuzzles up to politics, that the thing turns rancid.

Against them stand the local bankers, mining operators, merchants, and real estate men who form the Republican contingent, and when matters of law and order have become paramount, those men have looked to Wyatt and his brothers to field their cause.

Now I know what you must think, and I am not insensitive to your feelings.

I understand you may well consider it a form of betrayal that I might side with Yankee speculators against loyal southerners, however unseemly their disposition.

And I can attest that the Cowboys and their allies accuse the Republican faction of being nothing more than money-grubbing outsiders, opportunists — carpetbaggers.

All I can offer in my defense is a newfound understanding of how the march of history obscures the past, rewarding bold confidence, not sentiment, and how quickly even a noble ideal becomes outdated in the face of harsh but vigorous realities.

That is the West, Mattie. That is what it is like here.

In any event, that atmosphere formed the cauldron in which my troubles began to brew. Again, I will not belabor details except to say I have been accused of taking part in both a botched stage robbery and the murder of the driver, charges which, I assure you, are utterly meritless. That does not mean, however, they have not gained traction in certain quarters.

Ironically, one such quarter is inhabited by none other than my counterfeit wife, Kate.

We parted ways before I arrived here. The woman simply cannot abide any serious connection I share with any other living thing. She consigned to the fire more than a few letters I composed for you, and her relentless attempts to drive a wedge between me and Wyatt finally outlasted my patience.

She had gone off to Prescott to live, only to weary of the place, since it contained no scapegoat but herself for her daily aggravations. That and boredom obliged her to seek out my company, if only to recover her most reliable focus of disappointment and blame.

Meanwhile, accusations against me here rose from whispers to shouts as Kate returned to town, and when I failed to rise to the bait of her tantrums, she took to waltzing through every saloon that would serve her, drinking and jabbering with equal exuberance.

Naturally, this did not escape the attention of the Cowboys and their lawman friends. Pouring liberally from a bottle as they sat Kate down for a chat, they goaded her into the most absurd, acrimonious, and patently false "testimony" ever concocted since the Pharisees railroaded Christ.

I was arrested, but a mere four days later the prosecutor himself, having reviewed the bill against me, asked that the case be dismissed. He told the court that nothing resembling viable evidence could be mounted against me.

Kate tried to justify her betrayal as a desperate, last-ditch scheme to pry me away from Wyatt. How having me hang for killing a man I never harmed would somehow enhance our chances of being together escapes me, but such are the impenetrable workings of her mind.

Regardless, I may have been free from custody but not from scrutiny or suspicion. I told Wyatt I realized my troubles were driving a wedge between him and his more respectable allies in town. I said, if he needed me to do so, I would leave to spare his reputation.

To his credit, Wyatt did not accept my offer, but did beg me to "pack that woman off and soon." And so I told Kate we were through, this time for good. Hopefully, she will stay away, though God knows that woman has a way of creeping back, like some insidious infection.

That is where matters stand now. Once again, I apologize for this litany of misfortune, which I am sure must vex you. I know you believe me to be a better man than what my life out here might suggest. I know, as well, that you mean that to inspire, not condemn.

Have no misgivings, I have peered within my soul relentlessly, seeking the truth about myself and my nature. I do not believe, however, that what I have discovered bears too great a resemblance to the man you think me to be.

And yet, I cannot help but believe that who and what I am reveals any less the handiwork of God than the rest of creation, for even the Devil's mischief is preordained — thus Lucifer's nickname, the Lord's Left Hand.

Perhaps, however, if God indeed forgives, can we not hope that acceptance of our true if lesser natures is not just permissible, but justified?

In particular, does there remain a chance that you might find something within my soul worthy of your own forgiveness?

With a hopeful heart,
John Henry

———◇◇◇———

October 26, 1881

My Dearest John Henry:

I have read with great interest – and, I must confess, heaviness of heart – your most recent letter.

In particular, though it appears you have ended, once and for all, your arrangement with this other woman, you no longer ask that I join you, merely forgive. It would seem that the distance you have traveled these past eight years should be measured in something other than miles.

Regardless, your decision to remain away has sealed mine. I have, perhaps, held onto an illusion too long, without even clearly knowing it. The prospect that this separation might someday end and you would return home became a kind of invisible companion, always there, even if I was not aware of its presence.

I can no longer afford to be so blithely ignorant. I need to shake off all false promises, and commit myself body and soul to my own calling. With that in mind, I have begun preparations to join the Sisters of Mercy at their convent in Savannah. I will begin as a postulate, then enter my novitiate, gradually ascending toward final vows.

This will all take time, of course, not merely because of the arduous spiritual regimen. There are currently no openings here in the South, and I refuse to pursue one in the North. I have no trouble summoning the patience to wait, for reasons I am sure you can countenance.

I have not forgotten what Union troops did to our home and the land, nor what imprisonment at their hands did to my poor father. They broke him, destroyed him, it is as simple as that.

Ask me to forgive you and all you have done, in an instant I can oblige. But forgive them, and that? No. Never. And I have confessed as much to Our Lord.

That is all my news — far less perilous than yours. And yet no less dramatic, perhaps.

I fear for you, John Henry. From your own report, your life is in perpetual danger, and attributing these misfortunes to an atmospheric abstraction, this insidious trouble that hangs in the air, strikes me as evasive, even glib.

I will not, however, play the nag and beg you to return. You have chosen this path. Judging from your words, you have done so after peering honestly into the mirror of your soul.

I have done the same. That is all that can be asked of either of us. Yes, God forgives, but do not test Him. There is no greater sin.

I will pray for you.

Oh, if only we could have found a way.

Love,
Mattie

$$\sim 37 \sim$$

A dry night wind scraped dust off the desert floor, peppering Lisa's eyes, parching her throat. She tried to swallow regardless, a reflex from fear as much as thirst.

The high ragged scarp of the Dragoons lay faintly visible in the distance, like a giant wall of shadow beneath an infinite mist of stars. No moon as yet. Coy moon. Shy moon.

She felt especially small, an afterthought in the universe — tottering a bit in her tasteful pumps, still dressed in the slimming black suit she'd worn to court, though the tails of her blouse had worked free from the waistband of her skirt.

Hard to keep prim and tidy when men grab you, blast you with a snakebite of paralyzing current, shove you into the back of their big black shiny SUV.

She'd broken free just a moment ago, here in front of the mansion in the desert where they'd brought her—Littmann's place, presumably. He was crouching somewhere nearby, along with Rankin, the two bodyguards, and maybe a dozen other losers.

Check that: heavily armed losers. Good old boys with guns, rabble for rent, terms negotiable, apply within.

Apparently, they'd intended to use her as bait, a hostage. Comical notion—who of sound mind and clarity of purpose uses a lawyer as a bargaining chip?

She'd shaken off the judge's hold as he and everybody else hit the deck to avoid a sudden laser-strike of incoming fire, shattering a nearby windshield, leaving behind the telltale spider web in the glass. Then she simply started to walk, daring Littmann and his roughnecks to follow her up the long gravel drive, drag her back. Or just shoot her.

Glancing up through the dark at the distant mesa again, she noticed flickering lights along the ridge, about 100 yards apart. It conjured something, a memory, a thought—first the image of Elan Wingfield, standing beside her outside court, then the echo of his words: Gideon, the Mannaseh, the Midianites, the coveted central highlands of Canaan . . . That was it: the 300 warriors hand-picked by Yahweh for battle. They'd stood along the hill crests encircling the enemy camp, then broke open their clay lamps, blew their terrible trumpets, seeming like a multitude ten times their real number, an army of specters, horrible ghosts, striking terror into the enemy.

I've stepped into the Bible, she thought. The Parable of the O.K. Corral. Her foot brushed something fleshy—she jumped, thinking: snake!

Almost instantly, she broke into helpless laughter. How utterly, cosmically beside the point, fearing a rattler with a dozen or more misfits with guns behind you, taking cover behind their big-wheeled vehicles, while another gunman, a sniper, one of Rayella's marines no doubt, hides somewhere in the large dark house a couple hundred yards straight ahead.

No one terribly invested in sparing your life—*al contrario, piccola querida*—just about everybody pretty much okay with you dead.

Another glance up—so many stars, like brushwork across the trance-inducing emptiness. Was it really so wrong to wonder if all that lovely light, shimmering in her eyes, didn't somehow bounce back across the nothingness, a message: *Hello. My name is Lisa. I'm a double Scorpio, I love to sleep in on Sundays . . .*

She realized, finally, what she'd nearly tripped over: a body. Glancing around, she made out two more similar shapes in the dark. Three men dead, or dying, cut down by the invisible shooter. Who no doubt has me in his sights now too, she thought, some kind of night vision scope on his rifle. A killer's killer.

She resumed walking toward the house—Hell, why not? *Apply within.* Better the murderer you don't know, she supposed, than the ones you do.

The egg-sized gravel made each step unsteady so she took off her shoes, gripping one in each hand. A hint of the day's sunlight lingered in the smooth round stones, a few degrees warmer than the air, a strange but welcome touch of comfort against the tender flesh of her bare feet.

Go ahead and shoot, she thought. Front, back, somebody, anybody. Be my guest. Kill the afterthought.

~ 38 ~

IN the hours between Wander's stabbing and nightfall, Rags had felt the stranglehold tighten, then stop, as though whoever it was out there intended merely to toy with them, pin them down, maybe nick or even cripple but not kill. Not yet.

Maybe reinforcements were on the way, cowboy killers to the rescue, and that relief squad would be the outfit to finish the job, claim the victory, saw off scalps.

Either way, whatever chance remained for escape lay with darkness, and Rags knew from hard experience that night's principal advantage lay in surprise. Otherwise, its capacity for adrenalin mania, stumbling confusion, and outright chaos outweighed all other factors.

Unfortunately, surprise required a sharp, steady, active wakefulness, and whether from weariness or the tick-tock of uncertainty or sheer raw despair he couldn't quite tell, but every idea or hint of a plan that came to him whisked away like windblown dust before he could bring it to bear.

Here's how it had gone.

First, the sniper on the ridge proved eerily accurate despite his perch lying almost a click away. The faceless sharpshooter—probably a hunter like Chalky, born to his skill then drilled to perfection, military most likely, maybe SWAT— finally drove BBK off the roof with a shot that chipped off a thousand razor-like shards from the chimney a mere inch or so overhead.

Momentarily blinded, his face cut up like he'd been clawed by a feral cat, the big man scurried across the tarpaper daring his nemesis to take his kill shot, dodged a giddy-up round as he scrambled over the edge and dropped down into a twiggy bed of verbena, then took up position in the garden, belly- crawling along the dense wall of Indian laurels until he got into position, doing so behind the massive sandstone pedestal of a birdbath the size of a satellite dish.

From there, pointing the barrel of his Belgian weapon through the hedge down-range across the wide bajada with its carpet of chuparosa and brittlebush, he made sure no one made a move on the house from the rear.

<hr>

For most of the afternoon, Chalky served the same role in front as BBK at the back, though the two traded off now and then to stay frosty. He'd fashioned himself a decent hide by covering himself in an off-white bedsheet a slight shade lighter than the pillar he curled around, then chambered a round into his

M40A5 with its customized trigger, its Schmidt Bender scope, and traded the occasional potshot with the posse stationed at the gate, letting them know: You move, you pay.

Every half hour or so, he scrambled back inside to check on Wander—clean the wound, change the dressing.

Having lost more than a pint of blood, Wander had semi-stabilized in a ghost land between consciousness and delirium, thrashing at an unseen enemy from time to time, licking his lips, asking for water only seconds after his most recent drink.

Twice he opened his eyes, stared straight at Chalky, and muttered both times, word for word, like he'd been practicing it over and over in his mind, "Don't let me down, brother. Make sure it's you, not them. You know what I'm saying."

After the second round of that, Chalky, hands and cammies streaked with dried blood, told Rags, "He'll last a couple hours at most, we don't get him to an ER."

And who goes in to make sure he doesn't just lie there and die on his gurney, Rags wondered—which one of us stays and risks arrest for the four men dead already, who knows how many to come? Who explains to the intake nurse what happened? It has to be me, he thought. That's an order, no volunteers.

And yet he also knew Rayella would never let him stay behind alone. After all this so far? She'd dig in her heels, stick by his side, stubborn and loyal, and that just wasn't fair. He couldn't let her take the fall like that.

But he also couldn't just let Wander die.

Figure it out when you get there, he decided, then went to the back door, whistled BBK in from the garden. Once the group was assembled he told them all to pack up, it was finally time to make a break for Tuck's rental car parked out front. If that worked out, they'd see if they could slip past the sniper, dodge his shots, and outrun the posse that would no doubt follow as they made a run for the Middle Pass.

They lifted Wander to his feet, limp arm hooked around Chalky's shoulder, bloody washcloth duct-taped to his neck, the skin that sickly evil gray. Rayella clutched her satchel of letters. Rags and BBK got ready to lay down cover fire for the others when, after a count of three, they'd race out the door and down the steps and hustle into the car.

This was a little after four or so, about an hour and a half before sunset.

Maybe the time had nothing to do with it. Maybe the gunmen at the gate, somewhere between two and three hundred yards away, were simply watching, waiting, ready to fire in the blink of an eye should a door fly open.

Regardless, Rags and BBK made it out to the pillars okay, but no one else got the chance to take so much as that first bold step onto the porch before a barrage of gunfire peppered the entire front of the house, like a giant had spat out a truckload of nails. None of this bunch of gunmen seemed to possess the skill of the man on the ridge, but the fusillade still drove everybody back inside.

That accomplished, the shooters apparently felt inspired and turned their freshly aggravated hive mind to the car. Within a matter of seconds, they blasted out two tires, made short work of the windshield, and riddled the rest of the thing with what seemed like a thousand rounds, leaving it a perforated hulk, listing to one side and barely fit for scrap.

Why they hadn't thought of that before, God only knew. Maybe they'd been waiting all along for the chance to spring that little trap. Maybe they just snapped awake and opened fire.

Suddenly Tuck was there, easing forward from the back. He'd been sitting alone in the living room last time Rags checked, head in his hands, trying to come up with his own plan out of here no doubt, him and his haywire love from Way Back When. Inching past the others, trying to hide the drag in his bad leg, then peering out the beveled edge of the vestibule window, he remarked with that irritating air of smugness, "I told you those boys would know their business."

Rags snapped. On his feet in an eye-blink, grabbing the man's shirt in his fist, he backed him hard against the wall. If anyone here deserves, really truly deserves to die, he thought. Shaking off the impulse, he pointed through the window's frosted glass toward the blurred outline of the massive, four-door garage maybe fifty yards away, a third of the distance between the house and the empty stables. It had seemed irrelevant earlier. Not so, now.

"How many cars they keep out there?"

"The Littmanns?"

Rayella barked, "Who the fuck else would he mean, genius?"

Tuck closed one eye, the better to see through the prism of clear glass along the window's edge, studied the low-slung structure—white clapboard, pitched roof, big as a VFW hall with thick, wavy glass brick windows, impossible to see through.

"Can't tell if any cars are in there."

"Find out," Rags said. "If so, get the keys."

"Not to be overly negative here," Tuck said, "but which one of us is spry enough to hoof across that open ground without getting mowed down for the privilege?"

Rags said, "Just come back with the keys."

—◦◇◦—

Tuck found Meredith sitting at the dining room table, staring at the body of the youngster, the one named Seth. She'd winnowed the hair away from her face, braiding it absently, and a coiled strand lay loose to one side, perched in the freckled crook of her neck.

The bodies of the other three guards, still bound hand and foot, eyes fixed in their distant death stares, lay not far away in surprisingly minimal pools of blood, meaning they'd passed on quick. Give Rags that, Tuck thought. He's a capable killer.

He pulled up a chair across from her and sat. "None of this was supposed to happen."

Her breath was even, but shallow. "Well, isn't that a comfort."

"You can't imagine I wanted it this way."

"Imagine? No. No. Not at all."

"Meredith—"

"If only that were the point."

She turned toward him finally — her dull eyes, like wells pumped dry of caring.

He said, "They want to know where the keys are. For the cars. Out there in the garage."

She reached one-handed for her loosely knotted hair, began absently braiding it again. "Yes, but everyone wants everything. All the time. Don't you find that to be true?"

"I said it already—"

"Assuming for just a moment we could get beyond this." She gestured to the four dead men, like they were statuary, an exhibit. The Museum of Unwanted Consequences. "Suppose we could forget it all, pretend it never happened, run away, whatever . . . "

The drift of her voice into silence conveyed the chasm between this and that. "We won't get another chance," Tuck said.

She waved that away. "Here's a thought. Maybe you can just make this all un-happen."

"Meredith, please, listen to—"

"Bringing back the dead these days? I imagine that brings a pretty penny. Even better than forging the occasional masterpiece. Which is, admittedly, in its own way, conjuring the dead, no?"

He leaned forward over the table, lowering his voice. "You're right. I can't make any of this go away. But one of those marines took a knife in the neck, he most likely won't make it neither. Let's not forget that. But your boy there, he gets a free pass?"

"He was trying to protect me."

"Or himself. Or maybe he was just plain stupid, who knows?"

"No." She shook her head absently.

"What about those men out at the gate, or the ones up there on the ridge? Think they don't want us dead? Think that's to protect *you*?"

He reached a hand across the table, opening it for her to take.

"Not one single person on this earth, not one, can ever, will ever—"

"Don't say it." Pinning him with her glassy stare. "Not now. Not after all—"

The sound of someone clearing his throat: Rags, in the doorway, with his unnerving, disfigured face. He held a pistol in his hand.

———◈◇◈———

"We're running out of time," Rags said, doing his best to contain his impatience. Take a look at these two, he thought. "The cars you got parked out in that garage, we need the keys."

The woman, Meredith, glanced his direction only briefly, then turned back toward the room. "Given the issue with my eyesight," she said with that air of backwater aristocracy, "my husband denies me the privilege of driving. Call it a condition of my confinement. So whatever cars are there and wherever the keys are kept—"

"You know where they are. Get them."

She turned to face him. "Or else what—you'll shoot me? Don't be tedious. We've been through this."

And that, Rags thought, takes care of that.

He strode forward, grabbed Tuck by the hair, slammed his face hard against the tabletop, then pressed the pistol's barrel against his neck. "Tell ya what—how about I shoot him instead?"

She studied Tuck with a dispassionate expression. He struggled, though not all that aggressively—clenched teeth, a breathy grimace, eyes clenched shut.

After what seemed like far too long a pause, she murmured, "That would be redundant. He died a long time ago."

Rags took note of her eyes, like staring into a dark room. He let go of Tuck, came around the table in three quick steps, fought through the crazy batting of her hands and windmill arms then gripped that knot of loosely braided hair, dragged her up and out of her seat, forced her to her knees directly on top of the nearest body.

"You wanna talk about dead? Seth's his name, have I got that right?" He shoved her head down, drove her face into the lifeless neck. "Well, let's get a good look. Don't be shy. Believe me, you get used to it. And here's a little secret—he's gonna stick with you. Don't worry. He's gonna be right there with you till the goddamn end."

"Rags, whoa." Tuck stepped forward, hands held up. "Like you said, she's not well, there's no—"

The barrel of the pistol swung up and leveled, a bead on Tuck's breastbone, though for an instant what Rags saw was a black cloak and turban—a Taliban elder, the man shoveling dirt into a deep narrow hole, the hole containing a weeping girl, a girl who would get stoned to death for hiding a book she'd hoped, one day, to learn how to read.

In revenge there is life.

The Rankin woman's arm flailed vaguely toward the vestibule, she was saying something, but the words were muffled, her mouth pressed hard against the dead kid's flesh.

Rags turned to glance over his shoulder in the general direction of her gesture, then let go and stumbled to his feet. Pushing past Tuck, he went out into the entryway, the marble-top table beneath the mirror, pulled open the drawer—lo and behold, several sets of leather-bobbed keys.

Honestly—how hard was that?

"We still gotta wait till dark," Chalky said, sitting on the floor, Wander's head tucked into his shoulder. "Only way we can make it all the way to that garage, unless you wanna offer them a decoy, sacrificial victim—know what I'm saying?"

Yeah, Rags thought. I do.

"Give them Queen Crazy in there." Rayella's two cents, reading his mind. She was sitting on the floor as well, across from Chalky and Wander, a stranglehold on that satchel of letters.

Rags mopped the sweat from his face. "Given what she said on the phone, first to the guys out front, then to the lawyers, the judge, her old man, I think she's pretty much worthless as a hostage."

"Yeah." Rayella again—just like that, deflated. "Wack-job wife, who cares?"

Rags glanced toward the dining room, wondering if even Tuck had given up on the woman. "Regardless, you're right. Sit tight till dark. That's our only chance."

"They're making a move," BBK said. He was crouching near the front, peering through a bullet hole in the frosted glass window. Reaching up for the knob, he eased the door open just a crack, then slid out onto the front porch. From a prone position, he waited, aimed, fired three stuttered bursts on full auto—the chugging roar of his weapon, ejected brass chiming as it hit the porch.

He scrambled back inside. "Using the trees along the drive for cover." He dislodged his clip, put it aside for reload, pounded a second against the floor to clear any jams, whomped it home. No expression, half-mast eyes. Face etched with the cat-claw scars from the sniper's near miss earlier. "Got one for sure, maybe two, trying to inch in closer. Now they know—we ain't the only ones pinned down."

⸺◦◇◦⸺

That's how the stalemate remained through sunset, twilight. Up on the ridge, as darkness fell, someone built a series of fires along the bluff, and Rags had to give whoever it was credit. Was it just one man up there? Several? A dozen? No way to tell.

Chalky had switched places with BBK at that point, and so he was lying there using the Indian laurels for cover, siting through his scope, as the fires got lit.

For a long, voluptuous second a clear shot presented itself—he caught the man's silhouette brought into focus by the sudden eruption of flame. He took his time, pretty sure of the distance, clicking the sight's turret as he adjusted the reticle to compensate, as best he could, for the crosscut winds.

Hard to tell how close he got—not cocky enough to claim a hit—but it drove that man and any others with him away from the edge, which was all the advantage they could hope for.

A short time later, he and BBK exchanged places again, and resuming his position beneath the front porch bedsheet, Chalky traded out the Schmidt Bender for his night vision scope, then settled in to take out anything that moved in the dark out near the gate.

Rags with Rayella's help had taken over caring for Wander, whose drifts into unconsciousness seemed to be accelerating. He needed to be reliably alert before they could risk a run to the garage. If they had to drag him, that simple element of delay could prove lethal. Not just for Wander.

As it turned out, the delay already in-hand proved costly enough. The reinforcements he'd feared would likely come showed up about a half hour after nightfall—a Mercedes sedan and a Chevy Suburban. Not the law, interestingly. It seemed the law wanted no part of this fight. Maybe they'd been warned off, given the judge's influence. Maybe they were out there already—street clothes, civilian capacity, rogue-cop-gone-minuteman.

Rags had already ordered all the lights inside turned off, so the house sat utterly dark. He scrambled out onto the porch, took up position behind the pillar opposite Chalky, and donned his NVGs. Waiting for the headlights at the end of the drive to go out, he focused on movement, saw a figure—smaller, long-haired, dressed in a skirt—getting dragged from the back of the SUV.

"They've got Rayella's lawyer, looks like."

Chalky, siting her in his scope, replied, "That change anything?"

Rags saw another of the newcomers dig something out of his breast pocket, press it to his ear. "Guess that remains to be seen."

The phone in the vestibule rang—once, twice. "Suppose I should get that," Rags said.

He scrambled back inside, checked briefly on Wander who offered an eye-swimming thumbs up, then grabbed the phone off its table and put the receiver to his ear, lying on the marble floor since he feared presenting a target if he stood.

Before he could get out a word, the voice on the other end said curtly, "Meredith?"

Rags glanced toward the living room. He'd duct-taped the woman to a chair, sparing her the indignity of a gag once she seemed agreeable to behaving. Tuck sat nearby. Judging from their expressions, the romance had taken a southerly turn.

"Lady of the house is occupied. You deal with me."

"And who the hell are you?"

Interesting, Rags thought. He didn't ask if she was safe. Or even alive. "I'm the Killer of Christmas Present, Scrooge. Sorry it took me so long to get here. Better late than, you know."

"There's no way out—you realize that, right?"

"I know nothing of the kind. Here's what I do know— we're much better at this than your boys are. Count the bodies on the ground, Scrooge. That's not all of them, trust me."

"You're outnumbered—"

"Says who? You've got no idea how many of us are here. Besides, point is we're not outmanned. That's the difference. I'll put mine against yours any day of the week, screw the numbers. Now, you want to put something on the table, start talking. Otherwise, I'm hanging up, and we move on to Phase Two."

"You'll never—"

His voice broke off, then came a garbled scramble of voices until Chalky said, "The lawyer broke free. She's walking toward us. I've got a clear shot."

"Not her. She's the bait. Nail anybody tries to grab her though."

Chalky obliged, driving back the one man foolish enough to expose himself. Another round for good measure, shattering a windshield. Drive the point home: leave her be.

Through his NVGs Rags could make out in the distance the blurred, vaguely feminine shape. She cringed with each whistling miss, but didn't fall to her knees or scramble back for cover. Instead, she just kept totter-stepping forward across the driveway stones. Good for you, he thought. At least somebody out there's got some honest-to-God spine.

A moment later, he caught the sound of an engine starting up, revving out at the gate. Shortly the thing lurched forward—headlights dark, but from the general shape and outline he could tell it was huge—a long-bed, four-door, Mega-Cab SUV, six-wheeler, meant to pull an Airstream trailer up mountains. The gunmen rushed to fall in behind, like infantry using a tank for cover.

"Gimme a go on the driver," Chalky said.

"No. Windshield's tinted, Christ, could be bulletproof. Don't waste the shot. But tell you what—from what I can tell, there's a big ol' lumpy tarp in that truck bed, and I'll bet you anything those lumps are humps."

No sooner were the words out than Rags started to laugh—a sudden tickle of insight. Fresh hope. The plan came to him just like that, the tumblers of its mad logic slipping into place.

"They're doing us a favor, Chalkers. That's our ride outta here."

~ 39 ~

L ISA heard tires crunching gravel behind her as she reached the first bend in the tree-lined drive. No headlights—the huge rumbling vehicle fell in behind like a massive hearse, matching her pace as she walked.

Glancing over her shoulder, she saw maybe ten huddled shapes scrambling forward to use the big truck as cover, positioning themselves so it shielded them from the gunman at the house.

Littmann was presumably among them—or maybe he called out *Shotgun!* and scrambled into the passenger seat, the dick.

Either way, look at me. I get to lead the parade.

She resumed moving forward, one shoe in each hand, the raking wind making chaos of her hair, blinding her from time to time as one strand or another whiplashed across her face. What in the world did she hope to accomplish? Nothing, really, or something she couldn't quite place as yet. For now, just another step, another after that. Let the killers work out their own differences.

A voice from behind, only recognizable as Littmann's after a moment: "Once you get close enough, tell them: Put down their weapons. Otherwise, no deal."

Lisa wanted to laugh. There's a deal?

⟡

Inside the house, Rayella and the marines smeared on nightblack—even BBK, because skin is skin and light makes it shine—coating their faces, necks, throats, hands, then wiping their tarry fingertips on their pants, their shirtsleeves. Once he had his own skin darkened, Chalky bent down to work on Wander, who perked up a bit with this new round of prep, readying himself with his squaddies—his eyes clearing a little, that mercurial grin.

Catching a glimpse of himself in the entryway mirror, Rags noticed that the heavy streaks of black grease had all but obscured his disfigurement, and for just a moment, eyes bright white in the darkened face, he thought he detected his former self.

After the war paint, those not already wearing a Kevlar vest strapped one on—Wander, in a semi-conscious fog of chivalrous deference to the lady (who, after all, unlike him, could stand and fight), surrendered his to Rayella.

Next, they loaded their magazines with the rounds they had left—would that be enough? If all went well, Rags supposed, a possibility lying somewhere between dream and myth. Left unsaid, because every man already knew: Make every shot matter.

As they were wrapping up, Tuck ventured in from the living room. Rags glanced up, then the others.

"I understand how you folks feel about me," Tuck said. "Can't say as I blame you. But there's only two sides in this fight, and I'm sure as hell not on theirs." He nodded to convey what lay outside. "You don't put me to use, you're doing yourself no favors. You're short a man, looks like. Well, I ain't no stranger to a firearm. Hunted from the time I was five. And given all I been through, working rodeo to federal stir, I don't scare easy."

Rags glanced at Chalky and BBK, who offered no objection. Even Rayella could only shrug—after all, she'd seen him in action that morning at the gate.

By way of answer, Rags held out the tin of nightblack.

Tuck just shook his head. "Let me stand out, present a clear target. After all, if Littmann wants anybody dead, it's me."

Rags remembered what the woman said: *He died a long time ago.* "I'm not a big believer in walking targets," he said. "Suicide mission's just an ass-backward kind of surrender. I'm gonna need you to fight."

"Trust me, I'm all about the fight. Had my shot at killing myself a long, long time ago. Every day since been borrowed time." He seemed to get lost in some private stream of thought, then chuckled. "Suicide mission. Christ. Life in a nutshell."

Rags said, "We need to hurry."

Tuck nodded. "Time comes, you let me draw their fire. A man can withstand a gunshot or two, vest or no. Besides, don't forget, I rode some mean bulls. Got what's known as a high tolerance for pain."

⚬◇⚬

Chalky and BBK slipped out on opposite sides of the house, stealing into the thick desert darkness, each man jogging in a crouch along a shallow arc through scattered scrub, one left, one right, hoping to outflank the incoming group.

Rayella still had the pistol Tuck had given her that morning and held it in her lap atop the parcel of letters as she sat with Wander, clutching his strangely cold, feverish hand, watching his chest saw in and out with each rattling breath. Her job: not one stranger gets through the door. No matter what else is happening outside. Not even if he's wearing a badge.

Rags gave the Benelli to Tuck. "Just like any other shotgun, same range and kick, except it's semi-auto, no need to pump—you've got nine in the extended mag, one in the chamber, if the fight's still on after that—and God help us if it is—find cover and reload if you can." He handed him a box of shells. "Otherwise, turn to your pistol."

For himself, Rags took Wander's M4, standard weapon back in the 'Stan—the dink little brother you love to hate—set it on single-fire, to preserve his rounds, thinking: a marine and his rifle. No better fighting machine in the world.

341

He waved Tuck forward, opposite side of the door, then on a silent three-count threw it open. They scrambled out onto the porch and dove behind the pillars as the strange procession of killers, the barefoot lady lawyer out in front, made the final turn toward the house, flanked by the well-spaced cottonwoods, sycamores. As the big SUV pulled within five yards of the broad concrete slab abutting the porch, Rags whistled softly to Rayella.

That was her signal. She threw every switch on the doorway panel, clicking into service every single light along the front of the house, including a pair of high-beam spots that caught the visitors by surprise.

They seemed a motley bunch—older, younger, pudgy, lean, dressed in everything from jeans and pearl-buttoned plaid to hunting cammies, jeep caps, boonies, a variety of well-worn Stetsons, and they carried an equally haphazard array of weapons—deer rifles, pump guns, wicked looking semi-auto carbines, military grade—with only two, maybe three at most wearing Kevlar. Good sign. At last, a little luck.

The strangers stood exposed, wincing in the sudden glare. To their credit, it took no more than a heartbeat for common sense to click in. One by one, some quicker than others, they crouched even lower behind the SUV, which just kept advancing, engine a droning throb, gravel crackling beneath the massive tires.

Given this sudden shift in preoccupation, they failed to notice the two marines, Chalky and BBK, slipping into position a little behind, twenty yards to either side, ten-and-two o'clock, just beyond the perimeter of darkness.

The wind had died. As though the sky itself could sense this was it.

⸺◇◇◇⸺

Lisa lifted a hand against the sudden shock of light but kept walking, easing forward tentatively until she stepped with relief onto the smooth concrete skirt at the foot of the stairs leading up to the porch. Like a slo-mo base runner tagging home. If only that meant she was safe.

The stairs were broad and white and, on any other day, under any other circumstances, would have seemed utterly welcoming. At this particular moment, however, the barrels of two guns pointed out from behind the thick white pillars at the top — not at her, thankfully. For the moment, anyway.

Lisa called up to the invisible gunmen, "I've got nothing to do with these . . . guys, yokels, men, what have you . . . behind me. Frankly, I haven't got a whole heck of a lot to do with you, either. Not anymore, I guess. Unless you want to use me, lie to me, one more time. Anyway, for now, I'm just kinda-sorta stuck in the middle, right? So, question of the hour, what's it gonna be — do you guys shoot me or do they?"

From behind, Littmann's voice hissed through a narrow opening in the SUV's passenger-side window, "Tell them to throw down their weapons."

She resisted another impulse to laugh. He sounded like an angry playwright hiding behind the curtain, tongue-lashing an ingénue paralyzed with stage fright.

From the opposite direction, up the stairs, the one with the scalded face, Rags: "Tell them: weapons on the ground, step out from inside and behind the vehicle, arms in the air. Ones in the truck bed, too, come out from under the tarp."

Progress, she thought. We're negotiating.

She called out, "You probably heard — what he just said, I mean, Littmann — about you putting down your guns, too. First. Whatever."

A soft spate of laughter, then Rags said, "Oh, yeah?"

"Pretty much. So I gather."

"Well, if you can hear me, so can he. Not gonna happen. All due respect."

"I'll pass that along."

Littmann thundered through the gap in his window, the words muffled by the thick tinted glass. "They've already killed three men. Maybe more. That makes them murderers. Tell them!"

"They say — "

Rags cut her off. "Yeah, yeah, I heard. There's blood on both sides. Besides, we plead self- defense. His guards when we got here, that man up on the ridge, they can claim their pelts too, how about that? One more time, and only one: Weapons on the ground, hands in the air, everybody out where we can see."

"They put down their guns first! I'm done talking."

Adrenalin — or maybe it was testosterone — crackled through the air like a kind of current, at which point she came to grips with her lone source of power: acceptance. What can they do? Beyond the obvious, of course. Sooner or later, nobody gets out alive. Dig it.

A few seconds passed, minus an eternity or two, and then a voice—Tuck's voice—called out quietly from the porch, "Walk on up the stairs, Lisa. Nobody in here wants you hurt."

Imagine that, she thought.

"Honestly? You weren't the ones I was all that worried—"

"Just walk!"

"Okay then."

She put the first foot forward, lifted the second—then Littmann's voice, quieter than before, almost intimate, like a bullet in the back. "Last chance, Ms. Balamaro. Get them to hand up their guns, or you can blame yourself for whatever happens after that."

Oh, screw the bunch of you, she thought, shivering with rage. "Somebody's going to have to put down his weapons first, or everybody's going to die. Who wins then?"

Not that it would matter at this point. Men never take death seriously.

"How about this? Everybody aim at me." She dropped her shoes and raised her arms, turning in a slow circle. "First one to shoot loses. After that, do whatever the hell you want. Like I'll care at that point."

That was when she heard the two telltale sounds. First a dull ping. Then a slow ratcheting click.

Or was it the other way around?

From what ineffable instinct, she didn't know, but something drove her to her knees then pressed her flat to the concrete. She curled into a ball, knees tucked up to her waist, arms wrapped around her head.

⟨⟩

BBK had taken up position behind a weed-stubbled knoll on the gunmen's right flank, so close he could smell their bad luck. He had free access to the target, not only for the men hunkered behind the giant SUV, maybe six in all, but whoever popped up from beneath the tarp in the truck bed.

Done right, done to plan, no surprises, a firefight shouldn't last half a minute, he thought, and that includes mop up.

That's when he heard the unmistakable sound of someone clearing the chamber of a single- action rifle. Not Chalky. Closer than that, and Chalky wasn't that dumb. Someone who'd walked up unready for the fight. And from the slow soft sound of the bolt sliding back it seemed the shooter was trying to hide his mistake, be sneaky.

All warfare is based on deception.

Wait's over, BBK thought. Spot your target. Commence fire.

With his Belgian weapon on full auto, he sliced down the three nearest men in the first short left-to-right arc, the rest on the return. Whining yelps of stunned pain and full-throated screams. Weapons hitting gravel just before the men themselves. He'd aimed for the knees first, knowing a few of the men had vests, wanting to take them all to the ground, then made short work of the tangle of fallen bodies with follow-up fire, quick bursts, aiming for torsos, crotches, then heads.

Sure enough, the tarp in the truck bed fumbled to life — like a tent had collapsed on a pack of bears — and he dropped his spent magazine, jammed in another, let rip. These screams were muffled by the canvas.

With plans dark as night, fall upon the enemy like a thunderbolt.

Every man outside the vehicle was down, some finished off by Chalky, working from the opposite flank.

Now for the cowards inside.

He changed out the second clip for a third, and as he checked to make sure the magazine had clicked in secure he felt a round cut into his shoulder, spinning him sideways with the impact.

The sniper on the ridge. So far away, but no slouch, a bona fide killer. He'd spotted on muzzle burst most likely, or he had a night scope like Chalky's—why wouldn't he?

Chalky would be safe—the house provided a barrier from the sniper's line of fire. Good to know. No need to shout a warning.

A second round hit—the hip this time, knocking him down.

He tugged his pistol from its holster and prepared to take out any survivor who managed somehow to rise up from the gravel, stagger out from beneath the tarp, step out of the SUV's four-door cab.

Keep focused, keep fighting. Stay frosty.

The third round was the kill shot—side of the head. By that time Cardale Shipman, Black Buddha Killer, was already inwardly reciting his death chant.

⊰∘⟡∘⊱

The instant he saw the muzzle burst from BBK's weapon, Chalky had begun his own methodical slaughter from where he'd found cover beneath a cottonwood tree. The men froze for just a second at the first recognition of incoming fire, then hit the deck. Like that could save them.

One by one, with speed resulting from long practice and sheer hunter instinct, he sighted each target in the scope's reticle, searching out movement, exhaled, squeezed the trigger, registered the cushioned slug of kickback in his shoulder, slid back the bolt to eject the spent casing, slid it home again to lift the next round up from the magazine. Five more after the first kill, six in all. Enough.

He aimed for the groin if the man wore a vest, easier to hit than the head—unless, of course, the head in that instant presented the fatter target.

When things at last seemed still, he rose, left the M40, now spent of rounds, where it was, drew his pistol, cupped his left hand to the base of the grip, supporting his right, and eased forward in a crouch toward the oversized SUV.

A soft grunting thud to his distant right distracted him momentarily—BBK, falling. The distant bark of a rifle's report echoed across the valley from the fire-lit ridge.

Chalky crouched lower, sped up his gait, headed for the SUV, now more intent than ever to make them pay, all of them. Then get over there, tend to the big fella. Mind his wound.

Sudden movement from one of the men on the ground—no time for thought, Chalky put a bullet in him. Which was why he reacted an instant late as the driver's door swung open.

The long barrel of a vintage Colt six-shooter appeared in the gap between door and cabin.

They fired more or less simultaneously, though Chalky realized he'd lagged just enough to have his shot sail wide due to the impact from the incoming round creasing his temple. He recovered quick, refreshed his aim though one eye stayed blurred, and charged forward. Move to contact. He got three shots off even as the driver dove to the side, down onto the center console. Chalky reached the door, swung it back, two more shots. The man cried out like a kicked dog, catching one right beneath his bearded chin.

Glancing up, Chalky saw the judge, Littmann, still dressed in his suit, necktie loose at the collar, aiming his own pistol. Last round in the clip, he thought, make it matter. He caught the man square in the ribs, though at that point he himself was already trying to grip the door, falling from the second hit, the one in his eye, courtesy of an unseen shooter in the back of the cab.

The door, gripped with his left hand, helped steady his fall, which allowed for a soft landing in the gravel about the same time he noticed the towering circular web of lights, the swaying carriages, the faceless giddy nighttime screams—and in the distance, the wheezy oom-pah-pah trumpets and tinny cymbal-crash of a calliope in the sugary heat.

Grunting slam of a wind-milled sledge, the mocking silence of the untouched bell.

And the girl, of course the girl: wheat-brown hair held back with a ribbon, pink dress with the white scalloped collar—narrow at the waist, flaring around the thighs—turned-down cotton anklets and scuffed saddle shoes, about ten yards ahead in the sweaty, laughing, hat-fanning crowd, glancing over her shoulder, a gimlet-eyed smile, tongue arching out like a serpent's toward her glistening strawberry cone.

Tuck watched the bloodbath from his perch of safety, feeling a rush of spiteful hope as the bad men fell. Like spraying poison at a nest of wasps, he thought, admiring the marines, their talent for mayhem, one eye trained on Lisa curled up into a ball at the foot of the stairs.

Then came the helpless, heartsick fury, seeing first the one they called BBK, then the other, Chalky, fall.

At least they died like men, he thought. Meaning what—killed in a pointless cause?

Okay then—two against whoever's left, all of them inside that fat-ass glorified pickup truck.

Including and especially You Know Who.

First, though . . .

He called out, "Lisa, stay put, lie still. I'm coming down to get you."

From the opposite side of the stair, behind his pillar, Rags signaled no. Stay put.

Tuck said, "I'm not letting her lie there during what comes next." He shouldered the semi- auto shotgun, dragged himself up and onto his feet, hip aching from its ancient wound. "Now I told you, let me draw fire. You get ready to take out any dimwit that pops his head out."

He trained the Benelli on the passenger-side door, hoping Littmann would be arrogant enough to come out firing, then began easing down the steps, moving crablike, one step, then another, slow, easy.

The door that opened wasn't Littmann's — opposite side, and rear, not front. One man, or was it two — dropping to the ground, scrambling out of sight, using the vehicle for cover. From behind, Rags opened fire to pin down whoever it was, then hissed: "Speed it up."

Tuck did his best, scrambling down to the foot of the stairs, reaching for Lisa's nearest hand, locked tight to its opposite atop her head, tangled in her hair.

"Quick now," he said. "Come on. Up. Gotta get you inside."

She didn't budge—her body stiff, like fright had inflicted a kind of premature rigor mortis. Or had she been hit?

"Seriously, I mean it, Lisa. Please. Move."

He didn't see it at first, the inching open of Littmann's door. By the time the movement registered in the corner of his eye, the first bullet had carved its way into his shoulder, lodging deep into the muscle, knocking him down.

That's when the second unwelcome fact registered — it had been, indeed, two men who'd crept out of the SUV. One popped up and managed to nail Tuck a second time, this wound in the side. Rags took that man out a mere second later, but that emptied the M4's magazine. He dropped the carbine, letting it clatter down the steps as he went for his pistol, just as the second man swung around the back of the SUV for a better, clearer angle of fire.

The bullet entered Rags's thigh with a scary eruption of airborne blood, but he didn't fall—using his pistol to return fire, three quick shots. Having chosen to expose himself, the man had no chance.

Neither, as it turned out, did Rags. As he leaned down, pressing his hand to the gushing wound, Littmann unfolded his tall rangy body from behind the passenger-side door. Firing first at Tuck, if only from spite—and being a solid shot, hitting his target square in the chest—he then trained his pistol on the brave, quiet, love-struck marine with only half a face.

The judge's bullet entered the skull, throwing the head back helplessly.

⸺◦◇◦⸺

Dropping the parcel of letters from her lap—they meant less than nothing now—Rayella struggled to her feet, rising from behind the door where she'd watched and suffered the bloodbath's rise and fall, trying her best to honor the command to stay put, guard the door, protect Wander— who'd slipped into unconsciousness almost the second the others left him alone. Lifting her pistol, holding it in both hands, she marched through the doorway onto the porch, face streaked with nightblack, tangled hair a ratty fright, aiming at the man who'd just shot dead the only person she'd ever really loved.

Littmann raised his own weapon as she began to empty hers—one, two, three, four shots, at least one hitting home before his bullet buried itself in her brain.

⸺◇◇◇◇⸺

At the first eruption of gunfire, Lisa found herself not just physically curled into a ball but psychologically and emotionally as well, as though she'd withdrawn beyond a high wall into a garden of inner abstraction, taking comfort in the illusion of tranquility even as she realized, at some level, that she was dissociating.

The sound itself was something she'd previously known only through film or TV shows, and how different it was in the here and now—so much louder, like a train rattling past only inches away, but more menacing, terrifying, wrong.

And yet at the same time, it seemed strangely hollow—or was that a trick of the mind, a distortion caused by the closing down of consciousness, the narrowing of the aperture to the outside world—the closing of the garden's thick gate?

She entered something not unlike a wakeful dream, except she was fully aware of not being asleep. A sense of self-reckoning hovered in the background, and she could sense her own presence just outside the frame of her thoughts, a phantom skimming the edge of things.

This created an uneasy sense not just of duality but weightlessness—utter anonymity, no gravity of self. None of us are who we think we are, she thought, identity's a trick, a contrivance, a hoax.

With that, she suffered a sense of being trapped inside an elaborate illusion, the impression that she and everyone else, not just here but everywhere, throughout all of history since the first spark of time, weren't real. We're just pieces in some pointless game the universe can't stop playing, over and over. Why? We'll never know. But there's no way out. To be alive is to be a shadow wandering a maze. And to die? The dissolution of that shadow, nothing more.

Then the inner atmosphere seemed to shift. If there were such a thing as sunlight of the mind, she detected a tenuous ray of it leaking in through a crack somewhere, even as the impression of outside violence intensified, growing nearer, and—unless she was mistaken—a rough hand started tugging on her own.

There is just life, and it must be lived.

With that, as though waking not from her own dream but that of a twin, she gradually emerged from the imaginary garden. After a moment, opened her eyes.

What she saw was the back of Gideon Littman—same suit as in court, a little the worse for wear. He was standing only a few feet away, holding a pistol in his right hand, aiming it at Tuck, who lay gritting his teeth near the bottom of the stairs, blood-soaked shirt marking the wound in his chest, another in his side. A shotgun lay just outside his reach. He wore a strange smile, half hateful, half resigned, while Littmann clenched his free arm against his side—at which point Lisa realized he, too, was bleeding.

"There's someone I want you to meet," Littmann began.

She didn't hear the rest. From some inner reservoir of hatred and bloodlust and bitter pride, she dragged herself up, gained her feet, then leapt onto the man's back like a banshee straddling a wrecking ball.

He almost fell with the impact, staggered for a second, gathered himself, began trying to shake her off—but she'd wrapped her legs around his waist and locked her ankles, raking his eyes with her nails, smelling his rank sweat as she bit his ear as though meaning to rip it from his head.

Shoot to kill.

Roaring from rage and pain, he finally spun and flipped her off—she landed hard, head against concrete, stunned into a second-long blackout. When things cleared, she lay right where she'd started, only flat on her back now, not curled up, Littmann hovering over her.

Let's be adults about this.

His eyes brightened. Blood laced his teeth as he grinned and raised his pistol, point-blank range.

Deafening blast, a mere six feet away—Tuck, having gathered the Benelli, fired twice, the buckshot entering Littmann's back, exiting his chest like a miniature meteor shower, leaving behind a gory shred of flesh and fabric and a stunned expression, locked in place as he fell.

<hr>

Lisa hurried to kneel by Tuck. Closing his eyes, he let the shotgun slip from his hands into his lap. His breaths came shallow and quick as she took his head in her hands, waited for him to look at her. He didn't, couldn't, and what he tried to say got swallowed in an empty hiss.

She held his head against her chest, stroking his gray-brown hair, feeling the weight of him slump against her, suddenly limp and heavy, wanting to tell him goodbye, let him know it was okay, all was forgiven—well, maybe not all. Enough.

It took a moment for the smell to register—something burning, the oily tang of sparked accelerant, the thicker scent of wood smoke. Glancing up at the house, she noticed a flickering zig-zag of light beyond the window curtains leading off to the right. Puzzling at first, so seemingly out of place, then reality set in: flames. One entire wing of the house was on fire.

⋙◦◇◦⋘

Using her teeth, Meredith had managed to chew through the duct tape pinning her wrist to the arm of her chair as the first wave of gunfire began. One hand free, she unwrapped the other, then her ankles, finally able to stand for the first time since . . .

She eased toward the entry as the gunfire intensified and came nearer the front steps, not far outside the open door.

The intruder that poor dumb Seth stabbed in the neck lay slumped against the wall, dead presumably. Leaning down to check, she waited for some sign of movement, breathing, a tremor in the eyelids — nothing. Maybe there's some meek justice in this world after all, she thought.

The parcel of letters lay beside him, raising the question: Where was the snippy little half- breed who wanted them so badly?

Two nearby shots, quick succession shatteringly loud — no farther than the foot of the stairs.

Then the soft clatter of metal onto concrete — the weapon, presumably — followed by silence.

She waited, wondering: Is that all?

Finally, she inched her way through the vestibule to the doorway and onto the porch.

The one with the horrible face lay dead on the stair not far from his slutty mulatto. In the distance a dozen or more others lay motionless in positions only death could arrange, scattered about a gargantuan SUV, engine still throbbing quietly as it idled in park.

At the foot of the stairs, a young woman in a business suit — the lawyer she'd spoken with via FaceTime earlier in the day — clutched Tuck to her chest, his arms awkwardly limp at his sides, head thrown back, eyes gazing emptily upward. Gideon lay in a morbid tangle nearby. The men in my life, she thought.

Leaving the rest to me.

She gathered up the parcel of letters from the entryway floor, went to the closet at the top of the basement stairs, collected what she wanted — turpentine, furniture polish, paint stripper (ah, yes: acetone) — and a large box of wooden matches.

As she stepped cautiously through the debris in the hallway leading to her room, she doused the ravaged paintings with the flammables, trying not to inhale the heady fumes.

Once she reached her doorway, she tossed the final tin, emptied of solvent, onto the top of the wreckage.

The first match hissed into flame, only to promptly flicker out. The second had more moxie—it caught, flared, and held.

She tossed it onto the nearest painting, the fake Maynard Dixon, now soaked in Old English. A second of smoldering, then pop—the flames erupted nearby at first, then rippled to life all along the hallway, creating an almost instantaneous curtain of heat, roiling and greasy and massive, driving her back into her room.

But we're not finished, she thought. The letters. Gideon wasn't exactly wrong when he said they'd been destroyed. Merely premature.

She untied the shabby ribbon, letting it fall to the floor, then reached in for the first brittle envelope. Venturing toward the doorway into the hall, which now lay convulsed in ragged flames, she pushed herself into the scalding wall of smoke, then flipped the letter into the fire, watching as it caught. She dug into the velvet satchel for the next letter, followed suit, the next after that, one by one, throwing the worthless invaluables into the hypnotic flames.

Were they genuine, or fake? Small matter now, she thought. If you want to calculate what they were worth, look outside. Nothing tallies up value like the dead.

PART V

The more you struggle to live, the less you live. Give up the notion that you must be sure of what you are doing. Instead, surrender to what is real within you, for that alone is sure. As stars high above the earth, you are above everything distressing. But you must awaken to it.

~ Baruch Spinoza

September 15, 1887

My Dearest Mattie:

I shall be brief, and may need to break off writing for spells of rest, making for a disjunctive narrative. I now live in a web of lassitude and weakness from which, I realize only too well, there is no escape. And yet I need to write to you, if only because I lack all conviction I will find the strength tomorrow, or the day after, should it come.

As the jigsaw nature of my cursive indicates, I am having increasing difficulty containing the tremor in my hands. Every morning, my first activity, once I have coughed up enough pus, is to summon the bellboy and slip him two dollars, one for the whiskey I need to soothe my lungs and control the trembling, the other as a tip, which earns me my first smile of the day.

The symptoms I mention are but two of those that reveal to me the affliction is impatient — galloping, as is often said — to progress to its natural end.

Every indication is there. Sores have opened up on my skin, which never feels warm anymore, no matter how close I huddle next to the fire, even as I break into rivers of sweat from the fever. My cheeks have hollowed out as my weight plummets, to the point I resemble a sack of rags. I doubt I outweigh the boy who brings me my whiskey — did I mention him already? Ah, so I did. My apologies. I will try to pay more attention.

At all hours of the day and each endless night I find myself remembering how you and I and your sisters hovered at Mother's bedside near the end, holding her hand, watching as the sickness clawed its way through her, as though hoping to dig out her soul and slip it to one of the dogs.

My bed beckons like the grave. I know that there, on those damp sheets, white as a shroud, I will draw my last ragged breath. Pitiful, but appropriate. Vain to believe otherwise.

I am done perfecting grievances and escalating quarrels. I have spent my life trying to honor what I believe to be the truth — the truth about myself, about the world. From my present vantage point, however, I can attest that truth has given me no peace, and it is peace that I crave now.

Please do not interpret what I am about to say as indictment or complaint, but ever since word reached me that you did at last enter the convent, my fortunes have spiraled downward, dragging my body with them. It is not your fault. Rather, it is testament to how greatly I deceived myself.

I believe I squandered my chance at a life my heart would find worthy. In particular, I did not live up to the one affection that meant most to me.

I hope to rectify that in the next life. There is a priest here, Father Edward Downey, a good sturdy Irishman, I think you would approve. I have submitted to his guidance and accepted baptism into your faith, our faith, the Roman Church. I can now say, as I might have said long ago had I only been wiser, that I can reach out my hand to you as a fellow Catholic, and accept yours in mine.

I do not mean I intend to lie down and give in. Quite the contrary. One, it is simply not my nature to do such a thing, no matter how strong the temptation. The coward's way out, et cetera. Second, surrender of that sort indicates despair, and that, like suicide, I know to be a mortal sin.

I will not stain my soul in such a way, for I intend to see you again in the next life. I know, absent catastrophe, that I will be the first between us to pass on, and so it will be up to me to wait for you to follow.

I will do so gratefully. As Uncle Phillip so often sang, "And I will sleep in peace, until you come for me."

Yours forever,
John Henry

$$\sim 40 \sim$$

ON the plane trip home, Lisa read an article in the airline magazine concerning the recent discovery of a long-lost Caravaggio, *Judith Beheading Holofernes*, found by a couple investigating a roof leak in their house in the south of France. They entered the attic, traced the leak to a spot behind a door they had never opened, and broke the door down. They found the forgotten masterpiece waiting like a dotty uncle who'd wandered off after lunch—excellent condition, untouched in a century and a half. Experts placed its value at nearly $140 million.

There are times, she thought, when the entire universe seems to have formed a massive conspiracy to make you the butt of a joke.

She had remained in Arizona for three days, seeing to the disposition of Tuck's and Rayella's remains. The others were the coroner's concern.

Meanwhile, she endured the predictably endless onslaught of questions, posed by every law enforcement agency imaginable: Tombstone Marshals Office, Arizona State Troopers, Homeland Security, even Veterans Affairs.

The most poignant encounter, perhaps, was with good old Jim Preston, head of the Investigation Division for the Cochise County Sheriff—the man who originally told her that the theft of the letters was "a civil matter." He entered the interview room with the same Tony Lama boots and Stetson and revealed that same hairband halo in his crewcut as he placed the wide- brimmed hat on the table between them. The flinty voice seemed a bit more subdued, though not exactly chastened, despite the fact—as it came out in the media—he knew personally two of the men left dead at Littmann's ranch, one a former deputy, the other off-duty. He conducted his questioning with an air of meticulous abstraction, like he was puzzling through a theorem in advanced calculus, then thanked her quietly, left the room, and never reappeared.

As for the other agencies, each had its own particular ax to grind—and unique exposure of rear end to cover. It turned out the Cochise County Sheriff wasn't the only outfit left holding a sizable bag. Also among the dead were several vets, a rogue agent from Border Patrol, and a fugitive from Texas wanted by a veritable alphabet soup of law enforcement bureaus—ICE, ATF, DEA, IRS, DCIS, FBI, Arizona DPS, Mesa PD—for trying to acquire Stinger missiles for a Nomad chapter of the Hells Angels.

The one saving grace, if it could be called that, was the appearance of U.S. Marshals sent by Judge Numkena, with an encouraging nudge from Elan Wingfield. They were the first to arrive at the scene that night, with Elan riding along — the Navajo woman at the parking garage had tipped him off to Lisa's abduction — and he stood by her throughout all the ensuing interrogations, assuming the role of protector, confidante, adopted big brother, secreting her away at night in the home of a friend in the hills to escape getting badgered by the media.

He made sure she was fed and left alone, unless she wanted to talk, which by and large she didn't. If anything, she was worn out by talk.

Sleep was what she wanted. Not that sleep obliged.

At least four times a night, she snapped awake, disoriented in the strange bed, frightened by the darkness, remembering what happened.

She'd been standing at the gate to the Littmann property — clutching herself against the cold as the sprawling house burned to the ground behind her — when the spinning strobes of the Marshal's vehicles appeared in the distance, nothing but them and the dark.

She sat in the back of one of their vans, wrapped in a disposable foil blanket, submitting to a gunshot residue test and sipping coffee from a thermos, watching as the various forensic crews arrived, some local, some federal, big badges flashing at little badges, until finally they hammered out an overall approach, treating the scene like the crash site of a commuter aircraft given the sprawling range of the bodies, the number of dead, the relatively few survivors — four, excluding Lisa, all critical.

Over the next hours and days, she was shown a lot of pictures, faces of the fallen, asked to identify this one, that one, provide whatever background she could. More than once, she got asked point-blank—good cops, bad cops, sympathetic men, steely women—how many of those fatalities were hers to claim. In one form or another, her answer typically amounted to, "Depending on your perspective, none of them. Or all."

She chose to embrace candor—naïve approach with John Law, perhaps, but she stuck with it, like a dog that has finally mastered its lesson. Remaining steadfast in her commitment to the truth, the whole truth, nothing but, she waived her right to counsel—Nico offered to come down himself but she told him no, look after the practice, she'd be fine—and repeated what she knew *ad nauseum* as though by rote, correcting misinterpretations, countering accusations, wiggling out of traps. They wanted so badly someone alive to blame.

Meanwhile, a search party of local volunteers found Meredith Littmann wandering barefoot along the valley floor, picking wildflowers out near the dirt-pack airfield at the foot of the Dragoons. She confessed that she had, of course, yes, destroyed the Holliday letters—less than a day after testifying to Judge Numkena she hadn't. Almost immediately, her two adult children materialized and whisked her away to a private clinic, where it was said she was recovering—from what, exactly, remained unclear.

On the third day, the questions at last seemed exhausted. What more was there to say, really? People are angry and jealous and greedy. They want to hold onto the one good thing they've got. Add guns. Stir until ingredients are dead.

She gave the lawmen her contact information, agreed to submit to any and all further inquiries, then collected her carry-on from the house overlooking the city where she'd been staying and let Elan drive her to the airport, cracking a window to escape the lingering miasma of cigarette smoke in his car.

As he dropped her off, he said in that slow, distinctive, rumbling tone, "What I am hearing through the grapevine—tribal cops talking to local cops talking to the feds and so on—is that everybody kinda feels like they're standing out on the freeway, pants around their ankles, you know? Gotta answer to higher-ups, who have to kowtow to the guys over them, clean up the mess, or shovel it over the fence so it's somebody else's problem. But except for a few hardliners—you know, the kind that think everybody oughta be in jail yesterday—just about everyone involved is pretty much convinced that if anybody's innocent in this, it's you."

"What a relief," she said dryly. "Though I think 'innocent' is a bit of a reach."

He finally reached for the cigarette he'd so thoughtfully denied himself during the drive. Lisa took that as her cue. Opening her door, she collected her bag from the backseat, got out.

She was about to walk away when the passenger-side window slid down. Elan, leaning across the center console, said, "If they really do call you back, contact me ahead of time. I will make arrangements. For everything." One last smoke-scarred chuckle. "At least, everything I can think of."

"Thank you," she said, bowing so he could see her face, the genuine warmth in her smile. "You're a very unique and wonderful man, and I'm grateful for all you've done. So don't take this personally, okay? But I kinda hope to God I never see you again."

⸻ ◇◇◇ ⸻

A man in a black suit bearing a cardboard sign with "Lisa Balamaro" blazoned across it waited outside baggage claim at San Francisco International. He was a decoy, in case any reporters caught wind of Lisa's travel arrangements.

Nico, who'd thought up the scheme, met her upstairs just beyond the final security checkpoint and hustled her out to the actual limousine waiting for them.

How gallant, she thought. How Nico.

"Phone's been ringing off the hook," he said as they headed up the Bayshore Freeway toward Candlestick Point. "I've just let everything go to voicemail, but that means for every message left by an honest-to-God client I've had to plow through a dozen requests for callback from reporters."

Lisa resisted the impulse to say she was sorry. Strange, how that was getting easier, despite so much to feel guilty for. *There is just life . . .*

"Thank you," she said. "For everything."

"No need to thank me. I've been worried sick. Glad to have you back."

She wondered if he'd mind if she curled up, lay her head in his lap, and fell asleep. She'd found herself imagining that a lot the past few days.

"By the way," he said, "did you hear about the Caravaggio they found in an attic in the south of France? Worth how many hundreds of millions?"

One hundred forty, she thought. "I read about it on the plane, yeah."

"Couldn't help thinking about what your letters might have been worth, if . . . "

She flashed on Tuck hanging limp in her arms, Rayella lying dead on the stairs a few feet away. "They were never my letters."

He seemed to flinch. "Of course not, no. I didn't . . . " A sigh. "You know what I mean."

Yes, she thought, I do, but I don't want to talk about that now. Or ever.

"You shaved off your soul patch."

Almost blushing, he ran a timid finger under his lower lip. "Yeah." A shrug. He was wearing his long hair loose as well, no ponytail. Silk shirt, Italian blazer, linen slacks, handmade Duke & Dexter loafers. He looked good. Chic hipster with those saintly eyes.

"What possessed you? To get rid of it, I mean."

Still caressing the freshly naked spot with his fingertip, he said, "Not like you're going to miss it, right?"

I hated that ratty little lip beard, she thought. Mincing affectation. Magnet for soup.

"Makes you eminently more kissable," she said. "Or so I would imagine. What does your latest girlfriend say?"

The finger came to rest. Finally, he did indeed blush.

"I'm sorry, that was rude. And it's none of my business."

She looked out the window at the hills, green from recent, much-needed rain, walling off the city from the peninsula, like a line of battlements. The cultural frontier. Beyond which lay her adopted city, Babylon by the Bay. Home. Of a sort, anyway.

"Want to hear something odd? After everything that's happened, I think I finally, actually understand why someone would want to become a nun."

He leaned back a little, as though she'd slipped out of focus. "You're not seriously considering—"

"Me? No. I can't imagine there's an order that would have me."

"From what I hear, they're in no position to be picky."

"Not really my point."

"And aren't the twelve steps a kind of spiritual regimen anyway?"

"I just want to know where I belong. You know? And with the way things are, the way the world is, I mean, why not? Why not God?"

"Why not virgin sacrifice?"

"No, don't be glib."

"Why not art? I'm not being glib, by the way. Seriously, it's why we do what we do."

"It's not the same," she said. "Not really. I mean, imagine it, every day, same routine—devotion, contemplation, service.

Knowing, not guessing." She shrugged emphatically, like a child. "It just seems, I dunno, attractive."

He studied her for a moment, then tapped on the glass partition between the front and back seats, gestured for the driver to close it up. Once their privacy was assured, he turned back and said, "What's going on?"

"Nothing. Excuse me?"

"You seem different. I mean, of course, given what happened, you'd—"

"I've just had time to think. You know. Despite all the . . . business."

His eyes narrowed, as though once again she'd started to blur. "Okay . . . " He drew out the vowel, a prompt. Lisa took a moment to fuss with her purse, tucking it finally between her hip and the door. There. Now. Ready.

"Insomnia's not the awful bother it's cracked up to be," she said. "Great time to work things through, actually, figure out your life, middle of the night."

She glanced up, suddenly mesmerized by the back of the driver's head. For whatever reason, she also felt a sudden flicker of appetite, first time in days. Maybe she was relaxing. Or her nausea had developed protective camouflage.

Nico, gently: "And what did you figure out?"

Okay. Fine. Deep breath. "I spent all those years . . . trying to live up to what my father . . . "

"Ah." Nico reached out for her hand. "That."

"Yeah."

"He called, by the way. Left a message."

"Yes. He's good at that."

"For what it's worth, he sounded . . . concerned."

"Let me finish, okay? I'll call him back. Maybe. But my point—I gave up trying to earn his respect a long time ago, only to catch myself doing basically the same thing all over again. With Tuck. Older man, couldn't say yes, not really, always one more thing for me to prove."

"Lisa—"

"Never caught that before, not really. It's dreary. And spooky. So unconscious—"

"Lisa—"

"You were right, I had a crush. Not a client crush, either. It was stupid, worse than stupid. He used me, played me—I should've known better. I've been there before. Except this time people are dead."

That catch in her throat. The burning sensation in her chest.

"You're not to blame."

"Aren't I? I want the truth."

"The truth," he said, "is that you're not to blame. Look—"

"Not about that. About everything. I want the truth, and I want to know where I belong, and that's why I get it, I do, I really truly understand why women enter the convent."

"Because they've had bad luck with men?"

"It isn't bad luck. That's the point, Nico. It's me."

Outside, the hills gave way to a maze of intersecting freeways, like a massive tangle of concrete ribbon. She imagined herself, like Gulliver in Lilliput, waking up. Tied down.

Nico emitted a bottomless sigh. "Don't flatter yourself."

Her head snapped back. "What—?"

"Guilt doesn't make you special. You screwed up. Deal with it."

"What do you think I'm trying to do?"

"You honestly think nuns—or anyone else for that matter—you think anybody's got it figured out? Shortcut to paradise, secret sign. Did Sister Mattie—"

"Melanie."

"Did she ascend bodily into heaven? Perform a miracle from her deathbed?"

"You're missing the point."

"The point," he said, "is that nuns are no different than anybody else. They go through the motions, stumble around in the dark, make stupid mistakes, hoping someday it'll all click into place. Boom, puzzle solved. Except it doesn't get solved. That's what death is for."

"If you're trying to cheer me up, try harder."

"Cheer you up? No. Wise you up, maybe."

"Oh please, Daddy. Yes. Make me wise."

"Don't call me that." His face turned red again. Not from embarrassment this time. "What the hell—Daddy?"

"It just slipped out."

"No fooling."

"I'm sorry."

"I told you before, no more 'sorry.'"

Right. *Shoot to kill.* Except . . .

"What do you *want* from me?"

"Know why I never tried to get together? With you, I mean."

Lisa's jaw went slack. She felt like she couldn't get air. Why was he being this way? "I can guess."

"You'd be wrong."

"You like women who scare you. To a point. I don't scare you."

"You scare me plenty. Trust me. More than anybody."

"You're fucking with me."

"The way I feel about you scares me. You want the truth? Try that."

Don't do this, she thought. Don't give me what I want. It will only make me want more—and with that she teared up. All the stress, she told herself. "If you're saying what I think you're saying." She shook her head. "Bad idea. Business partners, like first cousins. Just wrong."

He looked both dismayed and about to laugh. "Good God. What won't you do to keep from being happy?"

Just about anything, she thought. I suppose. "You're right. Yeah. But I'm working on that."

Using his thumb, he gently wiped at the dampness beneath each eye. She felt ashamed at just how much she enjoyed that. Being touched. By him.

"Just give me some time, okay? Last couple days, I mean. Really. They've been, you know, a bit intense."

"I can only imagine."

"And this. I mean, come on. This is, like, new."

Beyond new. Uncharted territory. The wilderness. The West. "Where did all this come from?"

"From not knowing if you were coming back. Not knowing if you were alive or dead."

I get that, she thought. I get needing a miserable scare to figure things out. Being haunted, begging your ghosts to explain.

"So all this time, all I had to do was flirt with death, and you'd have flirted with me."

Oh, if only we could have found a way . . .

Shaking his head, he looked out across the city at the downtown skyline. "How about we let it go for now, talk about it later."

Fair enough, she thought. But shortly the silence felt terrifying. Her mind was boiling, churning with words, none of them true, none of them right, mistaken, maudlin, missing the point, over and over, each time different, each time wrong. But maybe that was okay. Maybe that's how you knew you'd found it, the place you belonged. Knew you were close to home.

The silence. The fear. Like just before daybreak, as you're waiting for that first show of light.

END

ACKNOWLEDGMENTS

THE author wishes to extend a hearty expression of gratitude to the many people who helped bring this book about. Thanks to John and Shannon Raab, Amy Lignor, and everyone at Suspense Publishing for giving this humble little book a second chance, and for all their professionalism, courtesy, and support. Special thanks to Ellie Searl at Publishista and Michael Torres at Square Tire books for allowing this book to once again return to print. Tom Jenks, Carol Edgarian, Jack Schiff, and Mimi Kusch provided a deeply appreciated shot in the arm by publishing an excerpt of the novel in *Narrative Magazine*, perhaps the finest online literary journal in America. Marge Elliott, proprietor of the Tombstone Western Heritage Museum, and Timothy Fattig, biographer of Wyatt Earp, both patiently indulged the author's tedious and often muddled questions. Jennifer J. Hagan, Esq., provided invaluable advice on legal matters addressed in the book. Thanks as well to Victoria Willcox, author of the definitive trilogy of biographical novels on the life of Doc Holliday, for her gracious and enthusiastic support for this project.

No book addressing the Tombstone era could even be considered without the three pillars of devoted scholarship on which this author relied: *And Die in the West*, Paula Mitchell Marks's impeccably researched investigation of the shootout at the O.K. Corral, which set the standard for scholarship in this domain, and countered the generally hagiographic folklore that surrounded the Earp brothers (and by extension, Doc Holliday) up to that point; Casey Tefertiller's equally exceptional *Wyatt Earp: The Life Behind the Legend*; and last but by no means least, Gary L. Roberts's definitive biography, *Doc Holliday: The Life and Legend*, a must-read for anyone interested in this archetypal true-life American antihero. Also invaluable were Karen Holliday Tanner's *Doc Holliday: A Family Portrait*; David Roberts's *Once They Moved Like the Wind: Cochise, Geronimo, and the Apache Wars*; and *The Valiants: The Tombstone Rangers and Apache War Frivolities*, by Lynn R. Bailey. Additional sources on other matters that proved especially helpful included *On Consumption: Its Nature, Symptoms and Treatment*, by Richard Payne Cotton; *Caveat Emptor: The Secret Life of an American Art Forger*, by Ken Perenyi; *Detecting Forgery: Forensic Investigation of Documents*, by Joe Nickell; *Techniques of the Artists of the American West*, by Peggy Samuels, et al.; *Chasing the Rodeo: On Wild Rides and Big Dreams, Broken Hearts and Broken Bones, and One Man's Search for the West*, by W.K. Stratton; *Civil War Letters: From Home, Camp & Battlefield*, edited by Bob Blaisdell; and *Searching the Heart: Women, Men, and Romantic Love in Nineteenth Century America,* by Karen Lystra.

I would also like to extend a special thanks to a trio of friends who unknowingly provided a composite template for the novel's female protagonist: Lisa Iaboni, Kim Addonizio, and Allison Davis, three of the most generous, funny, talented, and formidable women I know. And, of course, there is my wife, Mette, to whom the greatest and most profound debt is owed, for without her, the entire enterprise would be impossible.

ABOUT THE AUTHOR

D AVID CORBETT is the author of seven novels, which have been nominated for numerous awards, including the Edgar. His second novel, *Done for a Dime*, was a *New York Times* Notable Book, and Patrick Anderson of the *Washington Post* described it as "one of the three or four best American crime novels I have ever read." David's short fiction has twice been selected for *Best American Mystery Stories*, and a collaborative novel for which he contributed a chapter—*Culprits*—was adapted for TV by the producers of *Killing Eve* for Disney+ in the U.K. His non-fiction has appeared in the *New York Times, Narrative, Writer's Digest* and other outlets. He has written two writing guides, *The Art of Character* ("A writer's bible") and *The Compass of Character*; and he is a monthly contributor to Writer Unboxed, an award-winning blog dedicated to the craft and business of fiction.

For more about David and his work, visit his website at
https://davidcorbett.com.

PRAISE FOR DAVID CORBETT

The Mercy of the Night

"Tierney and company are so real they seem to step off the pages."
—Booklist (Starred Review)

"Corbett doesn't stint on either narrative or psychological complexity."

—Kirkus

Do They Know I'm Running

"Corbett delivers a rich, hard-hitting epic … an unforgettable journey."

—Publishers Weekly (Starred Review)

"A major work of literary art that breaks all genre borders."
—Bestselling Author Ken Bruen

Blood of Paradise

"Corbett, like Robert Stone and Graham Greene before him, is crafting important, immensely thrilling books."
—George Pelecanos, Producer, *The Wire*

"I would say of *Blood of Paradise* what I said of *Done for a Dime*: it's an example of the best in contemporary crime fiction—or, if I may be so bold, in contemporary fiction, period."
—Patrick Anderson, *Washington Post*

Done for a Dime

"Corbett's fluid pace is enhanced by his elegant writing and his focus on characters."

—South Florida Sun-Sentinel

". . . one of the three or four best American crime novels I've ever read."

—Patrick Anderson, *Washington Post*

The Devil's Redhead

[A] compelling, shocking and beautifully written tour de force."
— The Irish Independent

"Corbett's prose dazzles, cutting across the page with passionate force."

—Publishers Weekly